MW01030500

OUR
SISTER'S
GRAVE

BOOKS BY B.R. SPANGLER

DETECTIVE CASEY WHITE SERIES

Where Lost Girls Go

The Innocent Girls

Saltwater Graves

The Crying House

The Memory Bones

The Lighthouse Girls

Taken Before Dawn

Their Resting Place

Two Little Souls

B.R. SPANGLER

OUR SISTER'S GRAVE

bookouture

Published by Bookouture in 2023

An imprint of Storyfire Ltd.
Carmelite House
50 Victoria Embankment
London EC4Y 0DZ

www.bookouture.com

ISBN: 978-1-83525-509-4
eBook ISBN: 978-1-83525-171-3

This book is dedicated to my family, friends, and readers enjoying the Detective Casey White series.

With much love, thank you for your support.

PROLOGUE

Before the dive, Karol Witney took deep breaths and checked the scuba gear. She squinted past the sunlight toward her friends and followed the guide's instruction to inhale deep and exhale hard. When he signaled again, her eyelids fluttered with one huge, final breath, the air tasting salty as the guide lowered a mask over her eyes. Without hesitation, she tipped backward and quietly splashed into the waters off the coast of the Outer Banks. That's when she let go of the breath in her lungs, never knowing that it was her last.

———

There was freedom beneath the ocean's surface. Freedom and solitude. Two things that had been missing for a long time. How much time had passed? Karol looked at her watch as the ocean stirred around her. The underwater currents gently carried her body, making her rise briefly. She drifted down again, the sound of bubbles filling her ears. Weightless and floating, Karol checked the tank, reading it at three-quarters empty. She snugged her mask, bumping the regulator with a spot check while bubbles paraded in single file over her cheeks. She swam past a wall with a ledge, the stones cobbled and rising in a stagger. There were pairs of beady eyes staring from one of the dark nooks, the surroundings edged by green plants and long spaghetti strands made of thick seagrass that danced mindlessly.

Forever. Distant thoughts crept forward about staying in the Outer Banks and not returning home. Where else was there peace like this? She'd never find it with Jim. He was the main reason to get away this week, to take the girls up on their offer. They'd always been there, her earliest sorority memories having the same faces that were with her today. She felt a pang. A sadness for the years lost, friendships drifting, the memories an afterthought. A reminder to text or to call, but never doing so. He checked the bills. Checked everything. She saw Jim beneath the water then. Saw him trying to ruin the tranquil pool of blue and green. A gifted black and blue bruise in the shape of his hand that circled her arm, evidence he was always with her. He'd given it to her when she told him about the trip. Who saw it? Tina certainly did. A side-eye and then a sad look. A knowing look. Nothing ever got by her. What about Janine? The dive suit with the long sleeves would have been better. There'd be talk. Maybe a few words once the drinks flowed tonight.

Jim isn't here. That's that, she told herself and moved on, a round fish brushing her leg, its slender body moseying without a care. Her tank gauge read over twenty minutes. The visibility to the boat was grainy, the hull bobbing on the surface a hundred yards away. The guide had promised a remote location that hadn't been explored in a long time. The math was simple enough, figuring how long it would take to get back. She had time. Enough to go further, to go deeper and to see more.

Slippery algae coated the lip of a rock wall, fingertips sliding against it with a push. The jutting rocks dropped into a darker pool, the nothingness beyond seeming to go on forever. It was vast and gave her pause. An image of Chicago appeared, another image of her home, and then one of Jim with a can of beer swallowed by his thick fingers. What was there to be afraid of? A little darkness wasn't going to stop anything. Another check. Just under twenty minutes remaining. That was still enough air.

The ledge opened to a recessed floor that was sand and stone, and a large reef that was the color of ash. Beyond the blanched coral was a faint glimmer. A lost bracelet perhaps. Or a watch. Tall plants clung to the rocks, the tips swaying, sunlight shimmering between the blades, their touch silky as they brushed her legs. She eyed the surface, finding the sun in the sky, a rusty coin that was barely recognizable. Their boat bobbed, its anchor lines holding it in place. But for how long? The legs of her sorority sisters were near, feet paddling the water and bunched together in a tight group. A selfie no doubt. They'd been more interested in conversation than exploring anyway, which was fine.

The muffled sound of bubbles came with a start. Someone else's regulator? Someone was following her. One of the girls? Who was more adventurous than the others? It could be Janine or Tina maybe. They'd be the ones to follow if the curiosity suited them. Karol waved, uncertain if they saw her, the visibility dropping. She rolled with a flush of cooler water, passing in and out of a thick ribbon of cold water, the dive taking her another twenty feet down, temperature dropping. She was closer, the glimmer she had seen was now brighter and shinier. Fifteen minutes. The trek back to the boat was five.

Her hand disappeared into the cool sand as she reached for the mystery object. It was solid metal, the first glimpse showing something that couldn't be. *Impossible.* It was the size of a business card and a quarter inch thick. And it was heavy. Shockingly so. Her fingers closed around it; bubbles raced across her face as her breath moved faster than it should. Excitement climbed like an ocean swell, but she had to relax, tell herself this wasn't real, tell herself that the mind can play tricks. There simply was no other explanation.

Karol slowly unfurled her fist. She filled her lungs and held a breath, the bubbles vanishing. It was real! She closed her fist again, letting the corners dig painfully into her palm as she drummed it against her chest. It was a treasure amidst the sandy blanket of the ocean's bottom. She let the current lift her and spin her around. Disbelief making her search for her sorority sisters, but they were nowhere to be seen. How could this be here? Every shipwreck around the Outer Banks had been recorded. There were thousands of them. All of them had been searched a million times. Fright pinched her heart like the point of an icy finger. It had to be the oxygen mix! A leaky tank? Nitrogen narcosis causing hallucinations?

Don't get your hopes up, Karol! Hope leads to bitterness. This was like the lottery. What was it Jim told you? He'd said that the lottery was how the government stole money from stupid people. He was calling you stupid. Remember?!

Karol dismissed the notions, the nitrogen sickness. Instead, she dared another look. She felt like the kid in the Willy Wonka book. Charlie, his name was. The anticipation building as he'd opened the chocolate bar, peeling the wrapper a little at a time, and then seeing the edge of the golden ticket. That's what this was. Gold. And it was all hers. It was her ticket. It was enough to leave Jim. She'd finally get as far away from him as possible. And it would be warm all year too. No more Chicago winters with the raw cold that gets set deep in your bones. Hawaii maybe. That'd be home. Was that far enough? It had to be.

She swam forward, one-handed, heart thumping like a drum so hard she felt it in her head. A band of cold water rushed over her, the underwater stream thin but strong enough to move her sideways and carry her to another rock ledge. She grabbed hold of it, hand slipping through, its touch mushy and falling apart in her grasp. It wasn't a ledge or rock or even sand. It was old wood, the hull of an old boat. Just a portion though, barely noticeable with it hidden beneath a foot of sand. But what was inside burned into her brain like the afterimage of the sun. It glowed like a dream that was clearer to her than any memory she'd ever had.

Pain suddenly rifled into her leg. Karol spun around, her stomach shooting into her throat as images of sharks flashed in her mind. But it wasn't the teeth of a shark. It was someone's hand. She kicked, a gut reaction, bubbles stirring. Was it one of the girls grabbing her? Were they in trouble? She'd learned before about the dangers of being close to a diver who was panicking. It wasn't intentional, but a drowning person would kill for air. The pain came again, a jolting white light in her ankle, sharp enough that it forced her to drop the bar. She watched it tumble from her fingers, moving away from her the way things move in the water. It seemed to slowly glide back and forth toward the ocean floor. There *was* a diver nearby, two hands wrapping around her ankle and holding her in place like an anchor.

Ten more minutes. There was no time to waste. Every second now was a second without the oxygen reserve stored in her tank. Arms wide, waving at the surface, stirring the ocean floor into a cloud. She couldn't move. The hands held her tight. She clutched their arm and gave them a shove, the effort feeling useless as she fought against the current. Their grip grew tighter, painful fright filling her with a sense of what they wanted. They wanted her dead. But who? Why? Was she overreacting? One of the hands let go suddenly. She swam around to see who it was. But any relief swiftly turned into a nightmare when fingers clutched her mask. Karol grabbed their wrist, but she was too late, the mask tearing from her face.

Her eyes blurred instantly, stinging in the salty water as her mouthpiece was ripped out of her mouth with dizzying force. They were attacking her. Arms flailing, she eyed the sun through the ocean and kicked at her attacker. They kept their grip firm. An urgent burn kindled in her chest. The need to breathe a suffocating drive. Karol swung mercilessly, batting at a black diving suit, the figure like a shadow. Her attacker had become like a ghost holding her in place, a gravedigger readying freshly tilled grounds for her to sleep. She took hold of a hose and jarred it until it broke like a bone. Was it their mouthpiece? Water rushed past her face, hair flying around her head, the pressure against her eardrums threatening. She was being dragged below, dragged deeper, the sunlight dimming.

Her left ear popped like a gunshot. A sickening sense of water rushed in as though a hole had been bored into her skull. She'd always had weak ears, the kind not meant for these depths. But it was her chest that struck with deadly fright, a burn expanding like a wildfire across the deeper lobes of her lungs. She had to fight, fists clubbing something hard like rock. While everything was slowed beneath the surface, death was racing forward with unrelenting speed. She glanced once back at the boat, at her sorority sisters, their legs still bunched in a group while they talked about life after college.

The body can lie to you. She'd been told that once by a scuba instructor. She'd been young then, and still fit. Eighteen? She couldn't remember. It was the class where she met Jim, where she met who she'd thought was her soulmate. The scuba instructor was right. The body can lie to you. It can tell you that it's okay to breathe. Even when there was a million gallons of seawater pressing against you. The body will lie. She heard the lie. It told her to open her mouth and take a deep breath. It told her there wasn't anything wrong with the air, she'd breathed it her entire life. It was just wet and salty but wouldn't hurt you. Go ahead, breathe some more and free that fear laboring in your head.

Karol forgot about the fight as weightless buoyancy took over and her limbs turned numb. She forgot about the treasure which had been a brief miracle, its bounty giving her hope to leave a marriage that had lied to her the last seven years. The ocean filled with sharp, darting lights. They had long, wispy tails and flew like comets across dusky purple skies. They grew dim as the burning in her lungs was forgotten too. When the last of the lights was barely there, an unsettling thought came. This was happening because of what she saw. Wasn't it? Who attacked her? Whoever it was, they were going to go after her sorority sisters next.

ONE

With a homicide case, a crime scene is like a map. It shows us the dead. It might also show us the where, the who and with what as well. When we're lucky, it can even show us why. We read the crime scene, we process it, and we interpret every detail to tell a story about the homicide. If we're lucky, we'll see enough to decipher and map the events of what exactly happened. Unfortunately, that's rarely the case. Most times, we're following clues, some hidden or found without us knowing what they are. My name is Casey White, and I am a detective in the Outer Banks of North Carolina. And I know one thing for certain, every case begins with a crime scene.

So when word came in about a possible murder, my immediate question was where? Thoughts stirred next with the list of who to text and call. There was Tracy Fields, a crime-scene investigator on my team. And then the medical examiner, Samantha Watson. We also had a new team member, a first-year investigator with a background in computers and cybersecurity, Sherry Levin. When I pressed our station manager about the location, text messages already drafted, there was a pause. I learned that there was no crime scene. There was only a body and an explanation about the circumstance of how the woman died. Why did the medical examiner need me?

Hot water rained onto my shoulders as the endless patter of bare feet ran around the bathroom and up and down the apartment hallway. The clamor of pans and kitchenware rang out with calls about breakfast being ready. My eyelids shut, I swam in a hazy gray light while the water drummed against my head. When distant laughter erupted with a playful squeal, I couldn't help but smile at the sound of happy children and my soon-to-be husband.

"Coffee in five," Jericho told me, his voice nearby.

"Coffee!" Tabitha shouted with a lisp, her front baby teeth having gone missing. I peered around the shower curtain in time to see the top of her head disappear as she chased after my fiancé.

"Come on, Tabs," I heard him say.

Tabitha had taken to following Jericho everywhere since coming to live with us. Her brother Thomas, two years older, liked to watch morning cartoons, which was another sound I was still getting used to hearing. I'd been used to it once before. A lifetime ago it seems now. I was a cop living in Philadelphia and had a husband and daughter. Our happy lives ended one afternoon when my daughter was kidnapped. She's a woman now, and it was years before I was reunited with her. It was also how I ended up living in North Carolina's Outer Banks.

"Thank you, Tabitha," I yelled after her. We were foster parents. A decision that didn't come lightly. But a decision I'd had no regrets in making. Especially after learning how alone in the world the two of them were. "I love you!"

"Love you too," she said, returning briefly to give me a toothy grin, the front two baby teeth in the possession of the tooth fairy.

"Tell Jericho I'll be right there," I asked her. She was gone in a flash. I toweled off fast, preparing myself for a morning in the morgue. How is it we had a body and no crime scene? The beach? A body washed up? As a homicide detective, my life hadn't changed much with Thomas and Tabitha moving in with us. But I

couldn't say the same for Jericho. He'd been a major in the Marine
Patrol, his hours cut back to a fraction so that he could be a full-
time foster dad.

I think he was okay with that. I think he preferred it. I'd fallen
in love with this rugged, whiskery man who wore scars like they
were badges. He'd also had a presence that everyone revered. But
when I saw him with the children, I think I fell head over heels in
love all over again. His demeanor softened, they'd turned him into
a cuddly and playful goofy teddy bear. Phone in hand, I quickly
texted the team:

I'm hurrying

I needed coffee. The biggest mug we had. The idea of an
uninterrupted night sleep had become a distant memory to me
and Jericho. It was the nightmares. Mostly Tabitha, her screams
jarring us out of bed. Thomas had his share too, but they were
fewer. The children had seen their mom and dad murdered. We'd
caught the killer and put him behind bars where he'd never harm
another soul. But he was still free in their nightmares, and I could
only imagine the horrors they found there.

A body and no crime scene? I couldn't shake the questions as I
raced around the apartment to give the children kisses. I planted a
kiss on Jericho's lips too as he handed me a mug of coffee and
whispered loving words into my ear. Before I could leave, he
gripped my arm gently, his eyes telling me to be safe. I assured
him I would and got into my car, the radio clicking with a static
rasp as thoughts returned to the call. I'd seen people challenge
jigsaw puzzles by flipping them to solve without using the picture
on the box. If this was a homicide, then that's what we'd have to
do. We'd flip the puzzle and create a crime scene without there
being one.

"Detective," Samantha Watson greeted me outside the morgue, the bottom floor of the municipal building. We'd just entered the first month of autumn and, while the tourists had mostly gone and the temperature had dropped, there was no other place quite as cold as the morgue. She brushed my arms, clapping her small hands against them when seeing me shiver. "You know where the extra lab coats are."

"I do," I answered, eyeing the thick rubber doors, the plastic windows blurring what was on the other side. We were outside the morgue in a room with lockers and shelves stocked with booties and gloves and coats, everything that was needed to sterilize ourselves before entering. Samantha kept a clean house, a trait of her predecessor which I regarded fondly. And like her predecessor, she liked to remind us of it often. I put my things in a locker and dressed the part for the visit as the elevator doors opened, a bell ringing.

"Good, I'm not late," Tracy said, exiting in a rush. For a split second, I saw a deep resemblance to her father. I saw the likeness of him and of me and it stole my breath. Call it a miracle or a kind of godly gift, if that's your liking, but the daughter I'd lost years before was a crime-scene investigator working for me. Tracy was my daughter. She was in my life again. And though we weren't mother and daughter in a traditional sense, we'd become close, which was more than I could have ever hoped for. With light, baby-blue eyes that shined with the overhead lighting, she was lean and tall like me and shared my wavy brown hair. Nose wrinkling, she asked, "The report said there's no crime scene?"

"That's the word," I said and helped Tracy strip the jacket from her arms. "Just a body."

"The death?" she asked, goosebumps racing across her arms as I handed her a lab coat and gloves.

"Found unresponsive while on a dive," Samantha answered. "We received the body from the boat charter at the docks."

"This isn't an accidental drowning?" I questioned and held up a tin of salve. "Otherwise, you wouldn't have called us here."

"Shouldn't need the salve." Samantha shook her head and brushed the bangs from her eyes. She was on the shorter side and had straight black hair and a round face. Her skin was like ivory, thick eyeliner making her pale eyes stand out. She motioned to the door, waving us forward. She frowned. "It's best to show you why I called."

"Best to show," Tracy murmured while hurrying to slip gloves onto her fingers, powder drifting around her hands.

The temperature dropped twenty degrees or more when Samantha swung the resin doors open, a cloud of frosty air stirring beneath the doors. This was the room where the dead told their secrets. Like the puzzles of a crime scene, Samantha and her team teased through tissue and bone and stomach contents in search of answers. Without windows, the morgue's autopsy room walls were solid cinderblock, freshly painted a faded yellow. The floors were granite and reminded me of a chess board with their large black and white tiles.

We didn't need the salve, but the room was laden with death. I eyed the large body refrigerator to my right, the stainless-steel gleaming. It had eight doors that were about the width and height of a coffin, a deep tray on the other side, each carrying a body waiting for its turn beneath Samantha's blade. I followed Tracy to one of the exam tables as Samantha dragged a step stool from beneath and climbed it. Motors inside the table's pedestal hummed and large screens above the table flashed to show X-ray images and charts. On them I saw the weights and other measurements of the person's organs, the physical stats of their height and weight, as well as eye and hair color. But I did not see a cause of death.

"The autopsy was already completed?" I asked, my curiosity growing. The body was covered from head to toe with what was called an evidence sheet, an outline faintly showing through it.

"I finished it this morning." Samantha whisked the sheet from the body to reveal a woman in her late twenties, possibly early thirties, the stats would clarify an age later. She was attractive and had shoulder-length hair, reddish with blond highlights. Tan lines around her middle and her breasts indicated sunbathing, leading me to think she was a late season tourist visiting our beaches. Her chest had been parted for organ removal, the baseball stitching wide and spaced, the sight of them always making me uneasy. Samantha flipped a few switches, bright lights shining with a glare bouncing against the lip of the table. "Do you guys notice anything?"

"Safe to assume whatever it is we're supposed to find is why you called?" Tracy circled around the table, her shoulders hunched, head dipped as though there were a prize to be found. Samantha pinched her lips and made like she was locking them and then threw an imaginary key away. Tracy gave Samantha a hard look, indulging her in the guessing game. "A challenge? Okay then."

"The wrist." I lifted the woman's arm where I'd found a bruise. In the light I saw what appeared to be the shape of a hand with the index and thumb circling the woman's arm. The coloring of it was a few days older, a week perhaps. Though the woman's fair skin was grayed by death, the telltale signs remained. The bruise had colors that were a deeper black and blue with a shade of green, yellowing at the edges. I shook my head with a frown. "This isn't it?"

"It's not, but I do think it was worth noting." Samantha tapped one of the screens, zooming in on an X-ray, a bone in the woman's right forearm showing a mended break. "It's a few years old, recent enough for me to think two to three. I've already pulled records of her previous hospital visits."

Stomach sinking, metal clanked as Samantha worked instruments from a tray. She shined a light inside the victim's mouth, my asking, "Do you believe the woman was abused?"

"Previously? Yes." The inside of the woman's lower lip had an injury. I'd seen it before, the teeth cutting into the flesh when punched.

"Was that related to the cause of death?"

"It was unrelated. The cause of death was drowning. There was seawater in her mouth, throat and lungs." Samantha scrolled one of the charts to show the measurements. "From what was reported, she'd been scuba diving and was found unresponsive."

"I can't imagine dying that way. Her death must have come as a relief."

"Unresponsive beneath the surface isn't a good place to be," Tracy commented, the two of us having recently become certified to dive with Jericho's help.

I raised one of the eyelids and searched for petechial hemorrhages, thinking a bad air tank could cause asphyxiation and loss of consciousness. "Nitrogen in her blood?" Samantha shook her head. "Other contaminants?"

"Other than what is expected in a drowning."

Tracy waved her hands near her mouth. "What if the mouthpiece fell out? She could have panicked and then accidentally struck herself while trying to put it back in?"

"We bite down on them though." The mouthpieces Jericho had us using were made of a clear rubber with one end connecting to the air hose. The other end went into our mouths and had fins that were to bite on and hold in place. "What about ripped out? A possibility?"

Samantha glared at me with wide, shocked eyes. "Ripped out!?"

"We'd need to see it to know for sure." Tracy opened her laptop. "Even then, the mouthpiece might not show damage."

"How about the woman's scuba gear?" The morgue was empty of anything resembling gear, leading me to ask, "The docks? The boat she was on?"

"Must be," Samantha answered and looked to Derek, her

assistant. A tall, chunky man, he had thinning light-colored hair and was the muscle when it came to transporting bodies. "Was there anything when you received her?"

He shook his face. "Just the dive suit. The gear must still be on the boat."

"I'll get on that." Tracy motioned to Derek for the information, a trip to the docks likely to fill our afternoon.

We did have a crime scene, but I sensed this wasn't the only finding. "You wouldn't have called for a small cut on the inside lip. It could be incidental."

"It's down here." We moved to the woman's feet, the nail polish chipped and grown out. There were signs of lividity, the blood settling in the lower half of her body. Samantha raised one of the woman's knees, stiffness sounding while she worked the leg. With the shine from the overhead light, I saw why we were called this morning. It was another handprint, smaller in size, a fresh welt on the skin which was raised with an abrasion. "This happened just before death."

"Someone held her?" Without waiting, I studied the woman's fingers, the palm of her hands, looking for a bruise or any cuts. "There's no defensive wounds... then again, there might not be if she was struggling to get her mouthpiece in place."

"It was right to call you?" Samantha asked, uncertainty in her voice.

On the woman's left hand, I saw the shadow of a wedding band, a tan line, and thought of the hospital records and possible history Samantha commented about. We didn't have all the details, but this was a case to investigate. "Yeah. You made the right call."

TWO

Clouds blanketed the sky as a band of autumn air cut through us, the cold urging jackets to be buttoned and collars raised. It was a tell of winter's approach. The Outer Banks wasn't a place where snow fell regularly, but the forecast for the coming season suggested that a freeze would change things soon. That didn't stop the latest wave of tourists though. The fishing docks clamored busily with boots and rattling tackle, the boards standing room only as groups of all ages lined up for charter boats. There was mahi-mahi and wahoo and yellowfin tunas to be caught before the temperatures dipped enough to freeze their gear. Even then, I suspected there'd be more than a few braving the weather.

Our interest this morning was the charter Karol Witney was on. She'd left the touch of dry land and walked these same boards we were on now. After boarding the dive boat, she'd drowned a few hours later. Soon afterward, her lifeless body was returned to the docks. Who else was on the boat? Who was in the ocean with her? We had the name of the boat charter, a body and a cause of death. We also had what were considered suspicious bruises. There were past injuries too which added to the mystery of Karol Witney. We'd question everyone involved. If needed, we'd question them again and again until it was made clear to us what happened when Karol was beneath the surface.

Jericho knew everyone in the Outer Banks, his serving one time as sheriff. And most who called the barrier islands their home, knew him. That included Shawn and Patrick Rutledge, brothers and owners of the scuba and snorkeling charter that Karol Witney had been on. Families and fishermen made a path for us, rubber footsteps squelching, the gray daylight glinting from my badge. We waded through the crowd until reaching the far end, a smaller boat, the transom painted a dark, indigo blue, the name *Wanderer* painted in a faded and chipped silver. There were two men on the boat deck, the chill in the air having no effect on them, both dressed for summer in torn shirts and pants cut-off at the knees. Music thumped from a radio as one held a hose and the other scrubbed the deck, their faces sweaty, their bodies lean with deep tans.

"Captain?" I stepped closer, uncertain which of the two was the captain, the owner. When they both looked at me, I could see a resemblance. Their hair was bleached by a summer of ocean sunshine, and they shared the same high cheekbones and narrow chin, along with a broad nose and brown eyes. While they shared family resemblances, one was clearly older. He had creases across the forehead and the faint impression of crow's feet around the eyes. He was also taller by a few inches, standing up straight as he handed the hose to his sibling. He made eye contact and came to the edge of the boat, wiping his face with his shirt. "My name is Detective Casey White—"

"Shawn Rutledge. I'm captain and co-owner," he interrupted and extended his hand. The tide was low, the boat sitting below the docks. "We've been expecting you."

He motioned to come on board, offering his hands. "Thank you, Captain." Sunlight peered through the clouds, warming me instantly. I cradled the small of Tracy's back as she went first, stepping down while a younger mate quickly dried the deck. "Tracy, watch your step."

"It should be good now," he said and did a double take, eyeing Tracy briefly before turning away shyly. When she was closer, he spoke directly to her, saying, "It's okay, you can walk there."

I boarded next, holding the captain's hand and shoulder, focus already at work, taking a mental inventory of the boat's gear stowed. "Thank you."

"My name is Patrick," the young mate said, leaning in and offering his hand. In his mid twenties, he brushed the hair from his face and glanced at his brother nervously. "I'm the co-owner. And I am also the divemaster."

"It was just the two of you on board that day?" The younger brother nodded and then shared a look with his brother, as though seeking permission for answering. The motion made me naturally suspicious. I didn't waste a minute and jumped into why we were here. "Was there anything about the dive you want to tell us?"

"She just went off on her own." Another shared look, the older brother saying, "Maybe something scared her down there. It happens."

"Off on her own?" This was a dive charter which meant someone led the charter above and below the surface. "Who dove with the group?"

The younger brother raised his hand, reluctance weighing on it. "But I didn't know she'd been gone until it was too late," he said and shrugged apologetically. His face cramped and he glanced at the stowed gear. The sides were packed with air tanks that were lined up like dominoes, each secured for sea travels. I began counting the tanks, the younger brother adding, "We usually only go down with six people at a time."

"What do you mean?" Tracy asked, a breeze lifting her hair. She went to the stowed gear, the older brother nodding his permission.

"I'll get that," the younger brother said, metal clanking with the locks removed. He faced me answering, "They had two extra people with them."

Tracy's hand bounced while counting the number of setups available. "Is it a problem diving with eight?" She hoisted gear with the younger brother's help and then held two hands to show me there was enough for ten.

"We keep a few backups." The older brother's face dimmed with a brief scowl. "But, if needed, we'll handle up to nine, leave a spare."

"You had enough," Tracy said, taking notes. "Who does the inspections before leaving the dock?"

"Both of us." The older brother was quick to answer. They had a death on their tour. A single note of negligence in the news spreading about Karol Witney could destroy their business. "All certifications and licenses and inspections current."

"She just went off on her own," the younger brother repeated, voice pitchy. He lifted a tank in one hand and a regulator in the other. "This was her gear."

"It's been checked?" Tracy took a picture of the gear with her phone and proceeded to connect the hoses. The younger brother held the tank, handing her a gauge and mask.

The older brother approached and handed me printed copies of the charter Karol Witney booked. "We haven't cleaned or refilled the tank she used. We didn't do anything with the gauge either."

Tracy connected the regulator, fastener clanking, fingers moving fast. The young brother's lips parted as he stared, impressed by seeing her experience at work. When fully attached, she read the gauge with a frown. "It shows that there was ten minutes remaining."

"I know, right!?" he said, voice rising over a nearby motor. He shook his head then. "It doesn't make any sense."

"I think she must have gotten spooked." The older brother

took to a knee, bumping the mask. "When we found her, she didn't have her mask on, and the regulator wasn't in her mouth."

A gull's call filled my ears as I searched the mask's glass, looking for signs of fingerprints. It was clean. "You recovered the mask afterward?"

"I did." The older brother pointed toward the front of his boat, the wheel, and electronics. "Waypoints. It's all recorded."

"We may need to see that."

"I understand," he answered and looked uneasy. "What... what happens next?"

"We'll get to that—"

"I mean, it's the end of the season and we've got bookings through the month."

"There was a death," I said, leaning on death with emphasis. I was sure they were already facing other troubles. There was the state's licensing and insurance. Their divemaster certifications could be in jeopardy as well. Our interest was in Karol Witney and what happened to her beneath the surface. Which meant taking the time we needed to get some answers.

He stood up and placed his hand over his heart. "Apologies, ma'am. Of course, I know there was a death."

I faced the younger brother. "Let's talk about what you said." He looked uncertain of what I was referring to. "You said you lost her?"

His frown faded with recognition. "It was a charter for eight women, some sorority thing..." he began to explain. The mention of a sorority made me instantly curious. Which sorority was it? Who were her sisters? I wanted to hear more about it. I'd never been in a sorority but had a cousin who tended to drink and divulge. As she would tell it, there was no tighter group of friends, and there was none more messier either, especially when it came to the secrets they kept. I motioned to Tracy and saw that she was already writing it down. We'd talk to each of the women. More than once, I was sure. "...some kind of reunion of their sorority house?"

"Did you catch the name of the house?" Tracy asked. They did not.

I had names from the initial police report but wanted to reconcile it. "What about the other women? You have their names?"

"I can get that to you," the older brother said, wiping his forehead dry. The clouds had parted allowing the sun to break through, making sweat tick on the back of my neck. "It's on my tablet. I record names for insurance purposes. Can I text it to you?"

I opened my jacket, a breeze finding its way inside. I fished a business card from a pocket and handed it to him. "Soonest would be best."

The younger brother tapped the cages with gear, the front rattling. "They were all certified."

"It sounds like there was good diving experience between them," Tracy said.

Tracy's comment had me asking, "If Karol Witney was an experienced diver, doesn't it seem odd that she would have gotten frightened by anything. *Spooked* is what you'd said."

The older brother heard my tone, expression firming. A motor roared next to us, a fishing charter boarding. When the revving idled, he replied, "Listen, I've been doing this long enough to have seen legend divers get spooked. Like I said, it happens... to all of us."

"Anything can happen when you're down there," the younger brother added, his voice rising defensively.

"There was still ten minutes of air in her tank. How was the dive before she went on her own?" Tracy asked, jotting down the information about the tank's air supply, the time remaining. "Was there anything notable?"

"Clear weather." The older brother worked a rope as he

spoke, winding it back and forth in fast figure eight motions. "No swells to be concerned with. Nobody got seasick. The kind of dive we'd expect great reviews for online."

I faced the younger brother. "How about beneath the surface? Currents, visibility and temperature?"

He began with a shrug. "We got about five feet of good visibility to start. It was enough to explore the wreck," the younger brother explained. He stared at the sea as he recalled the day, sunlight turning the color of his eyes golden. "Then when we passed through a temperature change, the visibility cleared to over thirty feet."

"When did you lose her?" Tracy asked, her gaze still concentrated on Karol Witney's gear.

"I'm not sure when." Without a word, I pressed for a better answer. Eyelids widened, his seeming shocked. "I really don't know."

I looked to the older brother, his answering, "We were in a spot where we could snorkel. A few of them took to doing that instead."

"They split up?" I didn't understand what he meant, but saw the snorkeling gear stowed on the other side of the boat. "So you watched the group who went snorkeling while your brother stayed below with the group diving?"

"That's correct, ma'am." The younger brother tugged on his shirt, restless with the questioning. "She must have gone off by herself when I surfaced to make sure some of her friends got back onboard."

"A few of the divers returned to the boat?" Tracy asked, balancing as a boat's wake lifted the bow.

Both brothers nodded, the older one saying, "They switched gear to snorkel too."

"At this point you've got what, about three or so diving, the rest snorkeling?"

"Three?" The younger brother answered, his lips moving as he counted. "I had three, including Karol Witney."

"But you didn't check on her again when you returned below?" Tracy questioned.

I knew where she was going. When we dove with Jericho, he'd never left us alone. That included having us surface with him when needed. Although that was our dive with Jericho, I didn't know if that was a standard practice or not. "Is it required for you to stay within eyesight full-time?"

"They were experienced divers." There was heat in the older brother's voice, his upper chest and neck flushed.

"We *were* watching them." The younger brother continued to shake his head after answering. There was no mistaking that he was bothered by the woman's death. But was it an accident? I couldn't get the image of the handprint around Karol Witney's ankle out of my mind. My gut told me that at some point I'd be referring to her as a victim and not as an accidental death. Did the brothers know? I was about to find out.

"There's evidence that this may not have been an accidental death."

"Huh?" the younger one asked. Postures shifted and bodies went rigid as their faces emptied. "She was gone when we got to her."

"Foul play." I didn't sugar-coat the answer. A woman was dead.

"Murder?" the younger brother asked, voice cracking. He searched his brother's face. "They mean murder, Shawn?!"

Patrick's older brother crossed his arms and he went to stand closer to his sibling. There was a cautious look on his face. He whispered into his brother's ear, before facing us. "What do you mean!?" he asked.

Shawn's hand cradled his younger brother's shoulder, fingers slowly gripping it. "She… I thought she drowned?"

"The cause of death was drowning." I glanced at the gauge

and tank. "But there is evidence of a physical injury that was sustained in the moments before her death."

The younger brother's face lit up with shock. "Injury? What injury?"

"We're not at liberty to say," Tracy told him. She lowered her chin. "We believe it contributed to her death."

"An injury. Patrick, what are they talking about?" the older brother asked, his fingertips turning white as he squeezed. "Patrick?"

The younger brother's eyes were like moons, his jaw slack with disbelief. "We... I mean, I lost her."

"We?" The younger brother was reluctant but nodded. "Who else was with you?"

"It was my responsibility—" Patrick began to answer.

"Tell them who!" his brother interrupted.

Patrick's lips disappeared, turning in while he tried to recall a name. He finally blurted, "She was the other one who didn't go back to the boat."

"The other one? She didn't join the others to snorkel?"

"Uh-uh," he answered. He jabbed a finger in the air, adding, "I didn't lose sight of her. I remember waving her over to help me, you know, to help with—"

"Karol Witney," Tracy finished for him, emotion stealing his voice.

Handprints. I thought of the marking on Karol Witney's ankle and how we could assess the size of the hand used to create it. "We'll contact you when we have more questions," I instructed, nodding my head until they returned the nod.

"We'll take these with us." Tracy moved closer to Karol Witney's gear. There wasn't anything about the gear that had me thinking it was faulty, that it could be responsible for the death. We'd still apply a level of forensic to investigate it.

"You live local?" I asked.

"Yeah. All our lives," the older brother answered. His tone

changed, more callous now that we were speaking of a criminal investigation. "This was our pop's boat."

We slipped on gloves and began to gather the gear, the brothers retreating near the wheel, huddling in quiet conversation. "We'll be in touch."

I'd interviewed enough murderers and witnesses to recognize the difference. This morning, I saw who I believed to be witnesses to Karol Witney's death. If I was right, someone else was in the water with them and had grabbed the victim, took hold and ripped the mask from her face. There were more interviews needed. The sorority sisters at the top of my list.

THREE

There was a cracked rib in Karol Witney's first year of marriage. The hospital report stated that the woman had experienced a fall down a steep flight of steps. Tracy handed me a printout, the smell of toner fresh, its touch still warm. There were no other injuries in the report. I would have expected to see more with a fall like that such as bruising on the arms or her back perhaps. I went back over the first page, my head filling with images of the bruise Samantha showed us at the morgue. It was a week or more old and had occurred prior to the victim's death. That bruise was telling a story. And it was a story I'd seen before. More times than I cared to count.

Drumming footsteps filled the nook while we worked at the kitchen table. We had our laptops open, along with folders and a printer to add more pages to the new case. The apartment windows were raised to coax the cooler air in, curtains fluttering with an ocean breeze. The sun sank behind the western horizon, turning the sky red and orange with fringes of nighttime purple. There were stars and moonlight and the sight of them signaled that it was near bedtime for Thomas and Tabitha. They knew it too, a second or third wind fueling them just before going to bed.

We were still learning about them just as much as they were learning about me and Jericho. While they said they couldn't tell time, I suspected that might have been an innocent fib. They always knew when it was bedtime.

"Guys!" Tracy began, the commotion rising. Their footsteps ceased and their eyes grew with their smiles. Tracy ducked her head behind her laptop screen, soft giggles sounding. I grabbed another report from the printer while they began a game of Red-Light, Green-Light. Tracy never broke form, saying, "I think we know the source of that fracture Samantha showed us."

"A spiral fracture," I commented, glancing at the paper. In the second year of Karol Witney's marriage, a fractured arm was reported. Tracy found the record at an urgent care center which was five miles from the couple's home. This was the mended break we saw in the X-rays, Samantha's time estimate of when it occurred near exact to the date on the report. The doctor's notes were mostly generic, but there was one line which peppered the growing suspicions we had about the Witneys' marriage. The doctor had written that the type of fracture could not have been sustained in the manner the couple described. "We need to keep digging."

"Already on it." Tracy ducked again, laughter turning into shrieks, the children nearly at the edge of the table. I heard the printer whirring and saw the mail icon on my screen jump with a digital copy. Another icon on my screen contained a link to the laws governing a person's death, the disclosure of health information when suspecting there was criminal conduct involved. That meant the laws governing patient confidentiality were lifted, and we'd send the link whenever questioned by hospital staff.

"Okay, guys. It's time—" Jericho began, his voice cut short by groaning objections. He emerged from the hallway wearing a paisley apron that covered most of his front. He also wore a large pair of oversized construction goggles and a tight hairnet which created a tidy bun on the top of his head. Bright orange rubber gloves squelched when he tore them from his hands. He looked at us and sighed exhaustedly. "That... that bathroom is clean."

Tracy chuckled, asking, "What happened in there!?"

I shook my head. "You don't want to know."

"It was an accident," Thomas answered with a pout.

Jericho scratched his cheek, a week of stubble growing thick. "Don't worry about it. We'll pick up more shaving cream at the market."

"Ceiling too?"

He rolled his eyes. "Cleaned it off the ceiling too."

Tracy blurted another chuckle.

"Could you?" I motioned to Thomas and Tabitha, Jericho giving me a nod. Tracy's eyes shined with surprise when Thomas included her in our ritual of goodnight kisses, planting a sloppy one on her cheek. Tabitha remained standoffish though, shyly staying an arm's length from us while she watched. It broke my heart some nights, seeing her stand alone, fingers held in a tight clasp, her mouth twisting while contemplating. I tried not to let it bother me, knowing what they'd been through. And as Jericho had told me more than once, *time takes time*. I believed that. I'd wait. When Thomas returned to his sister, taking her hand, I told them, "Love you."

They were gone then, footsteps descending, replaced with muffled noise from their bedroom and the low chatter of Jericho's voice while he tucked them in. I'd check on them in twenty minutes, expecting to find them wide awake, still stirring as the nighttime excitement slowly drained.

Tracy pointed to one of the records, scanning the pages to develop a story behind that single bruise on Karol Witney's arm. My hope was that in understanding her past, it might lead us to identify what happened during her dive.

By the time we'd reached the Witneys' fifth year of marriage, their final year, we'd tracked down four more visits made to hospitals and urgent care centers. Aside from the X-ray images, there were no other pictures taken of the injuries. None. We'd also started to recognize some similarities across what the doctors wrote, each report telling a tale of clumsiness that involved a household accident. A few doctors did raise questions though but did not file reports with the authorities. Why? The question made my skin crawl. Surely just one doctor or nurse saw the spousal abuse, a developing history of it?

When I peppered a sheet of paper with addresses, I saw it. I saw why. Karol Witney never went to the same hospital or urgent care. The visits were made at different locations. The only reason we were able to connect the dots was the home address. It had remained the same. There was something else too. In all of the visits, Karol Witney was never alone. She was in the company of her husband, Jim Witney. Why visit different hospitals, different urgent care centers?

Should I shift our investigation to who Jim Witney was? It was a question I asked myself but a question I already knew the answer to. I needed to shift our investigation to who Jim Witney was, beginning with where he was at the time of his wife's death. How about warrants or a police record? Was there anything I could leverage if I wanted to question him? From the discussion and paperwork provided by the dive captain, it was only the sorority sisters on the boat. There were no husbands or boyfriends. Just the women. When I searched his name, I was surprised to find it appearing in police reports, some dating back years, his signature changing slightly over time. He'd been the reporter of them and signed each before filing them. Jim Witney was a patrolman for the Chicago Police Department.

Chicago was far from the Outer Banks, the distance making him an unlikely suspect. But with what we uncovered about the hospital records, that didn't stop the questions and I couldn't rule him out just yet. Did Jim Witney flash his badge when the doctors and nursing staff tended to his wife? Did he wear his patrol uniform to the emergency rooms. Was it to intimidate? Maybe it was to convince them that it was just an accident. Nothing more. Whatever it was, it must have been enough to dissuade them from suspecting spousal abuse.

This case was less than a day old and it was already making me sick to my stomach. It was making me sad too, Karol Witney's troubled life ending so tragically. How great must she have felt when leaving Chicago? Her heart and soul lifting with relief when boarding the airplane? The excited anticipation of days away from a toxic marriage, and the glorious rise when arriving in the barrier islands. I wanted to think it was an escape for her. That she was leaving him forever.

Speculation wasn't knowing, and at this point we couldn't know her plans. The belongings she brought included shoes and some slacks, a single beachy suit, and two dressier outfits for a night out. There was makeup and other cosmetics such as contact lenses, but she'd packed only enough for the sorority sister trip. Still, to be away from that house and from her husband. How wonderful. I think that was the part that sickened me most, the irony. She'd come to the Outer Banks for a respite from an abusive home, and somewhere in the tranquility beneath the sea, death caught up to her.

FOUR

Morning dew collected on the top of my shoes. The shortcut across the parking lot included a grassy knoll, workers pruning the trees, seeding the lawns, prepping the grounds for the coming fall season. I said my good mornings, my breath foggy, laptop bag weighing heavy on my shoulder. I wrestled the station doors open and flipped my badge shield-side out, overhead lights glinting off the metal. Our station manager waved me through as she attended to the visitors waiting on the benches. My desk was beyond the front, a gate separating the area made available to the public and the detectives.

"There's a visitor for you," Alice said, the gate clapping shut. She handed me a note. "I took the liberty of getting his information from the station sign-in."

I eyed the cubicles, seeing Tracy hadn't arrived yet. Long night. She probably overslept. My desk was empty too. "There's nobody there?"

Alice moved close enough for me to catch a whiff of hairspray, the smell of it always too strong. I wrinkled my nose, turning away as she tried whispering, "It's the husband of that Chicago girl."

"Jim Witney?" Alice showed me the sign-in sheet, the name at the very top in sloppy handwriting.

"Witney was her name, right?" she asked. When I nodded, she tapped her finger where the visitor put their license plate number, "He included his Illinois plates along with a CPD badge number and phone number."

"He's here already? We just contacted him." I shifted with surprise, thinking Jim Witney must have taken an overnight flight from Chicago. But Alice mentioned Illinois plates which meant he'd driven to the Outer Banks. How many hours did that take? The pause in my reaction had Alice looking wide-eyed. I had to be sure. "You mean *Karol Witney's* husband?"

"That's right," she answered sternly. She pointed toward the hallway, saying, "And I've already put him in interview room one for you."

"We know that Samantha called him as soon as his wife's body was brought to the morgue. That means, he must have driven straight through the night to get here so quickly." I dropped my backpack, feeling immediate relief as the strap stopped digging into my shoulder.

"Probably so." A stout nod, eyelids unblinking. "He showed up a half hour ago and asked to speak with you."

"He asked for me? I wonder if he saw Samantha already." I checked my notes out of habit, seeing the phone number recovered from Karol Witney's phone was the same as what was listed on the sheet of paper in front of me. But that was a day ago and Chicago was far. Nobody would have expected him to be here so soon. "Thank you, Alice."

"What's going on?" Tracy asked, entering the station, eyes puffy. I motioned for her to follow, passing our desks, bags dropping onto chairs with a plunk. We didn't stop and continued walking in the direction of the interview room. "Who's in there?"

"Karol Witney's husband." I handed her the sign-in-sheet before reaching the door to the interrogation room. She hurried to follow, her laptop perched in one arm, the sign-in sheet stuffed between fingers as she typed the plate and phone number with her free hand.

"Wow! He got here fast," she commented, a question in her expression. "Is he a suspect based on what we saw in the morgue?"

I shook my head. "We know Karol Witney arrived from Chicago alone. No husband or family. Just her. I'd think he was in Chicago at the time of her death. Then again, that doesn't necessarily mean anything."

The mystery of what was behind my comment swept the sleepiness from her face. "Murder for hire?"

"How about we just get a profile started." I didn't comment further. There was history of abuse, which instantly put Jim Witney at the top of the list.

———

Our interview rooms were used for interrogation. However, we weren't allowed to call them that anymore. Even if that is exactly what we were doing. It was our job to get to the truth. Sometimes that meant talking for hours. Many hours. I suspected Jim Witney of spousal abuse, the evidence clear. But his wife was in the Outer Banks while he was in Chicago, which meant that he had an alibi that was a thousand miles long.

"Mr. Witney," I said, extending a hand.

"Detective," he answered, standing briefly, and dipped his chin toward me and then to Tracy.

"It's a shame to come to the Outer Banks under such circumstances." When his hand touched mine, I died a little, revolted by how I suspected he'd used his status in law enforcement to get away with abusing his wife. I sat across from him, asking, "Have you been here before?"

"Never. My first time."

"Is that right?" I continued with the small talk. "Safe flight from Chicago?"

"I drove here, ma'am," he replied.

We knew that tidbit of information already, but I wanted to hear him say it. As he sat, I studied everything I could see, looking for defensive wounds. His hair was curly and light red in color, his eyebrows so fair they were almost nonexistent. His skin was fair as well, cheeks and forehead flecked by boyish freckles. His eyes were bright blue like sapphires, the whites of them reddened, which was probably from the fourteen hours of driving he'd done to get here. At just under six foot, he wasn't much taller than me, his build on the thinner side. To look at him, I didn't get the impression of what he was or who he became in the privacy of his home. Then again, it wasn't as though evil had a face. I knew it had a temperament but saw no evidence of that on his hands and arms. There were no wounds or bruising on his knuckles. There was nothing about him that spoke of cruelty or murder. But what I could not see, I felt. In his company, the hairs on the back of my neck stood on end.

As we took to our seats, he went on to say, "I hope it was okay to meet. I wanted to discuss my wife's death with you."

"You met with the medical examiner?" I scrolled through my phone, texting Samantha the same question.

He glanced at my phone and then to me. "Just the initial call is all."

"I am sorry for your loss." This was a courtesy meeting, my condolences important. Deep down, I wanted this to be an interrogation. "How can we help?"

"How did she die?"

I eased back in the interview room chair, listening to the shallow breaths of Karol's husband. Tracy sat next to me working her laptop, pausing long enough to show the opened medical reports in case our questions were to delve on the past.

He noticed the exchange and showed us his badge before

reframing the question. "Cop to cop. Is there any reason to believe the charter company is at fault for the accident that caused her death?"

"We haven't called it an accident," Tracy quickly said.

He reeled back in his seat, frowning. "I thought her death was an accident. That maybe the charter's guide was at fault."

Was he looking to litigate? My phone buzzed with a text response from Samantha, telling me she'd held a full conversation with the husband. That meant Jim Witney knew everything we knew about his wife's death. "Sir, as I am sure the medical examiner explained, your wife's death was a result of drowning. That is all we know at this time."

Jim Witney stared blankly at a cup of coffee which Alice must have gotten for him. It was clear that he didn't like our answers. He stared at a lump of powdered creamer circling slowly. When the clump fell apart, dissolving and becoming whatever it becomes in the presence of hot coffee, he looked up at us. He flashed a quick smile, lifting the cup with thankful regard. The politeness was brief though, his expression turning grim, asking, "Did my wife suffer?"

Silence descended between us, and after a moment, Jim Witney frowned. His expression eased as he glanced at me and Tracy, and to the folder beneath my hands. In that moment, I think I might have seen understanding in his eyes. He was aware that we'd already started an investigation. An investigation which included him. His gaze shifted to the door, questions about his wife's history of injuries perching on the tip of my tongue. We'd uncovered five years of medical records which strongly implied Jim Witney had abused his wife. And now he was asking if she suffered. The gall!

"When would that have been?"

Tracy's eyelids flicked briefly at my question. Unshaken by my response, Jim Witney sipped his coffee, steam rising into his face. I wanted him to know that we knew. I wanted him to squirm.

He didn't reply, knowing better. "You spoke with the medical examiner. You scheduled to meet with her today?"

"Not yet." He shifted, leaning forward as if to stand. "I'll do that. Thank you."

I wanted him to stay and offered some information. "I can't tell you the medical details about her drowning." Jim Witney sat back down, lowering himself slowly. "There was air remaining in her tank, but the respirator wasn't in her mouth. Her mask was removed too."

"None of that makes any sense." His frown returned, creating a rut above his nose. "She loved to dive."

"You do a lot of diving in Chicago?" Tracy's eyelids flicked again. I couldn't help the snark in my tone, a feeling of disgust driving my voice.

Jim Witney opened a pack of cigarettes and snapped them with a sharp clap. One appeared above the others like he'd performed a magician's trick. He gestured with the pack, asking, "Do you mind?"

"Actually, I do," Tracy answered before he could finish. There were some interrogations where we gave them whatever they wanted. Food. Drinks. A cigarette when the pressures called for it. She'd picked up the vibe of being firm, stringent even. Tracy bent the truth then, adding, "It's a smoke-free building."

He tucked the cigarette back into place, shifting uncomfortably. "We dove Lake Michigan mostly. Karol more regularly than me. She had enough experience that she'd been asked to work with some of the local charters."

"Lake diving?" Tracy asked, typing. "The ocean is different. Did your wife have any experience sea diving?"

"Oh for sure. Plenty of it." A faint smile. "We've been diving a while now. Last year was Key West. The year before that was the Jersey Shore."

Tracy sat up abruptly, shoulders straight. She handed me the station sign-in sheet and slid her laptop between us, turning the screen enough for me to see a traffic camera picture of a truck. I opened the note, the piece of paper with Alice's chicken scratch, letters and numbers scrawled hurriedly across it. I compared it to the license plate in the picture. They were the same. "Mr. Witney, when did you arrive?"

"Arrive?" He shook his head, confused by my question. Tracy tapped the keyboard to show there were no records of toll roads used in the last week. No records of his license plate numbers recorded on any major highways. "To the Outer Banks?"

"That's correct, sir." The muscles in my legs tensed as I sat up and stared.

Jim Witney continued to shake his head, his mouth shaped in an upside down smile. "I don't know exactly. There was the call about Karol. I guess I got some stuff for the car, the long drive, and then got on the road."

"When was that exactly?" He chewed on a reply, hesitating. Here was a man who went to great lengths to take his wife to different hospitals and urgent care facilities to hide his abuse. He'd continued that diligence in his travels to the Outer Banks, avoiding every toll road there was between Chicago and the Outer Banks. What he didn't know was that Wright Memorial Bridge traffic cameras picked him up just as he left Point Harbor to cross over Currituck Sound. So why avoid the toll roads? I zoomed in on the picture of his truck, the date and time of when the picture was taken. "When did you leave Chicago?"

"What? Maybe twenty hours ago," he answered, his voice breaking. He blinked fast as though his eyes were stung by tears. The smile that had appeared earlier when talking about how they met while diving wrecks seemed genuine. And I am sure that at some point in their lives they *were* in love. I didn't buy the emotion I was seeing now though. He nodded. "Yeah, that's about right."

"Help me out with something." I didn't show the photograph immediately, feeling like a cat with a mouse in its clutches. I didn't want to let the effect of its power fade. Jim Witney sipped at his coffee, playing it cool while I turned the laptop around and pointed at the windshield. "That's your truck? And that's you behind the wheel?"

"It is." He answered without noticing my fingers covering the camera's date and time stamp. When I moved my hand, his brow bounced with acknowledgment.

"This shows you arrived in the Outer Banks the day before your wife's death?"

This wasn't the first time I'd seen abuse in a relationship. Tragically, it wasn't the first time I'd seen murder resulting from it either. But it was the first time I had a suspect across from me who was a cop, a person who knew what to do and what to say to hide what he'd done. The picture of him was what I needed. Jim Witney was a suspect in his wife's murder. He didn't try to deny it or make up a story. I mean, anyone else would have said a hundred different things. But not another cop. Instead, Jim Witney tried to reason. "Look, I was here already. I came here to talk with Karol." His voice shook, and he might have even squirmed a little. It wasn't often I got enjoyment in questioning a suspect. This morning I did. "We had a bad fight last week before she flew down here."

"The bruising around her wrist?" I slid a picture from the folder across the table, handing the laptop back to Tracy.

Another shrug, uncertainty on his face. "Maybe? Yeah. I don't remember if I grabbed her." He took his cellphone and tapped the screen to place a call.

I motioned for him to put it down, glaring at it when he didn't. "Was that your cellphone our medical examiner called?" Karol Witney's husband stared blankly at it. When he lowered the phone, lips buttoned tight, I saw that he was refusing to answer. In his travels, he hadn't considered the cell towers. He hadn't considered that when in range of one of them, a cellphone will perform a kind of test connection, a ping it places with the tower which includes an identifier. There were more than a few cell towers for us to check in the Outer Banks. There were surely more in the thousand miles he drove to get here, all with dates and times of his travels. Between the picture of his truck, the traffic camera's date and time stamp, and the potential cell tower pings which Tracy was already querying on her laptop, there couldn't be anything for Jim Witney to say. Well, almost anything.

"You're trying to make me out to be a suspect," he said, voice raised. He raised his hand to say more, but lowered it, the emotion passing. Sitting back with a lean, he snapped his wrist again, a cigarette appearing. He didn't seek permission this time and struck a match. The tip of it turned to ash, a puff of sulfur and burnt tobacco reaching my nose. When he finished a drag, he added, "I'm not going to sit here while you imply that I killed my wife. So, the next time you want to talk to me, I'll have a lawyer."

FIVE

Jim Witney had come to the Outer Banks and to our police station to discuss his wife's death. But when did he actually arrive in the Outer Banks? On record, he'd stated getting here sometime after her death. He'd done well to avoid the highways with the toll roads. It was the cell tower pings that told us where he'd been as well as when. Tracy used his cellphone pings like breadcrumbs dropped in a forest, the string of them plotting his course from Chicago to the Outer Banks. We had accurate coordinates and times of his travels, which showed that Jim Witney was in the Outer Banks the day his wife was killed. Who saw him? Better yet, what was he doing? There was the abuse too. It was all enough to establish Jim Witney as a suspect, to provide a likely motive, the love he held for his wife having become septic. But it wasn't yet enough to hold him. For that, I'd need more.

Tracy got the names of the women in the sorority, the ones who'd come to the Outer Banks for a fun escape from their daily lives. There was a lawyer and a doctor in the group, one of them from California, the other from Detroit. Three of the women were married, two raising children. One of the sorority sisters owned a five and dime store that sold general merchandise. She lived in

North Carolina and was within driving distance of us. Janine Scott was another of the sorority sisters in the state and was a native to the Outer Banks. Born and raised near Kitty Hawk, it was her name on the charter's pink slip. Janine Scott coordinated the sorority sister reunion, choosing the late season beach sunshine, the boardwalk, and restaurants to bring her sisters together. With Karol Witney's death, I could only imagine how terrible Janine Scott must be feeling. Since Tracy did the heavy lift on the sorority sisters, this was her find and I gladly handed over the keys to the car. It was a rainy and dreary day, the type of day I'd prefer riding shotgun than driving south on Route 12.

Though traffic was sparse, Tracy's foot stayed light on the gas pedal, a few cars crossing the yellow line to pass us. There were annoyed looks coming our direction. Along with a particular finger gesture that was uncalled for. It disappeared when I lifted my badge to the window. I motioned to Tracy to speed up, thinking the rain was making her overly cautious. "Nothing wrong with doing the speed limit."

Eyelids rising, she glanced at me and then to the road. "Well, I *am* going the speed limit." Motor revving, she looked at the dash to see she was below it. "Okay, so *now* I am."

Plump raindrops ticked against the windshield and opened into small, watery blooms. The wind stretched the perfectly formed circles, the blobby shapes swept clean by the wipers. A moment later, fresh drops littered the view again, the wipers repeating with another cleaning. The monotony of it felt a little like this case. Not that the case wasn't important, but the conversations around it were the same. It was also all that Tracy and I talked about, and I think that bothered me. Not just a little. It bothered me a lot. I'd come to the Outer Banks to find my daughter. A last chance, a single clue bringing me east. I'd reached a point where I'd thought she was a million miles from any part of the world I was. I was wrong. Now that we were together, I couldn't help but want more.

I'm not sure how, but we'd gotten to a place where work was about all we discussed. She'd make small talk at times about Thomas and Tabitha, but nothing more. I don't know why that happened. Especially after we'd started getting close. Somewhere along the way, the momentum changed. I didn't like it. "Penny for your thoughts?" I said, borrowing one of Jericho's favorite lines. She glanced at me and then reached for her coffee. The top of it slipped, the car's cupholder greedily holding on to it. "I'll get that for you."

"A penny," she replied, taking a sip, steam fogging glasses that were new. She wasn't wearing contact lenses today like she usually did. They were shiny purple frames with square lenses. Her hair style had changed too. It wasn't as long as mine anymore, the waves relaxed and dyed a darker color. She wore a blouse and slacks with a pair of short heels, the business attire more formal. Her entire look was changing. How did I miss that? She took a shaky breath, answering, "Sorority sister case. That's what I've started calling this case—"

"Tracy," I interrupted, a hollow feeling dropping in my stomach. I couldn't help but think this was my fault. She had a bad breakup recently with a woman who was on my team. She'd moved to Philadelphia to take a job working for the FBI, the move ending her relationship with Tracy. That's when my daughter got quiet. Maybe quiet is the wrong word. Hyper-focused! That's what happened. She'd become more focused on all things relating to her career. I dared a touch. A gentle brush of my hand across her arm. "I was asking how *you* are doing?"

Eyelids fluttering. "Oh. As in, you want to talk?"

I bit my lip, hopeful she'd agree. "Yeah, if that's okay?" Hope turned to nerves while I eyed the phone, seeing we were ten miles from our destination. Had I just made the remaining miles uncomfortable? Perhaps. I drank my coffee, the burn growing in my chest. When Tracy said nothing, I added, "We don't have—"

"No. It's okay," she said, shaking her head. In that moment

with the sun fighting through the rain clouds, there was a shine that turned her face bright; in it, I saw Tracy's father. There were times when she looked so much like him that it hurt. He'd died before she ever got to meet him. He'd died after following me to the Outer Banks to search for our daughter. A pang thumped deep inside me like a gravestone toppling. It was grief for him. Guilt too, believing his death might have been preventable. "Casey? You're staring."

"Sorry." The break of sunshine was gone in a blink, the storm clouds swallowing the sun like a pill. "For a second, you looked like your dad."

"I was thinking about him the other day," she commented, the words giving me pause.

"You were?" My voice trembled with unexpected sentiment.

"Someday you'll tell me—" she couldn't finish, emotion catching her voice. She snatched her coffee, the magic elixir for all moments difficult or otherwise. When she was done, she added, "You wouldn't mind telling me about him. We could do dinner one night. A bottle of wine?"

"Two bottles." I held up two fingers. "I'd be honored to tell you everything about your father. Even about our first kiss."

"Yep, got it, I'm good," she said, the whites of her eyes growing with a laugh.

"Nichelle?" It was the name of the woman who'd moved to Philadelphia. Tracy's smile fell, silence filling the car, save for the wipers. "I was just curious if you've talked to her since the move?"

"Uh-uh. Not since she left." She chewed on the corner of her mouth and looked at me with hurt in her eyes. "You?"

A short nod, reluctant. I kept my reply to a few words. "We talked about a case she's working."

"That's good that she's busy." Tracy spun the wheel, turn signal clicking. It was the second to last street. "I'm glad for her."

"It'll take time, Tracy. Maybe you could get out more with your friends?" I cringed hearing the inexperience in my words.

Who was I to offer advice? I'd missed too many seasons in Tracy's life and had never mothered her through the firsts. No first dates. No first loves. Certainly not her first end-of-the-world soul-crushing breakup. Unfiltered, my lips kept moving though, spouting another cringe-worthy suggestion, "How about one of them apps you swipe up or right or down?"

"Really?" she laughed.

"God, I know." I rolled my eyes, embarrassing myself. "Terrible, right?"

"We're almost there," she said, bailing me out. When the car stopped at the next intersection, she reached across the center console and took my hand. "Thanks for trying though. I appreciate you for it."

"I'm still learning." Her eyes were glassy, the red traffic light shining in them. When it turned green, it cued her to let go. "I'll do better next time."

"You're doing fine," she replied. "I wouldn't want you to change a thing."

We turned at the next stop sign, my thoughts shifting to the case while searching house numbers mounted on the mailboxes. "That one there."

"With the silver car?"

"That's the one," I confirmed, matching the address on my phone. We parked on the street, the sorority sister's house stilted with two cars parked beneath, one silver, the other plum. It had cedar shingles covering the roof, curtains drawn in all the windows, the front door opened. Rain peppered my face and shoulders, the pavement gritty beneath my shoes. "Careful where you step."

A woman with a child appeared behind a screen door. They had matching blonde hair with auburn highlights in the curls. She put the child down, patting her behind, the girl giving us a curious look before running away. The woman wore sweatpants and white tennis shoes with an oversized flannel shirt that was partially unbuttoned. She jerked a kitchen towel from a shoulder and began drying her hands. Before we reached the steps, she propped the screen door and poked her head out, blinking against the falling rain. "Can I help you?"

I raised my badge to show who we were. She retreated behind the screen, the front door opening wider. It wasn't an invitation inside. There was screaming and yelling, children's voices pouring from behind her, the inside of the house sounding like a daycare. "Ma'am, we'd like to speak with you about Karol Witney's death."

"You're here for Karol?" she asked. Her lower lip trembled, chin quivering until a boy appeared from behind her. He was four or five and wrapped his arms around her leg. Another child followed, older by a year perhaps, her cheeks wet with tears. Mrs. Scott's thoughts about Karol vanished as she glared down at them, scolding, "Back inside. You can settle whatever it is yourselves."

"I'm sorry to interrupt your day." I felt like we were intruding. "It'll take a few minutes is all."

Mrs. Scott swiped her eyes and flashed us a welcoming look, saying, "Oh please. I could use the break." She opened the screen door, the hinges creaking. The inside foyer was small, the house a split-level with steps leading up to another level, while another staircase went down. There was a blur of children running, one stopping at the bottom step to look up at us. Mrs. Scott shooed them away. "Nancy, mind your brother and sister."

"We'll keep this short," I assured while following her up the stairs to a living room that was blocked off by a gate, the handle childproof.

She fumbled with the latch before it snapped open, turning briefly. "I hate these things. Adult-proof is what they are."

I shook my head and pinched a bruise on my fingertip. "I've recently become aware."

A warming smile. "You have! Boy or a girl?"

"Both actually," Tracy answered from behind me, helping to

ease into the conversation. "'Two Little Souls'. That's the name of the news story that went viral. You might have read it?"

Mrs. Scott turned to face us, unaffected by the hollering rising from below. "The brother and sister lost at sea?" I nodded with a feeling of bashfulness and pride. She covered her mouth with one hand and braced my shoulder with the other. "Bless you. My husband and I followed that story."

"Three?" I asked, having seen pictures of the children hanging on the walls. Mrs. Scott showed four fingers and placed a hand over her middle. "Congratulations to you."

"We just found out." She shook her head, adding, "I would have never gone on that trip if I'd known."

"Dangers when diving?" I made small talk as she led us to a couch. We sat, a spring beneath my bottom crunching. Mrs. Scott took to a loveseat across from us, crossing her legs and perching her hands on a knee.

"I don't even know if it's dangerous, but why chance it."

"The dive. All of you went scuba diving?" I held my phone, a list of questions based on what we learned from the charter boat.

She paused as if frozen, the moment lasting. "I... I still can't believe she's gone."

"I know this must be difficult—"

"It's just so surreal, you know," she interrupted, eyes glistening. Her focus returned then, asking, "I'm sorry, what were your questions?"

"Did all of you go scuba diving?" Tracy asked.

"That's right. We went diving first to see one of the wrecks." She shrugged at the comment and made a face. "I'd already been to all the wrecks."

"You and your husband?" Tracy asked, seeking clarification.

"Uh-huh," she said, getting up and leaving. She motioned to the kitchen. "Dreary weather. Coffee or tea? Something hot?"

"I'm fine, thank you," I said while Tracy shook her head. Mrs. Scott worked a coffee maker, the kind with pods that brewed instant cups. She turned enough to show a finger over her lips like it was a secret, saying, "A cup a day. Can you believe it. That's all I'm allowed."

"Is your husband around today?" I asked, thinking it rude to ask, but it was necessary. There were no pictures of him amongst the children's photographs. That wasn't uncommon though. Children have a way of becoming the center of everything in a house.

She shook her head. "Traveling again." Eyes rolling, she added, "Always traveling."

"If we could get his name and number?" Tracy asked. A look of concern washed across Janine Scott's face, Tracy clarifying, "In case we can't get hold of you."

"Oh, sure, I can do that." She worked the coffee machine, pressing buttons.

"When you were diving, did anything happen that encouraged your group to stop the dive?" The smell of brewing coffee warmed the room. Mrs. Scott saw me looking and dipped her chin with a nod. "A small cup would be great. The group's switch to snorkeling?"

Footsteps thundered below, rumbling through the walls and floor, a child squealing playfully. I'd expected it to be noisy, and it was noisy. But none of it fazed Mrs. Scott. She brought back a cup for me and for her, sitting as though we were in the complete silence of an interview room. "I think it was just the boredom. There was nothing more to it." She slurped with a wince, the heat touching her lips. "Like I said, I'd seen them all. Gracie and Sophia and Tyra didn't really want to go diving at all."

"They were who suggested to end the dive?" Tracy asked, typing the names.

Mrs. Scott mulled over the question, gaze shifting to the ceiling. "Probably Gracie. She can be pushy like that."

"The group then returned to the boat, along with your guide?" Tracy asked.

"That's right. We changed out of the gear and then hung out

in the water." She leaned forward and winked. "We didn't do much snorkeling. Too busy talking."

"Who didn't come back with you?" Her smile faded. "Besides Karol?"

Her gaze returned to the ceiling, lips moving while she considered who was where. "Wait! I've got pictures I can share." She grabbed hold of a tablet and opened a photo app. "I've got them all linked to my account."

On the tablet we saw pictures of the dive, dozens of them tiled across the screen. The first half showed the sorority sisters beneath the water, their faces covered with masks, and their bodies suspended by a string of bubbles spouting from the regulators.

"May I?" She gladly handed me the tablet and cupped her coffee with both hands.

"Scroll up?" Tracy asked, eager to see the next page. The tiled photographs were above the water this time, masks partially on, some worn like a necklace, the women grouped. Tracy pointed to a body behind them, saying, "I see the guide there."

"He's stayed in his scuba gear." The story the younger man had given us was that he'd brought the girls back before returning to Karol.

I counted the bodies, expecting a discrepancy. Mrs. Scott was taking the pictures, and we already knew Karol continued the dive. But there was one other person missing. I scrolled back to the previous pictures and pointed one of the scuba divers out. "Ma'am, this woman here. She has a similar hair color as yours."

"That'd be Tina Walsh. She was a year behind me in school. She lives across the bay on the mainland." When she finished answering, she frowned. "Why are you here? I thought Karol died from an accident?"

"The interviews are a standard practice in an investigation," Tracy answered, picking a canned response. Mrs. Scott half shook her head, half nodded, seeming to agree.

I showed the first set of photographs with all of the women scuba diving. "Everyone accounted for, including Karol Witney and your dive guide." Flipping the screen to show the sorority sisters together on the surface, I added, "Everyone accounted for except Karol Witney and Tina Walsh."

"Will you look at that?" she said, her tone questioning. Mrs. Scott took the tablet, paging back and forth to confirm it. "In all the confusion, I never noticed she wasn't with us."

"When did she come back to the boat?" Tracy asked.

She began to shake her head, her voice filled with disappointment. "Now I remember. Fog brain," she tapped the side of her head comically. When we didn't see the humor, she leveled her voice, answering, "Tina helped the divemaster bring Karol back to the boat."

Noise was building, footsteps ascending the lower stairs. "Thank you, ma'am," I began, feeling it was time to move on. "Would you forward the pictures?"

"Certainly, yes." Her voice shook. "Is Tina in trouble?"

I shook my head to ease her concerns while showing Tracy the time. "We'll give her a visit after this." Tracy agreed and began to work the directions on her phone. Mrs. Scott continued to look troubled, my wanting to answer her, *that depends on whether Tina did anything or not.* I didn't say what I was thinking, but instead answered, "We only need to ask her a few questions."

The miles from Janine Scott's house went by fast. Tracy was in the driver seat while I worked the case to catch up with Samantha. Based on what Janine Scott said, Tina Walsh was next on our list. Borrowing Tracy's sticker-covered laptop, I scrolled down to the map and directions to the sorority sister's home. The interview with Janine Scott bothered me like a nagging tune that gets stuck in your head. I couldn't put my finger on why either.

If anything, I should have felt more compassionate. She was a mother without very much support, her husband traveling. It was easy to see that she was busy and tired. With Thomas and Tabitha, a few meltdowns endured, I'd been on the brink of exhaustion. I know what that feels like. Still, her reaction to my questions? Karol Witney was her friend. Her sorority sister. Janine had also been there to witness the recovery of her friend's body from the ocean. There was a lack of emotion that bothered me. Maybe they just weren't as close as some of the other sorority sisters? Or maybe Janine Scott was simply just that tired?

"Make a left up here." The turn signal clicking, Tracy spun the wheel. "It won't take us long to get to Tina Walsh's place."

"I can do that." She rubbed her belly, adding, "Kinda hungry. Wanna stop after?"

"Sure." The mention of food stirred an awakening, a guttural rumble that made Tracy giggle. "What's your take on Janine Scott? Any thoughts?"

Her eyelids popped open, her head rocking back and forth. "There's no way I could take care of that many kids. Uh-uh! Can't even imagine it."

I felt a tiring laugh, the memory of exhausting diaper duty and cleaning crayoned walls. "Tracy, I meant about the case? Janine Scott's reaction about her friend's death? Not like I'd expect with them being sorority sisters. Take a right up here."

"Hmm. I mean, it's been like what, only a few days, right?" Tracy commented, chin rising to stare at the rearview mirror. "She's probably still in shock is all."

Tracy's hands tightened around the steering wheel suddenly, her muscles bracing.

"What is it—" But I never finished asking my question. A thundering boom swallowed the air and starry darkness jolted me sideways as glass shattered all around us. The blackness came next.

SIX

Blood. That taste. There was no mistaking it. It was like old pennies, the stink of metal wafting across my face. Eyelids fluttering, the seatbelt strap dug into my shoulder and across my middle, the edge of it like a blade. Was I conscious? The inside of my head felt congested and swollen. It pounded mercilessly with ungodly pressure. Temples pulsing, my eyes bulged like they were going to shoot across the dashboard. The inside of the car was all wrong too. The gravity of it flipped with the horn blaring as gray smoke floated around us. Pain rifled down my spine like a gunshot, a short scream spilling from my bloodied mouth. It wasn't the blood and the injuries that bothered me though. It was the stark blackness. A starless dream. I had no idea what had happened to us.

"Tracy?" She was driving. Wasn't she? An interview. We'd gone to talk to one of the sorority sisters. Tina? No. Her name wasn't Tina. Her name was Janine. Janine Scott. The roads were wet. It'd been raining and Tracy was driving. I dared to shake my head and clear whatever was plaguing the moments leading to now. "Tracy! Babe!"

"Huh," she coughed, a whimper trailing. She was conscious. Or somewhat conscious. "Wha...?"

"I think we were in an accident." Another cough, the back of my throat stinging with a chemical bite. I gagged at the thickening smoke, acrid like burning rubber. A fire? My heart leapt and my eyelids sprang open. "Tracy girl? Can you move?"

"Do you smell that—" she began to ask, an explosion silencing her words. Glass nuggets showered around us, clinking against the pavement and roof of the car. Someone hammered at the driver-side door, metal ringing as it was wrenched open. "Who are—?"

"Tracy!" Light shined through the hazy smoke, hands reaching into the car. An arm crossed Tracy's middle, fingers curling around the seatbelt strap binding against her body. A click, she fell hard onto the ceiling as another pair of hands tried cradling her head. Flames crackling, a tire blew with a boom loud enough to make my ears ring. "Tracy!"

"Cover her," a voice yelled distantly. My window disappeared in a gust of glassy rain, pummeling like hailstones that fell around my head. Heat followed and climbed fiercely as I saw Tracy dragged away, the heels of her shoes scraping, the left one slipping from her foot. "Get the other one!"

"Help me!" I screamed when the first burn visited, the belt buckle sticking. Yellow and blue flames danced close enough to blow me a kiss. The fire grew fast, stealing the air from my lungs, a trapped fright building like I'd never known before. I was alive for the moment, wriggling and twisting, gritting my teeth as the seatbelt used for safety kept me locked in place. In a moment, I was going to be cooked alive. "My seatbelt! It's stuck."

"Casey!" Tracy shrilled, her voice like a knife through my soul. A mother should never hear their child scream like that. "Hurry! Get her out, please!"

My eyes watered terribly from the fumes, blurring everything. There was oil and gasoline and who knows what else from the dozen other fluids in a car. A blade crossed my chin, daylight glinting against its edge, an arm placing it carefully beneath. It was a man's arm with a heart-shaped tattoo behind the wrist, the name "Clara" inside with two dates. As he began to cut the seat-belt, I read the inky months and years beneath the name. Clara was only three when she died. A toddler. Did this man lose his daughter? The strap tore free, and the roof of the car came at me violently. There were hands gripping my shoulders and upper arms, jerking me from the car I'd only just started making monthly payments on.

"Tracy?" I gagged and nearly retched. There were red and blue lights surrounding us, and fresh air blowing across my sweaty skin to cool me instantly. I looked over at Tracy and felt relief flood my body at the sight of her alive. Firehoses ran alongside me with firefighters bracing as they doused the flames. Fingers crawling, I found Tracy's and gripped them tight. "We're okay."

"We were hit!" she said, voice choked by the smoke. A memory flashed like a flame, her hands on the steering wheel, knuckles turning white. She sat up, pushing at a paramedic's hands. The look on her face took my voice, a new kind of fright setting in its place. "Casey? It was a white SUV that hit us."

"An SUV. It came from behind us." I sat up, a paramedic guarding against it, a bothered look appearing when I ignored him. Black smoke billowed, the height of the plume dizzying. The road was blocked on both sides, traffic standing still behind patrol cars. It was already impossible to distinguish anything resembling my car. Or what was my car, metal bending and the paint peeling. "There's no other car."

"It must have took off after it hit us." Tears stained her face, the incident fresh. Though it pained me to see her so agitated, the details of what happened were needed. She swiped errantly to dry her eyes, stare shifting with hard concern to my forehead. She motioned to it, saying, "Casey, there's blood. You hit your head."

"You saw them in the rearview mirror!" Another image flashed in my mind, a crash reverberating across my skull. A paramedic dabbed my head as the images became clearer. We'd finished the interview with Janine Scott and had gone to see another sorority sister. Tina Walsh lived on the mainland, which took us across the bridge. At one point after crossing, we'd made a turn. That's when we were hit. But I never saw the car. I turned around, looking at the road. It was narrow like our own Route 12, but we weren't in the Outer Banks. I looked at Tracy, nodding. "I remember it. Did you see a license plate?"

She shook her face, mouth twisting with a dimple showing. "Just the car."

I brushed the paramedic's hand from my shoulder and got to my knees, eager to stand. I braced the lump on my hip, the gun holster in place, my gun secure. My badge and identification were also safe from the fire. "Help me up!"

"My laptop," Tracy cried, firelight dancing in her eyes as she staggered to her feet. She clutched my hands and squeezed my fingers, turning them purple. The right-front tire burst, the rubber engulfed. She shook her head. "Shit, what caused the car to catch fire?"

"Looks like fuel spilled when it rolled," a firefighter answered, his reflective coat and boots stained with soot. He pointed out a section of road that had been scraped a few yards back. "A hot catalytic converter or the car roof throwing sparks."

I waved over a patrol officer, explaining, "We were hit from behind by a white SUV." I looked to Tracy to confirm, some of the memories still shredded, torn into pieces and not quite whole. "I want an APB on a hit and run."

"Plate numbers? Driver?" the patrol officer asked. She chewed on the end of a pen, glancing at me and then Tracy.

"Uh-uh. But there was no warning. No horns. Nothing," Tracy's voice was ragged with a heavy breath.

The tip of the officer's pen danced as she wrote, moving fast to keep up.

"We're okay." I held Tracy's head close to mine, a shudder rocking me. Glass shattering, metal whining. Heat from the fire forced us back. A team of two firefighters dragged a second hose across the pavement but it did little to help. What if we hadn't gotten out? I couldn't think like that and kissed Tracy's cheek before wrapping my arms around her. "You're okay."

The sound of shoes clopping in a run against the pavement made us pull apart to see who was approaching. "You're both okay?" Jericho's voice was pitched high and shaking. His face was sweaty with a deep frown. "What the hell happened?"

"How?" I began to ask, stopping as he looked for injuries. His focus shifted to the paramedic's, who gave her approval. I faced the paramedic, asking, "You know Jericho?"

She nudged toward my badge, saying, "I'm Outer Banks born and raised. Everyone knows the sheriff."

"Thank you," I mouthed to her as Jericho took hold, his hands gliding up and down to see if I was okay. He hadn't been the sheriff in a long time, but he'd always be my Jericho. "We're fine."

"Got a lump up there." He brushed my hair aside, tucking it behind my ear. "It needs ice."

"I'm fine too," Tracy said softly. Jericho opened his arms, inviting her, the three of us hugging a moment as Tracy added, "It really wasn't my fault."

"I don't care. I only care that you aren't hurt," he replied, his breathing labored. I looked up and saw the concern, the rigid fright. He stared at the remains of my car, yellow and orange flames dancing eerily in his glassy eyes. Not many things scared Jericho. But fire was one of them.

"By the way?" I thumped his chest to break his gaze and help rid his mind of what might have been. I knew the macabre rabbit hole he was circling. It wasn't a healthy place to be. He didn't budge until I pinched the dimple in his chin and gave it a tug. "If you are going our way, we could use a ride."

An hour went by, the icepack on my head nearly melted. My fingers were shriveled like prunes. Reports from the issued APB trickled in almost immediately. There seemed to be a million white SUVs in the Outer Banks, including some from clear across the bay in Point Harbor and Powells Point. None of them were suspect though. With the help of a colleague, we extended the APB further west to Elizabeth City. There, plenty of vehicles were pulled over, the drivers and passengers questioned, the vehicle bumpers inspected for damage. Some had bumps and bruises like me and Tracy, but none of the people were found suspicious enough to warrant further investigation.

As much as I hated to admit it, we needed more information. The word accident was thrown around the station, along with hit and run, and mention of the driver being a nervous teen perhaps. They'd commented that fear probably drove them to flee the scene, especially when seeing my car flip unexpectedly. One officer stopped at our desks and spoke for ten minutes about a similar incident. I don't think he took a single breath while speaking. He droned on and on until I finally had to make an excuse for us.

It could have been an accident like everyone was saying. A nervous teen bumping us and then taking off. What happened after the bump was a chance happening. A one in a million where every needed condition was present at the same time. That's what the patrol officer thought, and mentioned how the roads were slick enough, the speed was high enough, and that there had been a stormy cross wind at over twenty miles per hour. Add to that, the tires hydroplaned until the momentum tipped my car. It all sounded reasonable, but I didn't buy it. There was no bump. It was a jarring strike that shuddered me inside and out. I didn't see it happen, but felt it rock the car sideways hard enough to roll us. I told the investigating officer as much, insisting on the APB. I could see his reluctance, even feel the disbelief.

Before leaving the scene, I took as many pictures as possible, my focus on the rear bumper's passenger side where it was blackened, the neon blue I'd ordered barely visible. What I was interested in was the enormous dimple and the broken taillight. I'm not an engineer, but the damage had me thinking that it'd take a lot of force to do that. I rolled my chair into Tracy's cubicle, leaving the icepack behind. There was shredded cardboard and Styrofoam above and below her desk, a new laptop already docked and plugged in. The screen was a faded blue, white stars spiraling in the center with a *Please Wait* message.

"Any luck with that?" Bangs hung in front of her eyes as she cradled her head and waited.

"It's coming along." She didn't look up when replying. Didn't move either.

I brushed the hair back and lowered my gaze so I could see her eyes. "It's okay. Nobody got hurt."

Chair creaking, she sat up when the screen refreshed to show the default desktop icons and the generic wallpaper. "It's a county issued laptop," she began, typing fast, the screen's colors on her face. She looked at me with the slightest evidence of a smile showing, her dimples giving it away. "Which is good news. It means that everything I had on the other laptop can be restored to this one. Everything except any notes you'd been working."

"Cloud backup?" A nod. "That's great! I'll think of the notes. No worries there."

"Okay, then I only need to do this," she said, keys rattling with her typing. When prompted with a tile puzzle, Tracy clicked on all the pictures that included a bicycle. Her phone buzzed in response, showing a number to continue with the final level of the authentication. Folders appeared one by one, blinking onto the screen as her desktop and files were being restored. "Ya gotta love it."

"I'm glad you were able to get everything back." I sat back, watching the paper and folder animations.

"Good timing too," she said, digging into her bag. When her hand appeared, she handed me a micro-SD card, the kind used with cameras. She swiped a digital reader from behind a heap of unused equipment on her desk and snaked a cable to the laptop. "Now we can see what's on it."

I thought of the sorority sister we met with, the security cameras inside and outside her home. "This isn't from Janine Scott's house, is it?" I asked, instinctively closing my hand around the card.

Tracy shook her head. "No, I'd never do that." I opened my fingers slowly, handing her the card. She winked, adding, "Not without a warrant."

Her enthusiasm was contagious. It knocked on the door of my curiosity, but also made me cautious. It was a strong enough feeling for me to close my fingers again. "Then where?"

She smacked my fingertips, answering, "It's from your car."

"My car?" Not everything burned. I unfurled my fingers, poking at the SD card, searching it for evidence of water or soot. It was clean. "How?"

She nudged one of the laptop boxes, answering, "When I went to pick this up. I stopped by the junk yard where they'd towed the car."

"I didn't know there was a memory card," I said, a breath of surprise carrying my words. "What... I mean, where did you find it?"

"Easy. I googled the specs for that year, make and model." Her eyelids grew, the whites in her left eye bloodied. There was a slight bruise on that side of her face from where the airbag hit her. "Did you know that your car has, I mean had, cameras in the front and the rear? And the card was buried behind a removable panel in the trunk."

"The trunk didn't burn." I couldn't stop staring at the card, asking, "You got all of that online?"

She looked at me like I had two heads, answering, "You can get everything online." She took the SD card and plugged it into the reader. "If you had bought their options for cloud storage then we would have been able to pull the images directly, same as how I restored my laptop."

"I did get that option," I said, recalling the sales pitch and thinking it was wasted on me. I never considered cars as *being* online too. "There was a free trial period, but it was only for the first month."

A disk icon appeared on the screen, numbers and letters making up a list of cryptic names beneath it. "It wouldn't have mattered. Your car probably went offline when it was hit. It stopped sending data."

"But anything leading up to the crash would be on the memory card."

"Bingo," she answered, clicking on the icon. She fanned the air with her fingers like a magician, saying, "And here we go."

A list of files appeared, the timestamps showing us the files were seconds apart. "Sort on the date and time." She filtered the list. The top showing data and image files written. "Open one of them."

It was a picture of the road and showed what the officer mentioned, standing water. It was a puddle deep enough to hide the yellow center line and reflect the storm clouds. Tracy's shoulders slumped when she saw it. "Shit. I guess the tires did hydroplane. But I'm sure there was a white SUV, I know—"

"Keep going. Open another one." I inched to the edge of my seat, saying, "Screw it, open them all."

She did. Selecting the last minutes of the recordings. They popped onto the screen in succession, the layout reminding me of the old filmstrips we used to watch in school. In a few, the road was sideways, and then upside down where the sky should have been. "Casey!" she magnified the picture with the bumper. It was a shiny metal, a warped image of my car mirroring in the chrome.

"Before that frame. Before it hit us."

She clicked on the previous picture to show an SUV. It was the one she claimed hit us. Only, it was painted black, not white. "That's not what I saw—"

"It's not what we reported." I began texting to cancel the APB and issue a new one. I thought of the hard hit we took, the possibility her memory was hazy. There was the punch from the airbag deployment too. A hit like that was apt to turn everything stark white. In the next image, the rear camera's wide-angle lens showed the moment my car was struck. "Tracy, these are exactly what we need. Go back a few frames."

"The license plate," she said, excited we were solving a puzzle. The file opened, the car appearing much smaller than expected. "That's odd. I guess it's the camera's wide-angle lens? The license plate is too small."

A sick feeling swept over me like the fire that destroyed my car. My throat tightening, I told her, "Bring up the list of files again." She followed my direction, listing them. "The time on the images is every ten seconds."

"On the car's console, the video stream is live," Tracy explained. "I'm guessing the cameras are configured to keep a fixed number of static images, one every ten seconds?"

"Right. I get that." I opened the calculator on my phone, plugging in a time interval of ten seconds. "Look at the distance the SUV traveled from that frame to the frame before it hit us."

She pointed at the first picture, the SUV appearing tiny. "We can use the road's mile markers. They're placed every tenth of a mile." She pointed to the picture with the initial contact. "That means the SUV's distance from the first picture to this frame would be roughly a thousand feet?"

"A thousand feet. The SUV traveled a thousand feet in ten seconds." I plugged in the numbers to calculate the speed, adding,

"Tracy, the speed limit on that road was twenty-five." I turned my phone around to show how fast the SUV was moving.

"They were going almost seventy!" Her mouth fell open. "That means they were speeding up!"

"This wasn't an accidental hit. Whoever it was, they hit us on purpose."

SEVEN

Bumps and bruises and a couple of burns. We'd become a target but survived. The same couldn't be said about my newer car. It was a heaping mess of crumpled metal, broken glass and burned rubber, some of it scorched. What instigated it? Was it the visit to Janine Scott's house? The interview with Jim Witney? Neither of them really struck me as the kind to attack law enforcement. Certainly not without a suitable cause. There were the charter boat brothers too, Patrick and Shawn Rutledge. But why? There was no clear answer. What we knew was that this was no accident. My car was gone and the healing from yesterday's crash would have to wait. There was work to do. Work that took place below the ocean's surface. It was the place where Karol Witney died, the scene of her murder.

The hour was early and still dark, but there were signs of gold growing across the horizon as we approached the dock. The first beams struck my eyes and put Jericho in silhouette, the dive boat disappearing in a pool of fiery sunlight. I hoisted an air tank from the truck, metal ringing like a bell, the scuba gear's weight pressing on my shoulder. The dock was slick with dew, gulls pursuing, feathered bodies swooping and shouting. A family of pelicans were perched on the nearby pilings, our footsteps stirring the closest of them, beady eyes following lazily while their long bills stayed tucked. Before handing the tank to Jericho, I squinted and read the gauge, the needle pegged in green, the tank filled with compressed air.

I wondered if these were some of the last things Karol Witney saw and heard while her charter fueled and readied for its launch. This wasn't a recreational dive for my team though. Somewhere beneath the Atlantic Ocean's surface, somewhere in its darker depths, there was a crime scene. It was the place where Karol had been murdered. This wasn't like any other scene we'd investigated either. There was no knowing what we might find. Or if we'd find anything at all.

Thin steam drifted over the water, the shallows holding on to the last of the summer heat. A zipper shred the air as Tracy opened her wetsuit, which was long sleeved and had stirrup straps that looped around the heels of her feet. Mostly black, it was bright blue beneath the arms, the color matching her eyes, a point she'd made when we picked it out. Made of a flexible spandex and nylon, it'd keep us warm in the deeper parts of the dive. Mine was the same style and brand, only the blue was replaced with a green-turquoise color to match my eyes.

As for Jericho's suit, I'm not at all sure what we'd call it, other than being well past its time. Originally black, it was a faded char-coal with large patches of rubbery white, clumpy repairs he'd applied over the years to cover the holes. A ragged and sorry sight, I'd offered to replace it. He wouldn't part with it though, saying it had history dating back as long as he'd been diving. Not that he'd admit it, but that history was at least ten pounds ago, the suit fitting snugly. As long as it insulated him from the cold, a neces-sity considering the currents of cold rivers that ran beneath the surface, that was all that mattered.

"Let me help you with that," Emanuel Wilson said, his height towering over Tracy. He ducked to avoid the dive boat's upper deck, Tracy giving him a quick hug before handing him her wetsuit. A basketball star once, Emanuel moved to law enforcement when he was finished with that career. That's where he met Jericho, their work relationship becoming a deeper friendship. Later, Emanuel would become one of my best detectives. He was everything a good detective needed to be. Bright and strong. Witty and bold. And an in-your-face person when he needed to be. His time with me didn't last though. He was just too good. These days, he worked as a lead detective like me, solving homicide cases in Elizabeth City. Thankfully, the drive there is a short one so we could stay in touch. Emanuel held up Tracy's wetsuit, his muscular size looking comical next to it, like he was holding a suit meant for a child. He fixed the zipper and handed it back, saying, "I got my gear onboard in case anyone can't dive."

"It's good to have you here." I grabbed the tip of his large-brimmed hat and gave it a playful yank, a smile appearing beneath its shadow. Emanuel was Jericho's regular diving partner, the two having trained most of the new Marine Patrol recruits this past summer. His gaze shifted to the water, a fish chasing the sunshine with a jump. I could tell he wanted time diving, but his value today was working topside. We needed him to be our eyes and ears. We needed him to be our protection. There were sharks in these waters. And not all of them had fins and gills with the threat of razor-sharp teeth. There'd been one with hands and feet that killed Karol Witney. "Did you bring your sunblock?"

He peered down at his arm where a fresh scar was etched into his light-brown skin, the outline of it crusty. There'd been a small mole there which took on a life of its own during the summer of dive training. What had been a small speck changed, its shape resembling one of the barrier islands. At his wife's urging, Jericho's too, the mole was removed. It was cancer. Not the *it will be fine* skin-cancer kind either. Not that any of them are fine. Too often we become ignorant to the dangers we cannot see. That is, until disaster brushes life. He frowned at the scar, asking, "You've been talking to my wife?"

"Should I be?" I didn't wait for a reply and dug out my tube of sunblock. With my lighter skin color, I always carried fifty shades of armor. We had our wetsuits to cover most of us, but he wouldn't if he was working on the deck. When he grunted, I pressed the sunblock into his chest. "Let's not make this uncomfortable with an order."

"You're the boss," he sighed, taking it in hand while lifting another tank on board. He anchored the tank in the last cubby along with the others, straps creaking as they grew tight under the load. The motors revved, Jericho sounding a high-pitched whistle. Vibrations rumbled through my feet, Emanuel pocketed the sunblock and shouted, "That's our cue!"

I took a seat next to Tracy, Jericho handing over the wheel. The boat eased backward in the water while I closed every stitch of clothing. I told myself it would only be cold for a few minutes, and then we'd be deep into the dive. I was wrong.

———

The beaches of the southern barrier islands looked distant as we drifted to a slow stop, a wake trailing and water rippling against the bow. Emanuel announced we were at the location matching Karol Witney's charter. He also mentioned that there were three wrecks beneath us, explaining the history of them with a lilt in his voice, playing off the trip like he was our tour guide. I only half listened, fingers clutching my gear, the weight of it jerking me when the boat was rocked by a swell. A splash fountained port side with a hollow gulp, Jericho dropping an anchor to steady us and hold the boat's position. I unbuttoned my shirt, jerking it from beneath the belt of my pants, a shiver running through me when the winds touched my bare skin. Jericho joined me, tank and gear in hand, his gaze wandering from my belly to my face, a devilish smile appearing.

"What are you gawking at?" Goosebumps sprouted across my arms and chest, the single piece bathing suit beneath my clothes doing little to ward against the cool air. I gave him a hands-off frown, but then grabbed him to steal some of his body heat. I loved that he still looked at me like he did. I loved that he still wanted to. I planted a kiss on his mouth for luck before the dive, a habit we'd started when he first trained me. His lips were soft and wet but turned stiff. When I pulled back, he was looking deep into my eyes, the playful flirting replaced by rigid concern. When he didn't say anything, I assured him, "We'll be okay. You'll be with us."

He leaned over the rail and gave the watery chop a stare; the winds were opposite of the tide, causing the swells to roll. But the rough seas wouldn't be a problem since we'd work beneath them today. "Casey, it's deeper than you and Tracy have ever gone."

I lifted his shirt, urging him to change into his wetsuit. When he didn't help, I pressed my hand over his heart assuring him, "We've had an excellent teacher."

Jericho glanced over at Emanuel, and then the ocean again. He didn't look convinced but agreed hesitantly, "As long as we don't stray far from each other."

"You got it." I pushed a slow smile, relieved he didn't call it. On this boat, Jericho was our dive captain and for a moment, I thought I'd be working topside with Tracy while he and Emanuel took the dive. I unbuttoned his pants, jerking on them. "Let's get in the water."

"Yes! Let's!" Tracy said, teeth chattering. She wore a one-piece bathing suit like the one I had, her clothes heaped in a pile on the deck. The sound of wet kisses erupted from her bare feet as she jogged in place while Emanuel helped to sleeve an arm into her wetsuit. I took to sitting, our voices silenced by the spandex and nylon squelching against our skin, the boat rocking and the radio belching staticky conversations. When I was ready, I stood up and tested my gear, butterflies in my belly. It was time to dive. Tracy looked up. "You're done already?"

"Come on now," I told her, Jericho joining me, his suit on and a pair of tanks and gear at the ready.

"Coming," she groaned. Emanuel hoisted Tracy by the belt, lifting her onto her toes, tightening the straps for her air tank while she tested the regulator. She gave us a thumbs up, her mask down. "I'm ready."

"Ready," I repeated, voice garbled while biting down on the regulator mouthpiece. Emanuel clapped my shoulder, giving me the okay.

Jericho jumped in feet first, the ocean swallowing him whole, a splash reaching up like fingers in a come-hither too. There was a flutter in my belly while I positioned myself on the lip of the boat and sucked in a last breath. My lungs tightened and I pitched backward in a roll just as I'd been trained, hoses in place, hand held firm against my mask. The ocean shot up around me like a storm, a flush of white foam brushing across my face and through my hair. I forced myself to turn over and to swim away from the boat. The water turned clear, the colors a light blue like a dusky sky. My ears filled immediately, the dense sound of Tracy's splash coming from nearby. I dared a breath, never fully trusting that first one from a tank no matter how much testing I'd done on the boat deck. Clean air filled my lungs and bubbles glided up the side of my face.

When the bubbles cleared and there was ten feet between me and the boat, I looked for Jericho and Tracy. I could see them both, our visibility surprisingly good. It was great in fact, which was promising for the work we were doing. Jericho was already searching, floating buoyantly while scanning the bottom. Tracy oriented herself like I had, turning around to get a bearing relative to the ocean floor and the boat above. I waved them over for us to group before we began a broader search.

We'd never talked nationalities, family histories or the like, but I think Jericho might have been part dolphin. He swam like them, his legs together, fins paddling as one, propelling toward me in a gush. His face was near mine, pale blue behind the mask, his eyes bulging and oddly huge. Tracy followed, her pace slower, feet kicking the way I swam, arms stretched wide as air bubbles surrounded her. When we were together, I pointed to where we believed Karol Witney's dive ended. The brothers from the charter boat couldn't tell us an exact location, which meant we'd have to canvass the surrounding area, each of us going in a different direction.

I took the regulator from my mouth, salty currents touching my tongue while I squeezed the sides. Air spiraled upward in a steady stream, Jericho and Tracy agreeing with a wave. It was our underwater emergency signal. A beacon to use, telling us to come no matter what we were doing. We broke then, taking a different path down to the ocean's floor, swimming away, the paddling pushing from behind. The vastness of the Atlantic Ocean surrounded me, and the silence of being underwater reached my insides with a kind of peace that was only felt when beneath the surface. I was alone and descended deeper, the daylight that bled through the depths shifting, the quiet growing.

It wasn't long before I was joined by a school of silvery fish. They swam between my arms and legs, enveloping me like a cloud. A few regarded me with pin-sized eyes that didn't move, seeing me as another thing in their world that was of no threat to them. Seagrass slithered across my middle as another fish swam near my head, the silver school darting from sight. This fish was big enough to give me pause in the same way as when crossing the path of a large dog. When I became interested in scuba diving, I'd gone to the library and got as many books as I could carry. Among them was a book about the fish and I tried to memorize some, to learn the names and to recognize them when diving. This one was called an Atlantic spadefish and it was as big as a doormat. It was shaped like an angel fish and was striped silver and black. The spadefish grew more curious, its eye the size of my fingertip. It swam close to my face making me think it wanted to kiss my cheek. I swam deeper, having no idea if they were known for biting.

I'd give thanks to the spadefish later, his curiousness taking me past a reef that was caked in barnacles and patches of grass, to a wreck that Karol Witney might have been diving near. *The Grave-yard of the Atlantic*. That's one of the names given to the waters just beyond the Outer Banks coast. It was the deceiving shallow-ness that caused all the shipwrecks, boats having to travel miles and miles due east before turning north or south. What seemed a tranquil and peaceful paradise above the surface, could be treach-erous beneath, ripping through hulls, sinking ships without preju-dice. There was no care for what the ships carried or for what purposes they sailed. Over two thousand wrecks had been recorded, but there were many more. There were shipwrecks from before records were kept or lost, papers with names and numbers, a purpose long forgotten perhaps. Ships that had yet to be recovered.

Enormous timbers climbed above me. I recognized it as some-thing that had been made from shipbuilders tooling wood into planks and tenons and holding them together with dowels. Brown algae and green moss turned the once hard surfaces into a home for marine life, the soft currents acting like a breeze, plant tendrils swaying, tiny fish playing a game of peek-a-boo. To look at the wreck as is, I would struggle to guess that it had been a hull of a ship once, or that it had been a massive structure weighing a few tons and had defied gravity and floated effortlessly. However, there was no mistaking that this was something built by hands, and that it had been here a long time.

I rose enough to see past this part of the wreck and make sure Tracy and Jericho were still in sight. That was the rule: we could separate as long as we stayed within sight. A dozen yards away, a stack of bubbles floated to the surface. They weren't racing or teaming in a spiral of trouble, a blur of muted baby-blue colors beneath them. It was Tracy, she was okay.

Tracy gave me a wave, her hand moving in slow motion, our visibility dropping. There was plenty of light, but the ocean floor had been stirred and a cloud hadn't settled. Suddenly, there was no sign of Jericho. He was the most experienced diver, and was apparently allowed to bend the rules he applied to me and Tracy, but he was bending them a little more than I was comfortable with. I would have sighed deeply if the respirator allowed me to. I searched the rear of the wreck, suspecting he hadn't ventured far.

From my hip, I took my underwater camera, this side of the wreck strange enough to want to show Emanuel and Jericho later. Unlike the front, there was no vegetation, the wood blackened and lifeless as if it had been buried until recently. Considering how lively the front was, I didn't understand how that could be. The camera's flash was muted at this depth, but I could maybe adjust the exposure later. I returned to the front, taking more pictures for comparison. We'd review the photographs again and again, to see if we'd missed anything.

Strands of kelp stood on end, rooted where an octopus appeared like a magic trick, causing me to startle as it swam away. I'd nearly stepped on the poor thing when my foot touched sand, its legs stretched, its bulbous head unmoving, and its coloring a camouflage. I took a picture, the flash bouncing brightly against something in the cloud of sand, a shine catching my eye. I dove enough in the Outer Banks to know what was expected. This wasn't expected. I waved away the sand, grains of it falling around what looked like a gold coin. It couldn't be though. Not here. Not with the thousands of tourists who'd explored the same grounds.

When I heard the rapid bubbling, I knew it was my breathing. That my pulse was speeding up. A picture. I had to take a picture, and I framed the half-buried coin as best I could and snapped a photograph. Touch it. I had to touch it next and make sure there wasn't a poor mix of air in my tank that had me hallucinating. The camera dangled from my wrist as I buried my fingers behind the coin. The gold was the same temperature as the water. But it was electric, the touch of it sending a shock into my body that said this was real. Grains of sand drained from my palm until there was only the gleaming gold, a woman's face on the front with stars around the perimeter. The back of it had a denomination of twenty dollars.

Bubbles rose above me in a narrow spout, its volume looking too much like our warning beacon. I had to slow my breathing, but the excitement of what I held was too much. I'd floated fifteen yards while inspecting the coin but knew from the wreck where it was. I had to show Tracy and Jericho and spun around to find them. Tracy was nowhere to be seen, but on the other side of a reef I saw a faint column of bubbles. The closer I swam, the stronger the bubbles, a tornado of air forming, an emergency alert from one of them. They were in trouble.

I tucked my camera away, along with the coin, and began kicking as hard as I could. When I swam over a mound of sand, I saw Tracy holding her regulator, air spewing in a gush. She was distant but saw me approaching and put the regulator back in her mouth. That's when I saw the splotchy white patches of a wetsuit. Jericho's suit. But there were no air bubbles rising from his regulator. They were floating in the shadows of a dead ship's bow. Time stopped. It froze. The sea life around me ceased to exist and I only saw the two people in the world who mattered most to me. One of them wasn't breathing, his arms and legs hanging limp.

Tracy's eyes were enormous behind her mask, fingers working diligently on a strap holding Jericho's tank. Heart racing, insides burning, every fiber of my being was on fire. I raced to her side and circled behind to see the tank strap looped around a metal post. Bloody puffs billowed from a wound where a rusting spike cut into Jericho's suit. I looked at Tracy's face, both of us breathing fast and heavy, and squeezed her arm while shoving the regulator back into his mouth. He was unconscious though, every part of him dead to the world. How long had he been without air? Unconscious? Was he dead already?

Daylight glinted off my knife, my insides tearing to pieces. I didn't know if Jericho was dead or alive. I couldn't think like that and began to cut. Metal clanked against metal, the knife's sharp edge slapping against the rusty post. Tracy got beneath Jericho when she saw what I was doing and grabbed his middle in a hug. When the belt strap came free, I dropped the knife and took hold of his collar, fingers clutching harder than I'd ever held anything in my life. It was Jericho's life that I was holding now, the silhouette of our boat thirty yards away. Maybe more. I didn't wait for Tracy and began to swim like I'd never swam before. I'd known Jericho to hold his breath for minutes at a time, up to an impressive count of four when we went free-diving. But how long had it been? I cleared my mind and kicked my feet, Tracy's hand joining mine, sharing the grip, the two of us rising with Jericho's lifeless body.

EIGHT

Thrashing. Fingers splayed, arms swinging, and kicking feverishly while a sinking feeling turned cold in my gut. We broke the surface with Jericho between us, the boat far, the distance impossible to comprehend. Dread filled me with a threat to zap the energy needed to save him. I made a fist on Jericho's vest, the ocean breaking over my head, a white cap crashing into his face. A wishful thought came for a moment, of seeing him wake suddenly and telling us that this had been a terrible practical joke. But he didn't flinch. Didn't blink. He didn't react at all. A hard lump was fixed like a sharp stone in my throat while a heartbeat thrummed violently in my head. Jericho's head tipped back, his eyelids slitted, the sunlight bleeding inside. Not a blink. Not one.

Jericho's dead weight was significantly more on the surface than it had been beneath it. Tracy struggled against holding it, her face disappearing briefly and resurfacing with a spitting gasp. New concerns struck, the back of my mouth turning bitter. If not for the rush of adrenalin, I might have caved to the growing fright. There was no other hell like losing someone. I know. I lived that nightmare before. I wasn't willing to live it again.

"Gimme a sec!" I strained to lift Jericho's head and to get my arm cradled beneath his, taking more of his weight. Thighs pumping with long strides that burned, Jericho's dead weight shifted as Tracy reworked her grip. There was twenty feet of water between us and the ocean floor. It'd only take a few inches for one of us to die though.

Tracy finished adjusting, and cried, "He's not breathing!"

"Need to hurry!" I choked, seawater filling my mouth. We continued dragging Jericho's body, paddling and kicking, glaring at the boat while his legs floated behind us. There were no more words. Only the exchange of fright-filled glances while waving for Emanuel to see us.

What felt like a lifetime was another ten seconds before Emanuel saw us. Heat teemed in every muscle, the fibers of them like ignited kindling, the strain spurred by steeper swells pummeling us sideways. Without warning, a larger one crested and broke, splashing into my eyes and mouth, some of it stealing my breath. I choked and spat up the salty taste with a broken scream. "Over here!"

"What happened!" Emanuel yelled, the boat dipping behind a wave. It rose above us suddenly with surprising height, our bodies bobbing beneath. He didn't wait for a reply and dove head-first toward us. His body reappeared inside a swell moments later, dolphin kicking like Jericho, swimming fast until his head emerged in a gush of breaking foam. There was a hard look in his eyes as he grabbed Jericho's vest, jerking him from us with a command, "Get to the boat, I'll lift him to you."

"I found him like—" Tracy began to say, a sob in her tone. I couldn't hear it. Wouldn't hear it. Neither would Emanuel.

"Tracy!" he shouted, coughing and spitting water as we swam faster than we'd ever done before. "Not now. I need you to concentrate. Can you do that!"

"I... I can do that," she cried, climbing the ladder.

The rungs were in my hands, the stainless-steel glinting sunlight. The deck was beneath my feet a moment later, gear shedding from my body in a blur. "Tanks!" Tracy did as I did. Belts unclipping, vests slipping, the tanks clanking together. I leaned over the side with the crook of my arm wrapped around the ladder, demanding, "Hand him to me!"

Tracy knelt on the other side of the ladder while Emanuel hooked his arm around the bottom rung. Blood rushed into my head with the strain, Tracy grimacing and shouting out a cry. Together, we muscled Jericho on board, where he fell onto his side. I stripped the tank and gear, yelling, "Help me lie him flat on his back." When he was face up, I pitched his head, making sure his neck was straight. With my hands on his heart, I hammered into it as hard as I could, each compression pumping blood.

"How long was he out?" Emanuel asked, taking over, shoving his balled fist with a force that had me fearing it'd break through Jericho's chest. Hard and fast compressions. It was part of the training. "Casey! How long!"

"I don't know." Tears stung like a swarm of bees, Jericho's body lying still, his color gray, eyes remaining still. I breathed into his mouth, performing emergency resuscitation, his cheeks puffing with every breath. "A minute. I think."

"Tracy?" Emanuel demanded frantically. She shrugged and shook her head, lips blue and thin. "How about his regulator? Was it in his mouth?"

She regarded the question, eyes huge and filled with dread, and answered in a shout, "It wasn't!"

"Jesus," he grunted, his voice cold with heartbreak. I grabbed Emanuel's hands, stopping him so I could listen. Sunlight sparked from the droplets in his hair and on his face, his expression like stone. He got up and went to the cabin while I put my ear to Jericho's mouth and listened for a breath. I had to hear past the ocean, and the sea lapping against the hull and the call of gulls who'd decided now was the best time to make noise.

Tracy pressed her fingers against the side of Jericho's neck to search for a pulse. "Nothing!"

"Shock him?" Emanuel asked, returning. There was desperation in his eyes and a portable defibrillator in his hands. I shook my head, but then nodded, uncertain. Velcro tore through the air as he prepared the kit, Tracy grabbing the pads and wiry leads from the unit. Urgencies climbed, turning feverish with them moving closer, Emanuel's shoulder shoving mine, "Casey!"

"Just a second!" There was a twitch. I was sure of it. Heartbeat racing at an immeasurable rate, a tiniest sign of life in the corner of Jericho's eye. "I think I saw something!"

"We need to shock him!" Emanuel insisted, his voice like a growl in my ear.

I continued the compressions and waved for Tracy to take over. When my mouth was on Jericho's, forcing air, I heard a faint gurgle echo from deep inside him. "Come back to me," I whispered, despair leveling my voice. I squeezed his face, tears streaming down mine. "We were just getting started!"

A cough. "Holy shit!" Emanuel shouted. Another cough. Foamy water shot from between Jericho's lips. "Get him onto his side!"

"There you go!" I said, letting the tears come. We rolled him over, seawater spewing. It was followed by a heaving breath, Jericho's eyes bulging, a shade of pink flashing across his neck and face. "Can you hear me?"

"Wha—" he began. The words cut short as he sucked in air, the muscles in his arms tensing, corded like sinew as life slammed back into his body. When he caught another breath, he insisted on sitting up. "What?"

"Here, let me."

Jericho eased onto his knees, his hands clutching my arm like a rope as he climbed. I unzipped his wetsuit, peeling it back, blood rolling between my fingers. He made eye contact with me, the whites in them riddled with rivers and streams, vessels broken from nearly drowning. "We... were diving."

When he insisted on standing, Tracy came to his side, her arm supporting his middle, the three of us helping him. "I found you unconscious."

The top of his wetsuit pulled away easily while Jericho stood like a mannequin, his gaze searching the vast nothingness of open waters. He nudged his chin toward some boats a few hundred yards away. There was confusion on his face, "Who are they?"

"Just a couple dive boats," Emanuel answered, twin motors muscling the air as a few took off, three of them pulling away from the area. "I suppose they're done spectating. You put on quite a show."

"Quite a show," Jericho repeated, drops of blood falling around our feet.

It was the cut on his back. In a way, I was glad to see the bleeding. It proved life was with him and that I wasn't imagining he was okay. I dabbed it with a wad of gauze, eyeing the emergency medical kit, thinking we'd need more. "You're going to need a few stitches, a tetanus shot too."

He shook his head, jaw hanging slack and muttered, "I don't like those."

"Nobody likes them, but they—" I stopped speaking when I saw the alarm on Emanuel's face. "What is it?"

"It's this," he answered, backing away to make room. "You'll want to look at this."

I followed his finger, the tip of it pointing to a spot beneath Jericho's shoulder blade. "What is that? Jelly fish sting?"

"What's what?" Tracy asked, joining while Jericho swayed, his motion matching the boat's. When Tracy saw it, she commented, "They're not stings. Those look like burns?"

"Burns?" I didn't understand how burns could have happened during a dive. There were two significant burn marks, both the same diameter. "Emanuel?"

"I think I know what could have caused something like that." He raced back to the boat's cabin, feet slapping wetly. There was a clatter of wood latching and unlatching, a locker door slamming, my eyes locked on the burns. Emanuel returned with a pole in hand, the end of it with two prongs. I'd seen it once before in one of our dives but couldn't imagine what it would do if used on a person. "He got zapped with this."

"That's a shark deterrent tool?" Jericho was more alert and turned toward my voice, seeing what Emanuel held.

"It's the most popular one there is," Emanuel answered, handing it to me.

"Let me take a look." Jericho's body felt warmer than it had as I pressed gently with my fingertips. I lined up the probes, his body stiffening when they touched his skin, the distance between them matched his injuries perfectly.

"Don't zap me with that thing," Jericho joked, sounding more alert. That was good.

"I think you already were." I gave the shark deterrent tool back to Emanuel and held Jericho, knowing what stopped his heart. "We need to get you to a hospital."

Emanuel launched the boat toward land, the motors whining, the bow cutting through the wake with little effort. I held Jericho in my arms, my hand pressed against his chest. I felt his breath rise and fall, terrified that it would stop at any moment. He continued breathing and the boat docked without incident. When we were back on land, an ambulance was already waiting, and I slipped into my clothes and searched for the coin. It was gone.

My fingertips burned from turning my scuba suit inside out a hundred times. I stretched it every which way possible, but it wasn't there. A pelican eyed me as if warning of the dangers that the coin would bring to the islands. Only, I suspected that the danger was having found it in the first place, the attack on me and Tracy, and now Jericho, a dire warning. I had the image of the coin fresh in my mind. And that was all I would have. The coin was gone.

NINE

Antiseptic stung my nose. There was the faint odor of cleaning fluids too. The powerful bluish lights bleeding from the hallway reminded me most of what it was like when staying in a hospital. It was a place where the sick cannot rest because sleep was impossible. That is, unless it's medically induced. That was the case for Jericho. Sleep was provided by the doctors, throaty snores grinding as he showed off how well he could sleep. That's what he called snoring, showing off. And I think I was a little jealous of it. Just a little.

With my shoes kicked off, and a baby-blue hospital blanket covering my legs, I stole moments between his snores. They were brief stays in that place we go before falling sleep. But sleep wasn't waiting on the other side for me tonight. I knew deep down that I wasn't going to reach it. Not with the adrenaline which had kept me wired to the point of feeling like I was going to vomit. Whenever I closed my eyes, Jericho's body was there. Lifeless and dead-still. I mean, his heart had stopped.

I opened one eye to look at him again. To make sure he was still breathing. There were tubes alongside the bed, bubbles shimmering as fluids washed through them. I couldn't help but search whenever I looked at Jericho. If it was death he experienced, then would he be okay? Would he be the same? The doctors had given their okay after performing a full examination, the overnight stay a cautionary one.

If anything was going to happen, then it would have happened while we waited in the emergency room. That ordeal lasted hours before we were finally seen by a doctor. That was all Jericho. I'd raised my voice that this was an emergency, but he'd commented to a nurse that he was fine and that we were only here to treat the wound with stitches and a tetanus shot.

He got the shot, the needle digging deep into the meat of his shoulder while the young physician got an earful from me. When she heard about the near drowning and the emergency CPR we performed, she ordered a stay for the night. Though he objected, the physician insisted on a full evaluation. Jericho could have signed himself out and gone home, but there was a slur when he spoke. It wasn't much, but it caught my ear, and it caught the doctor's as well.

Tracy texted a picture of Thomas and Tabitha, their little feet standing in a lake of popcorn, a blurry cartoon on the television behind them. It was already late, but I didn't complain. I was just thankful she could watch them while I watched Jericho. I'd have to leave soon, certain the hospital policy wouldn't allow me to stay. The chair wheezed while I turned around, my bottom sliding against the vinyl. When I shut my eyelids again and drifted to that place before sleep, a throaty snore grated the air, loud enough to pull me back. At home, I would have pinched Jericho's chin, turning his head slightly. Not here though. He needed sleep more than me.

Heavy footsteps erupted outside the hospital room, shoes running, the direction hidden by the echoes. A blur of lab coats and light-colored scrubs passing across the doorway with a cart full of electronics, one of its wheels squeaky and spinning around. The ruckus was short, but enough to rouse Jericho. He spoke groggily, groaning indeterminable words before wiping his face. An IV tube followed his hand and crossed the bridge of his nose, his eyes going cross when he tried to focus on it. He shook his arm with a start, eyelids snapping open.

"Babe?"

He found me, the scowl easing.

"You're in the hospital," I told Jericho, the confusion in his voice scaring me.

"What—?" He spat his tongue out like it was bad food and licked his dry lips. The IV was meant to hydrate him, but wasn't helping to ease his thirst. The edge of his bed dipped beneath my weight while I held an oversized jug of water for him to sip from. He sucked on the plastic straw, grimacing as he swallowed. When finished, he said with a hoarse rasp, "My throat... it's sore."

"You were showing off again."

He smiled shamelessly as I cradled his face, whiskers scratchy. I motioned to the vents in the ceiling. It was that time of year when the mid-afternoon heat still climbed high enough to trip the thermostat, trick them into turning on the air-conditioning.

"Your mouth was open while you were sawing wood."

"Next time—" he tried saying, his words riding on a weak breath. He drank more water to clear his throat. The weary look about him told me this was going to be a short conversation. I'd seen when he was groggy and when he was tired from a long day of working on the patrol boat. This was different. There was a second bag on the IV pole. Its color was less translucent, the bag was tiny by comparison, with red and black lettering. I suspected it was what was making him a bit loopy, his gaze wandering. His eyelids closed and opened slowly. "Next time wake me."

"Try to get some sleep."

He shook his head and nudged his head toward the television. "I don't want to sleep. Maybe something to listen to?" His hand wandered to cover mine, fingers trembling as his breath deepened.

"I'll find us an old movie."

I clicked the remote, the screen filling with black and white pebbles, a raspy belch coming from the speaker. I flipped the channel to where two women and a man were discussing a can of what looked like ink, and how it would seal any hole. "How about an informercial?"

"I think I bought a can of that stuff," he commented with a giggle. "What happened on the dive?"

"You don't remember?"

"I know I used to have a good memory." His gaze searched up and down and around the room. "I just can't remember where I put it."

A smile. It was good to hear him joke, but his not remembering bothered me. "Do you feel up to it?"

A nod. Hair hung over his eyes, bangs growing long. I combed them back, a touch of nerves making my heart jump.

His face turned white and sorrowful like he'd just learned of a tragedy. It wasn't tragedy though. It was fear. Tears welled and he looked deeply into my eyes like he was peering at my soul. He found my hand and squeezed it. "I... I can't remember anything. What happened to me?"

"It'll be okay." I lowered my head onto his shoulder, my arms around him. My heart ached seeing him like this. The only thing I could do was tell him what we knew. "We think you were attacked."

Muscles tensing, they turned rigid, the fibers standing out on his arms, thick ribbons across his chest and shoulders. "What do you mean?"

"On your back." I laced my hand beneath him, fingers driving between his back and the mattress. I touched where I knew they were, telling him, "Two of them."

"Burns?"

He winced when I touched the bandages.

"Here and here." On the boat, we'd showed him what did this. Rather, what we suspected caused the injury. But Jericho wasn't recalling the conversation or remembering Emanuel with the shark deterrent tool. "We showed it to you on the boat?"

"Showed me what?" He sat up abruptly, tense.

I flipped through my phone to find a picture.

Shock and surprise replaced the fear, his defensiveness waning. A glimpse of recognition was there too, the beginning of his recalling the accounts after he'd been resuscitated. "Maybe? I think I remember that."

"Do you remember anything before that? Anything during the dive or before it?" I put my phone away and squeezed his hands. He searched the room and then my face, looking as if the answers would suddenly spring to mind.

Ever so gently, he reached up to touch the bump on my head. "Accident. You and Tracy." The scowl returned, his adding, "Not an accident. They hit you!"

"That's right." It hurt to see him struggle. I wiped my eyes dry. "I think they went after you. Jericho, they tried to kill you."

His eyes grew wide, the whites in them still bloodshot. "On the ocean floor, the wreck."

"The wreck we were diving to." His memory was coming back. "Anything else?"

"Emanuel captained the boat." His eyes narrowed as though the recollection brought pain. "I saw something that shouldn't have been there."

Did he see gold? "What happened?"

Jericho lifted one hand, closing his fingers to make a fist. "I think I tried to pick it up—" his expression twisted, the memory fading like an unfinished dream. "—it's gone. I don't see it."

I cradled the side of his face in my palm, the IV dripping silently behind his shoulder. "It might come back to you."

"Did anything else happen?" he asked, looking troubled.

I leaned forward and put my mouth to his ear, overwhelmed by the eagerness to tell him what I saw. "Jericho, I found gold." I sat up to face him, adding, "And I think that's what you saw too."

"Gold?" he mouthed. I nodded as he fought the medication with a slow-forming frown. "That's not possible. I *know* I would have remembered *that*."

"Not necessarily. It could come back. Let me show you."

I left the bed and pulled a spiral notebook from my bag, a few of its pages filled with doodles. I'd never been able to draw the way I wanted to, believing those who could held some magical ability. But there was enough on the paper to create a decent sketch. Jericho sat up, or tried to, his arms giving out. I helped him up, stuffing pillows behind his back, and flipped the cover open to show him the lady on the coin, the stars around the edge. "This! I found a coin that looked like this."

"That's a Liberty Head coin?" he questioned, moving the paper away from his face with a squint. A spark showing on his face with a change coming over him. Was it fright or fancy? "Where is it?"

"I had it, but then I lost it." Excitement was brief like a lightning bolt, disappointment following with a sigh. "I did get some pictures. They're not great, but you can see that it's gold."

"Let's see what you have," he said, sounding skeptical.

I handed him my phone, the camera images transferred. While the color was gold, the details were fuzzy.

"It's definitely got a coin look to it. You think you lost it on the boat?"

"I don't know where, but—" I didn't finish, the idea popping into my mind a wild stretch.

"But?" he insisted. "What were you going to say?"

"What if there's more down there?" I shook my head until he dipped his chin, compelling the thought. "Well. We were attacked on the road. Then today, you were attacked. I'm certain it's because of this." I held up the drawing of the coin. "What if Karol Witney saw gold down there too? It might be what got her killed."

"Plausible," he said with a cringe. He turned his head toward the burns and where he'd been stitched. "Has to have been someone from one of those boats that were nearby."

"You remember those?" A nod. "There were three."

I flipped the page to show the other drawings. He ran a finger over them, saying, "They've got to know something is down there."

"Do you think there's more?" I was already sure of the answer but didn't know the history.

He pegged the drawing of the woman's face, saying, "Uh-uh. If that is gold..." he began, eyelids closing and opening slowly, "then we are all in danger."

I let Jericho sleep, the news of the coin quickly forgotten. There was no denying the excitement of gold, the prospect of it, but this wasn't a treasure hunt. It was a murder investigation. One or more divers had to have been in the water with Karol Witney. Maybe they were the same people who'd gone after Jericho. I rested my head on Jericho's chest and felt the slow rise and fall of his breathing, the comfort threatening to lull me to sleep. He'd gotten lucky that we were there to save him. Sadly, the same couldn't be said for Karol Witney.

TEN

Pancake mix dusted the countertops and drops of gooey batter were sprinkled across the range. Bacon sizzled as Jericho flipped an almost perfectly round pancake. To see him up and about would make one think he was bulletproof. I could see it, though. See that he was hurting. I'd tried to keep him in the hospital bed for a few more hours but failed. The doctors couldn't convince him either. We almost got through the night, but he signed himself free of the hospital before the first beam of light struck the eastern skies. As he'd say it, his medicine was here. It was home with the kids. To see him with Tabitha while she watched eagerly from his side, her eyes huge and hungry, I think Jericho was right.

"The cakes ready yet?" she asked, licking her lips. That's what she called pancakes. The *cakes*, leaving off the first part.

"Yes, little-miss, they are almost ready," Jericho answered, flipping again, smoke rising. He bent down and kissed her forehead, "Didn't you eat enough of your dinner last night?"

"Can't like it," she told him and scrunched her face.

"What?" he asked sarcastically. He handed her a piece of pancake. "But everyone *loves* nuggets."

"Can't like nuggets," she continued.

"Want to help with the spoons and forks?" I asked and put the syrup on the table, along with butter and a small dish of powdered sugar. Thomas only ate the pancakes with a touch of sugar. He didn't care for the syrup like his sister did. Left alone, she'd probably guzzle the bottle.

"Um. Okay," she answered, mouth stuffed. She didn't budge though and continued watching Jericho work the grill, eyes following his every move. She was his number one fan. She pointed at me with her index finger, comically adding, "In a single minute, okay." The last word came out sounding like, *Ahh-K*.

"That's fine," I said, watching her and her brother, a wave of gratitude rushing through me like a wave. It had been a week. A hell of a week. My heart and soul stuck in a seemingly endless state of angst about Jericho, about his health. A puff of white smoke lifted from the pan, rising to the ceiling near a smoke detector. I turned on the exhaust fan, a rumble vibrating loud enough to make Tabitha jump. I coaxed her into a hug, explaining what the noise was before she ran off to join her brother.

"Hey there," Jericho said when I wrapped my arms around him. He looked at me briefly with eyes that were surrounded by puffy skin and gray pouches, their green and blue colors swimming in glassy red pools. Days of stubble hid the dimple in his chin, the past days having taken a toll. When he saw me noticing, he turned away and dished out the remaining batter, a thick glob dropping onto the skillet with a searing sting. He'd almost died, and I couldn't shake the idea of losing him. I squeezed until I felt his heart beating beneath my arms, the flatware clanking as he cupped my fingers beneath his hands. They were big and he covered my hands with a firm press. I nuzzled the back of his neck as he spoke, "Casey, I feel fine. But what about you?"

"I'm fine too," I assured him. There was the car accident, my muscles still aching with fresh bruises surfacing. An inch more here or another foot-pound of pressure there? Who knows what could have happened. We were lucky. I know the accident was related to the case and the treasure. Whoever targeted my car could have killed me and Tracy. Guilt reached the back of my throat with a bite as I peered into the breakfast nook to find Thomas and Tabitha setting the table. We risked not being there for them. That can't happen again.

"Look," I whispered into his ear, pointing. The place where I sat had five spoons while Jericho's place setting had four forks. I felt a chuckle rise in him, easing the guilt bothering him too. "It's crazy how much I love them."

"Yeah. The little thieves stole my heart," he said, eyes glistening. He flipped the last batch of cakes, the batter bubbling just the right amount. "That's the secret, you know. Wait until the batter bubbles just enough."

"Is that right?" I asked, a knock at the door quieting the clamor of dishes and flatware.

Thomas and Tabitha craned their necks, forever curious, sensitive to change.

"There's somebody here?" Tabitha announced. She dropped the remaining forks and began to go to the door.

"Tracy?" Jericho asked. "I can mix up more batter."

"Might be. One second, little-miss," I answered and raced ahead of Tabitha.

But it wasn't Tracy. I peered through the front window to see that a Toyota hybrid was parked. I knew at once who it was and had a sinking feeling. I knelt and braced Tabitha's shoulders, telling her, "I want you to go wait with Thomas for me."

"Who that?" *That* sounding like *dat*. Her hazel eyes were fixed on the door as though she could sense my concerns. And maybe she could too. I brushed my fingers through her light-colored hair, its softness gliding over my skin like silk.

"It'll be okay," I said and saw Jericho dish out the pancakes, his brow furrowed with questions.

"Tabs," he called, kneeling to coax her back to the kitchen. She spun around and ran to him, the fleeting patter of bare feet filling the room. He hoisted Tabitha onto the chair next to Thomas and captured her attention with a healthy pour of the pancake syrup. It was enough to keep her busy, a second and third knock coming louder.

"It's the woman from Child Services," I said when Jericho joined me. "Ms. Welts."

"Their caseworker?" He ducked to look out the window, his hand cradling the doorknob. "Well, that is her car."

"Open it." I hated the stirring in my gut. I hated that my mind immediately went to the possibility of bad news too. "It might not be anything."

Jericho looked me up and down, glancing at the bruises, and said, "Both of us had trips to the hospital this week."

"You think Child Services would step in?" The idea of what he said was shocking. "I mean, anything medical is protected. Privacy, isn't it?"

"I guess?" He shrugged at me, questioning, "It could be an unannounced welfare call? But Ms. Welts knows the staff at the hospital. What if someone told her?"

"Shit, she does!" I felt the concern work its way into my face, my nose and eyes stinging. I primped my hair, brushing it back neatly, and pinched my cheeks thinking some color would look good. He turned the handle. Before the first creak from the hinges, I clutched his arm. "We don't know what we don't know."

"Fair enough," he said in a low whisper.

When daylight struck his face, Jericho put on the biggest and brightest smile he could muster. "Ms. Welts! Come on in. How are you doing?"

"It's Patricia, please," she pleaded and wagged a finger, always insisting that we use her first name. The woman was smiling. A good sign. She was tall and larger than me and had silver hair which had grown since we first met her. What had been a short cut was now shoulder length and covered the sides of her face. In place of her usual denim jeans and black jacket, she wore a jogging suit and had on tennis shoes which looked newer, as if taken out of the box this morning. The lack of a Child Protective Services badge told me this might be an informal visit, the idea raising my hopes slightly.

Jericho swung the door open as we tucked in behind it.

"I hope you don't mind a short visit?"

"Never. You are always welcome," I heard myself say, trying to sound pleasant. My insides were crawling with wishful and selfish thoughts though. "We were just about to have breakfast. Would you like to stay?"

"Oh I couldn't, please," she gushed. "But thank you."

"The kids already started," I said as we entered the kitchen area. Ms. Welts followed, pausing as she looked around. Thomas was first to wave to her, powdered sugar covering his mouth and cheeks. I cringed seeing that half the syrup on Tabitha's plate was already gone, some dripping from her chin, and some in Thomas's hair. There was a sticky handprint on his shirt too. The sight was like a comical calendar picture which I would have normally swooned over and texted to everyone. But this morning, it had come at the worst time. At once, I felt the heat of scrutiny, North Carolina's Child Services monitoring our care. I put on my best smile, saying, "You just can't leave them alone a minute."

"No, you can't." Ms. Welts didn't give it another look, her focus shifting to the coffee pot.

"Can I fix you a cup?" Jericho offered.

"That would be lovely."

She helped herself to a mug with a cat picture on it, the words *Cat Lover* fancily written across the top. "Cute. I don't recall your having any cats?"

"A gift from a friend," Jericho answered, pouring steadily, Ms. Welts dipping her face close to the steam. When he offered her cream and sugar, he asked the question that was pressing, "How can we help you this morning?"

"Black is fine," she mumbled and took an eager sip.

"I... well... to be frank, I'm not here for the children. They look great. Messy, but great."

I found myself rubbing my left temple which was throbbing. "Is everything all right?"

"I don't want to sound like I'm intruding, but I am here to see how you two are doing?" She raised the coffee cup to her lips, steam clouding the small glasses she wore. She never looked away, eyes shifting from me to Jericho and back.

"We're great." They were the first words out of my mouth and I felt instant regret, the tone too forced. I nudged my chin toward the breakfast table to quickly add, "Some days are a challenge, but I was expecting it."

When her eyes didn't follow mine, I knew the visit wasn't cordial. She put the coffee cup onto the counter, lips thinning. "Please understand that when there is anything that might compromise the welfare of Thomas and Tabitha, I'm compelled to investigate it." She selected her words carefully, but I could tell she had to know about the hospital visits. It was the only reason she'd have for showing up at eight in the morning. "Your daughter, Tracy is it?"

"That's right," I answered, mind spinning up wondering what Tracy had to do with anything.

"She stayed with the children? Alone?" Ms. Welts asked. A spiral notebook appeared. It looked small in her thick fingers. "There were a few days where one or both of you were away?"

"The hospital," Jericho said without expression. My stomach rolled. "I had a minor accident while diving off one of the shipwrecks."

"There was a car accident too," I said, following Jericho's lead. "Just some unfortunate timing."

She didn't speak, but raised the coffee cup, a series of giggles rising from the breakfast table when she slurped loudly. "One of my responsibilities is to ensure there is stability in Thomas and Tabitha's lives."

"There *is* stability. Tracy is like a big sister to them," Jericho said, a touch of defensiveness in his voice as he scratched his chin. I'd never seen him looking so tired which didn't help to support his words. "We would do anything for Thomas and Tabitha."

A smile appeared, the sight of it easing the tension. "I don't doubt that at all." She faced the breakfast nook, smile broadening. "I know when I'm looking at happy children, and I see two happy children."

When her attention returned to us, I asked bluntly, "You knew about the hospital visits?"

She regarded my question a moment. "It's my job to know about anything that might impact the children."

"What happens now?" The edge of my words was filled with emotion.

"You finish eating breakfast"—she turned again, coffee cup in hand—"and then I'd guess there'd be some baths."

"How about what comes next? This won't have an impact?" I looked to Jericho to gauge his reaction, the discussions many and life changing. Ms. Welts's coffee cup clanked against the counter. Saying it aloud in front of her made it real, and so I did, "About adopting Thomas and Tabitha."

"We want them to be a part of our family," Jericho was quick to add, his eyes fixed on mine. "It's what we both want."

"It is," I said, answering him. I could have melted right then and there, my legs wobbly as we openly expressed a blueprint for the rest of our lives.

When my gaze returned to Ms. Welts, she'd braced the counter, a hand covering her heart. "That is wonderful to hear." Her face was flush as she jotted down something in her little notebook. When the top of the pen stopped moving, she looked up and said, "The stability for them. A consistent and stable home environment along with financials and support from friends and family."

"We can do that," Jericho said, chin dipping to his chest.

Ms. Welts took a breath, gaze shifting to the children, saying, "It would mean submitting a petition to adopt Thomas and Tabitha."

"A petition?" I asked, unfamiliar with the process. "Does that mean a hearing and court?"

"Family court," she answered, focus returning. She put on a reassuring smile, saying, "It's all quite the formality, but you two will do just fine. If you're willing, I can set it up."

"We'll make it happen," Jericho said.

Ms. Welts looked to me to join in Jericho's declaration. I nodded and said, "It'll happen." But inside, the questions blew up like a swelled balloon. We worked in careers that put our lives at risk every single day. I peered over to Thomas and Tabitha and the mess of pancakes in front of them. They'd torn the breakfast apart and fastened the bits and pieces into an edible jigsaw puzzle. My heart swelled. They deserved everything and more. I turned back to Jericho, sleeving my arm in his and giving him an assurance that I was on board. Inside though, down deep where secrets dwell, the thought of providing stability had me wondering if we could be who Thomas and Tabitha needed.

ELEVEN

I tapped the navigation on my phone, the map zooming out to show the bridge to the mainland. The navigation unit called out Tina Walsh's home address, the destination we'd attempted less than forty-eight hours earlier. She was the next sorority sister we were going to interview. From Janine Scott, we learned that Tina Walsh continued diving with Karol Witney while everyone else returned to the boat to snorkel. There was only one problem with the drive. A truck was following us.

It was faded yellow with mismatched door panels. One like eggshell and the other one brown like dirt. It was tall with dual wheels on the rear axle, something that I'd known to be called a dually. Its front bumper was mottled by chunky spots of rust, the bottom edge brittle with decay. I saw it first when we drove north out of Kitty Hawk but didn't consider it. Not until I turned left onto the bridge. Blue-gray puffs of smoke followed it as we reached the halfway mark of the bridge, the truck's motor clapping the air. My insides were like jelly that pulsed nervously. I gripped the steering wheel hard enough to make the leather creak, the muscles in my forearms strung taut like rope. I was convinced that whoever hit us the other day must have switched cars. They'd come back to finish what they started. They knew there was an APB, and they knew who I was and what we'd been investigating.

I tapped Tracy's arm and motioned to the rear. She loosened her seatbelt enough to turn and see what I was seeing. We said nothing as we exited the Outer Banks, crossing the bridge to the mainland. Outside the driver-side window, the road had a jaggy gouge in the asphalt that stretched across the opposite lane and into the shoulder. It was where my car had rolled to its death after being struck. We passed it and marked a single mile closer to Tina Walsh's house than we'd traveled the other day.

When we reached the first traffic light, the yellow truck pulled up alongside us. Instinctively, my hand drifted lower to rest on the butt of my gun. I kept it holstered though. Tracy jabbed at the controls on her door, the motor buried behind the armrest clicking hollowly, the window already raised as high as it could go. A band of sunlight put the driver's face in view. He was a man in his thirties, scruffy chin, short bangs with longer hair in the back. The knot of worry loosened when the light flashed green and the truck jumped into the intersection, blue smoke following. The driver gave Tracy a smile and a somewhat suave, 'How ya doing' type nod before leaving.

"It was nothing." I tapped the destination, the navigation unit calling out the miles and telling me to turn left at the next light. Tracy rolled her eyes as I went on to explain, "I guess we weren't the only ones heading in this direction."

"You're so keyed up, you've got me looking over my shoulder." She opened her laptop and continued working.

"It was a minor overreaction," I admitted. She side-eyed me as we pulled up to the address. "Can you blame me?"

Mouth twisting. "I suppose not."

She tapped the screen to close the navigation map, closing her laptop too. From the road, there was only a mailbox, its wood post beaten by age, the address numbers sitting askew with one of them missing. "You sure this is it?"

"It's it." I tried to see beyond a row of tall evergreens edging the property, but the overgrowth was too thick. I turned onto a gravel driveway, leaving the asphalt, the tires kicking up the stones. Past the row of evergreen, there was a house set back fifty yards, a red brick two-story home with a wood porch. "See. We're here."

Tracy searched the grounds, asking, "It doesn't look like anyone is here?"

"Let's hope she's home." I motioned to the porch where the front door was ajar, a dark ribbon showing in place of light. The stillness of the house was odd considering the mess on the patio. There was a chair turned over, and a potted plant lying on its side. A puddle of black soil was spilled around it, the plant's leafy remains smashed.

Tracy glanced at me, saying, "What do you make of that?"

"Stay close to me." We exited the car, the doors latching softly with my finger pressed to my lips. There was noise like furniture being moved, the echoes of glass shattering, the clamors deep inside the house. There were no voices though. No conversation or back and forth, which had me thinking there was one person inside. When I reached the door, I eased it open enough to see. A gray figure sprang to life on the wall like a giant shadow puppet. They went still, motionless, the wood beneath our shoes creaking. "Police—"

I never finished. Glass crashed through the door, chunks spilling onto the porch as footsteps stomped away. The front door was already open, Tina Walsh's life possibly in danger, I shoved it clear and ran into her home. The living room had been tossed. Bookshelves emptied. Couch cushions torn apart. Even the flat-screen television had been toppled from its perch. A shadow appeared in the kitchen, the blurry figure running toward the back. I gave chase, hurdling an overturned ottoman, sidestepping the flat screen as the backdoor slammed shut.

Tracy was gone, my heart sinking. She'd run around the side

of the house to help. But she was a crime-scene investigator. She wasn't a cop. She wasn't armed. I blew through the backdoor, the rear of the house a half an acre of tall grass, swaying with a westerly breeze, the tips budding with seed. Tracy was twenty yards deep and approaching a thicket, arms waving for me to follow. I saw a man disappear into the grove of heavy bushes and trees. He wore a blue shirt and denim jeans, his face hidden beneath the shade of a hat.

"Don't go in there!" I screamed to Tracy, having no idea what was on the other side. I holstered my gun, the field's grassy stalks whipping across my bare arms. The ground was mushy, soft enough to trap a shoe if I didn't keep moving. My heart leapt when Tracy reached the property line. "Stop!"

A scream. It was my daughter! She could be three. She could be ten or fifteen, or twenty-two. I'd always know her voice, and the blood-curdling sound of it stole my voice. I jumped the boggy remains of turned soil and broke into the thicket, stopping where the dense tangle sprouted from the ground. "Casey!"

"Oh shit!" I gasped, swinging my arms to stay balanced. I fell to my knees and belly, arm extended to Tracy. Tina Walsh's property ended with a fall of fifteen feet or more. There was a steep trench that was ten yards wide and filled with rocks and dead trees, the branches long and sharp and ivory bright like the tusks of an elephant. Beneath all of it, there was the faint sound of water trickling, a creek under the stones, a natural boundary between properties. Tracy was on her back, groaning, her hands covering her face. Birds flitted from tree to tree, watching as I tended to my daughter. "Are you hurt?"

"Just my pride," Tracy answered. She was shaken and looked as though she'd almost given up her ghost. But she was okay and that rested well with my nerves. She let out a yelp when moving, her face cramped. "Maybe an ankle too."

Footsteps approached, twigs breaking. "We've got company." I got up, hand returning to my gun.

"Ya know, it's easy to bust a leg down there," a voice said, a woman's face appearing from behind the shrubs. She had red hair and freckles, her skin pale and her eyes a blue-hazel color. She wore coveralls and rubber boots which were coated with the dried mud. She came up next to me and knelt to take hold of Tracy's arm. I joined her, the two of us grunting against Tracy's weight. The woman looked at me, saying, "You must be the detective who called."

Tracy raised a hand. "That was me."

"Detective Casey White." I handed her my card. She looked it over and stuffed it in a pocket on the front of her coveralls. "And you must be Tina Walsh."

"I am. I just got back from a workout." She hung a thumb over her shoulder, her voice breaking, "That's my place? You... you got any idea who trashed it?"

"We were hoping you could tell us."

A shrug. "Fuck if I know," she answered, swallowing a cry. She perched her fists on her hips, sadness eclipsing the anger. "I just got that flat screen too... I don't understand! What a mess—"

"Can we?" I motioned to her house.

When we turned to leave, a plume of dust rose from the adjacent property. There was a distant engine revving, the sound moving with the clouds, the tree line hiding any vehicles. Tina saw it too, saying, "That's strange. I haven't seen anyone on that land in forever. Must be finally selling."

"I don't think that was a real-estate agent." A hard look, she narrowed her eyes. "I think it could be the guy who trashed your place."

"Can you like call someone now!" she blurted, her phone in hand. The dust spiraled upward, the car impossible to make out. She lowered her phone, looking defeated. "I can't even see them."

We said nothing more as we returned, Tracy walking with a noticeable limp. At one point she gripped my shoulder, hopping, Tina Walsh consoling, "Let's take care of that. I've got some ice."

"Oh wow," Tracy gasped as we took in the level of destruction inside the house.

The look on Tina Walsh's face made me feel bad, especially when her lips quivered while piecing together a broken plate. She lowered it to the table, my offering, "If you've got a spare broom?"

Her voice breaking, "Maybe you can, like, get fingerprints or something?"

She cleared a loveseat for Tracy to sit, flipping the ottoman upright. There was compassion and concern, Tina Walsh's nature showing without her speaking. She braced Tracy's arm, helping her sit while I raised Tracy's leg. Unlacing Tracy's shoe, she glanced at the broken plate asking, "You know, that black powdery stuff they use on television?"

"Thanks, I got that," Tracy told her, shoving fingers beneath the laces. "Gloves. I'm certain that I saw them wearing blue gloves."

"Whoever did this was being careful." I put the cushions on the couch, shoving the material inside and zipping them shut. "Do you have any reason to believe someone would want to do this?"

"No idea!" Tina Walsh answered, voice raised. She went to the kitchen. I followed, cautious not to let her out of my sight. She slammed the bottom refrigerator door, the shelves broken, food containers piled in a heap, some spilled onto the tiled floor. Her hands disappeared into a freezer drawer above where she filled a plastic bag with half-moon shaped cubes. She saw me watching, and raised a hand, saying, "It's just ice."

"We'll do what we can to find who did this to your house, but we're here to talk about Karol Witney. We believe you were the last one to have seen her alive?"

She said nothing but closed the freezer door and returned to Tracy. She cradled the bag of ice onto Tracy's ankle, the sides of it puffy. Tracy flinched, Tina lifting it with a squint. "Sorry. I know it's cold."

"I got it," Tracy said, taking the bag. "Thank you."

"I'm not sure if I was the last one to see Karol alive," Tina answered, assessing the damages. She went to a fish tank along the far wall, and breathed a sigh of relief. It was one of the few things to survive the attack. There were neon and electric-blue colored fish swimming aimlessly. A pair of goldfish hovered near the surface, facing our direction, that seemed to be staring. One of the plastic ocean ornaments gurgled bubbles as Tina sprinkled flakes on the surface, instructing the fish, "Come and get it."

Tracy grimaced, shifting the ice pack. She wiped a bead of sweat from her forehead, and asked, "You didn't change out of the gear to snorkel?"

"Dunno why they wanted to snorkel," Tina complained. She knelt to adjust the ice, a certificate sitting askew on the wall indicating a medical background. "We were there to dive."

"Understandable. I prefer diving myself."

"Me too," Tracy added.

A slow nod. "Then you get it." Tina stood and turned over a chair, a wood leg striking the floor with a thud. "Damn, just refinished it."

I couldn't help myself and picked up another chair, righting it before tucking it beneath a dining table. It didn't occur to me until I saw the nursing certificate on the wall that whoever ransacked Tina Walsh's home may have done so completely unrelated to the case. "Do you keep drugs in the house?"

The whites of her eyes flashed like a car's headlights, a smirk following with a snicker. "Drugs?" she asked, couch cushion stuffing bunched between her fingers. She saw the certificate on the wall, understanding. "That was my parents' idea."

"You went to school to be a nurse?" Tracy asked.

She shook her head, saying, "To be honest, I could never get comfortable around sick people."

"What do you do now?"

"Administrative assistant... on and off." A deep sigh, of what might have been discontent. Her gaze drifted to a stack of unopened mail, a bold, red-lettered past-due stamp on one of them. "I got let go last month. Some shit about downsizing."

A job loss and then to have her place ransacked. "I'm sorry to hear that." A part of me wanted to tell her to contact the station. Alice, our station manager, had been looking for an administrative assistant. For another time though. "Can you talk us through when you last saw Karol Witney."

"It was the dive," she began and nudged her chin toward the other end of the flatscreen. I grabbed the edge, lifting it as she lifted. We placed the television back on its perch, the television stand adorned with several remote controls. The screen was black and clean of any cracks. "Karol swam ahead of me toward the wreck. I couldn't make heads or tails of it. Looked like a jumbled bunch of wood to me."

"How deep was that?" Tracy asked, telephone in hand.

Tina picked up one of the remotes and pressed the power button. Nothing. Her lips thinned with disappointment, chin quivering. "New too." She worked the remote batteries, swapping them and answering, "I dunno, maybe thirty feet down." The power plug dangled loose behind the television stand. I shoved my hand behind it, plugging it into the socket. She squeezed the remote again, the television turning on, the screen shining in her eyes.

"Just the power."

"Sweet," she exclaimed quietly. "Thank you. TV seems like the only thing my brain can focus on since the dive."

"Can't miss that." The screen was clear of defect, her television had survived the ransacking. "Thirty feet? That's when the group broke off and returned to the charter boat?"

"No, they left almost as soon as they started diving." She made a tsk-tsk sound, adding, "Didn't make sense to me to get all that gear on and then switch to snorkeling."

"So you were alone?" The younger charter owner hadn't mentioned losing sight of both women. He would have had to though, based on what she was saying. Tina cocked her head. I clarified, "After the other women returned to the boat, you were alone because Karol Witney already split from the group?"

Confusion set in her eyes, fingers tapping her lips. "Ya know, I don't remember when Karol left to go on her own and when the girls returned."

"Tell us about what happened next."

Tina thought about the events as I took to fixing one of the couch cushions, shoving the stuffing back into it.

"She went left. I went right, but I never left the sight of the divemaster or charter boat," Tina began. She returned to the tank, the colorful fish darting at the surface. "I was at the bottom and sifting the sand for shells and shark teeth."

"You were looking for a megalodon?" Tracy asked, sliding a book from the coffee table, the title including the word, *fossil*.

"Always," Tina answered with a grin. "It's like the holy grail of shark teeth."

"And then?" I gave Tracy a cursory glance. She slid the book back into place. "What happened next?"

"I saw the divemaster first. Shawn? Might have been Patrick." She considered the names, the fish tank bubbling. "Doesn't matter. Does it?"

"It'd help if you could remember." What we learned from the Rutledge brothers, it was Patrick acting as the divemaster that day. The older brother stayed on board. Her face twisted, the recollection not coming. "It's okay."

She waved a hand and drove her fingers into her hair. "Anyway. Like I was saying. I was at the bottom, sifting." She turned to Tracy and then back to me, adding, "We had great visibility by the way. But then I saw the divemaster kicking up a storm, like flying through the water past the wreck we'd anchored near."

"Do you recall which wreck it was?" We already had the name from the Rutledge brothers. She shook her head. "That's fine. You were saying about the divemaster?"

"Swimming like he was being chased by a shark. That's when he waved at me to follow. So I did." We could hear the excitement of the dive and see it on her face. It vanished. "When I got close enough, I saw Karol just floating there. I didn't see any bubbles or movement."

Her words stung. Tracy glanced over at me, and I imagined she saw Jericho's lifeless body in Tina Walsh's words too. I felt emotion rise in my chest and forced myself to take a second. I cleared my throat, asking, "You helped the divemaster?"

Nodding as the whites of her eyes flashed again. "Tried to." She started blinking to stave the tears, her eyes turning red. The nod turned to a shake, a tremble, answering, "But she was dead. I mean, like, already dead. I shoved the regulator in her mouth, forcing air, but—" Tina Walsh heaved a ragged breath and felt her way to a chair, dropping into it where she shoved her face into her hands. A muffled cry came as she continued, "—I'm sorry."

"It's understandable, and I'm sorry to ask these questions." From the kitchen, I grabbed a bottle of water off the pile in the refrigerator, snapping the plastic cap with a twist, and handed it to her. After she sipped it, I asked, "It is important for us to know where the divemaster was and if anyone else was around Karol."

"That's just it. I think we were alone." She tipped the bottle for a steeper drink. "The older one on the boat, he'd mentioned we were in luck to get a spot. There were other boats already on that wreck."

"There were other boats, but no other divers?"

She regarded the question while I paged through the pictures sent to us by Janine Scott. In one of them, the sorority sisters were huddled together and wearing snorkeling gear. I could almost read the names on the transom of the other boats.

"I can't tell you what the other boats were doing. Maybe they were snorkeling too," Tina answered. Annoyance edged her voice and she stood and continued to clean the mess. "I thought Karol's death was an accident?"

Tracy laced her shoe, keeping it loose. She stood with a grunt and handed the icepack to Tina. "Standard investigation," she replied.

"What can you tell us about Jim Witney?" It was a question that I'd waited on, wanting to spring it when least expected. A wry grin formed. "Something is funny?"

She chuckled, her gaze returning to her fish. "He's a slut."

I didn't know how to respond but questioned it. "A slut?" I asked, wanting clarity. From the look on Tracy's face, fingers pressed against her lips, she wanted to hear more too.

Tina looked at us with a nod. "A real dog if you know what I mean."

"Another girl in the sorority house?"

Her eyes grew bright with another laugh. "*All* the girls," she said, voice curving.

"Including you?" I had to ask the question and thought Tracy's eyeballs were going to fall out of her skull. I wondered if we'd hear similar when we interviewed the other sorority sisters?

Tina's smile grew wide, one brow cocked. "Yeah, quite a few times. But that changed once I introduced him to the girls. That's when he hooked up with Karol." Her expression turned serious, and she crossed her arms. "He was a lot of fun at first, but there was a dark side of him. Troubling, ya know?"

There was fear in her voice as she chased a chill, shuddering.

"Did you ever feel that your life was in danger when you were with him?"

She knelt slowly and picked up one of the books, its binder torn, a few of the pages falling. "Yeah, that's what I mean. It was danger. When I couldn't feel safe with him anymore, I ended it."

"The other sorority sisters?" Tracy asked, getting up slowly.

"Same," Tina answered. "We traded some stories, figured it was best."

"Except Karol? Their relationship continued after college."

Tina's mouth twisted, leading me to think she had more. "Not all of you ended the relationship?"

"Well, she'd never admit it," Tina began, a hand on her hip, neck bent like she was gossiping. "We all thought that he was still carrying on with Janine."

"Really?" Tracy said with a rise in her voice. She cleared her throat, writing it down. "I'll make a note of it."

I thought it odd that Janine Scott hadn't mentioned any of this. Perhaps she didn't want it discussed. Maybe she wanted to leave it in the past. "How about after the Witneys married?"

Tina shook her head vigorously as if I'd touched on a voodoo topic. "I've already said too much. Like I mentioned, we suspected Jim and Janine were hitting it, but nothing to substantiate it."

I added the names Janine and Jim to my notes, circling them. Was there something there? "Thank you for taking the time to help with the questions."

"And thanks for the help with my ankle," Tracy said. She motioned to the surroundings, telling her, "Take pictures if there's considerable cost. We can write it up for your insurance adjuster."

"Yeah?" Tina asked, looking more relaxed, relieved by the offer.

"Certainly," I assured her, taking Tracy's arm to help her to the door. "We'd be happy to help."

Tina followed, instructing, "You should stay off of it." She turned around to face a mess of books on the floor, asking, "Am I in danger?"

Nothing of value that I could see had been taken. "Whoever did this was clearly searching for something." I couldn't give her a straight yes or no response. But asked, "Do you know what it was?"

"I wish I did," she replied, broom and dustpan in hand. "I have no fucking idea."

"I recommend you come with us down to the station and file a report." I made the suggestion with the idea of asking more questions in the car.

Tina Walsh looked over the damages and then up at a clock on the wall. "It's okay if I go myself later today?" she asked, waving at the floor. "I want to clean some of this up first."

"Of course. When you get there, ask for Alice."

"Alice."

"Janine Scott and Jim Witney?" Tracy asked. She smirked like Tina. A cringe swiftly wiped the grin when she put weight on her foot.

"College romance?" I challenged, unsure what to make of it. "It sounds like Jim Witney was like an exploration or something to accomplish."

"Like he was some kind of freshman college course," she said, grinning. When we were back in the car, she laughed, "Jim Witney 101 for three credits."

"Funny girl." I let out a short laugh but changed the subject before we got carried away. I showed her the pictures sent by Janine Scott. There were three with names of boats, two of which were too blurry for us to read, and one with just enough letters to start a guessing game.

"What's your idea?" she asked, rubbing her ankle.

"First, I think we need to get that foot checked." She scoffed, the sound of it making my motherly instincts kick into gear. "Now hold on a minute. I can already see bruising. A quick check?"

"Fine," she agreed. She took my phone, zooming in on the picture. "Now, your idea?"

"Whoever was in the water with the sorority sisters had to have come from one of those boats."

TWELVE

The station was thankfully quiet. I gave our station manager a wave. She stood at the receiving desk, her face partially hidden behind a computer screen. There was a man and woman sitting on one of the benches, both handcuffed and wearing a face filled with dread that came with an arrest. Alice mouthed the words *shoplifting* and rolled her eyes. I opened the small gate, Tracy taking hold before it slapped shut behind us. When we reached our desks, we stopped across from the new team member's desk, Sherry Levin. Sherry had been in training, renewing her certifications, which kept her busy. We needed her help with the photographs and names of the boats that had been in the vicinity of Karol Witney's murder.

"The training went well?" Sherry looked up from her computer, a wall of monitors erected from her desk. It reminded me of Nichelle, the team member Sherry was replacing.

"Sorry? What's that?" she asked in a raspy voice. She stood abruptly, as if it was a requirement, and brushed her hands against her slacks and shirt nervously. Her height was just beneath my chin, she was thin with a round face, her eyes narrow, her nose petite. She tucked her long brown hair behind her ears and asked, "The training, ma'am?"

I cringed. "Call me Casey. Please." Ma'am made me feel older than I was, even though I knew it was used as respect. I leaned against the cubicle entrance, relaxing, and hoping she'd relax. "We're kinda loose on the formalities."

"Oh, okay, detective," she replied and flashed a grin. I decided that the title detective would do for now. When she was comfortable, she'd use my name.

Being nosy, I looked over her shoulder, curious what she was working on. The top monitors were covered with photographs from the dive, the ones sent to me by Janine Scott.

She followed my gaze, asking, "I just got access to the county's system. Want me to archive—?"

"Not archive," Tracy commented, appearing next to me. She looked at the walls of the cubicle, eyeing some of the science fiction memorabilia. This had been Nichelle's desk, the walls once covered with cat pictures with funny and motivational sayings. Initially, their breakup had been difficult, Tracy seeming frozen by the kind of pain that made it impossible to move on. But she was getting through it. I hope she'd heard me when I suggested getting out more with a few friends. The cubicle was a tough one, the station manager reassigning the desk. Tracy cleared her throat, moving toward the monitors, saying, "Do you know how to pull the names from those boats?"

"The names?" Sherry took a quick breath, uncertainty on her face. I followed Tracy, Sherry making room for me, the three of us huddling around her desk. She put on a slight grin and clumsily picked up a pencil and pad. "If you show me what you need?"

"We can do that." I tried to sound reassuring, but in my head, I couldn't help myself and was comparing. Nichelle had been unique. Like Sherry, she'd come to the station working as our main IT person. But she'd also been an online sleuther, investigating forgotten cases in the off hours, which had included my daughter's kidnapping. We couldn't expect the same with Sherry, who may have taken this job with one thing in mind, working the tech. Hand firm against the desk, I motioned to her mouse, asking, "May I?"

"Sure, yeah. Please do," she replied, an eyelid twitching. She rolled her chair behind me, instructing, "Please, sit."

Chair creaking, I clicked through the pictures until finding the one with the boat transoms in the background. The foreground of the picture was filled with sunshiny faces, the sorority sisters with their hair wet and slicked back, beads of ocean spray on their cheeks and shoulders and chest. There were seven of the sisters in this picture, a few blurred faces on the fringe, and all with snorkeling gear. It was the boats behind them that we wanted. "We want to find out who owns these boats," I instructed, shaking the mouse cursor over one in the background where boat transoms had names like *Little Miss* and *The Mystique*.

"The boat names," Sherry exclaimed, understanding. Her forehead wrinkled as uncertainty reappeared. "How do I do that?"

"I can help with that part," Tracy said as I zoomed in on a few of the boats.

"All boats are registered with title and hull identification numbers," I told Sherry. "But the names aren't."

"However, there are boat name registration sites which we can use," Tracy continued.

Sherry tilted her head to the side, asking, "And you need me to help with what exactly?"

"It's the ones we can't read." I panned the screen to the boat where the name was only partially visible.

Tracy let out a sigh, heavier than the usual, which told me she was growing impatient. She turned to Sherry, asking, "Do you have any image processing tools? You know, like the stuff to clear up the images?"

"I use Paint a lot," she replied, smiling briefly with understanding. When she saw Tracy's disappointment, "That's not what you mean though?"

"Tracy, you have some of the tools we've used before?" I asked while motioning subtly toward her desk. My pocket buzzed with a call, the phone's light blinking through the fabric.

"I do," she answered, catching on when she saw I had a call. I got up to leave, Tracy adding, "Sherry, let me show what I mean..."

I was gone without another word and left the area when seeing Alice's name on my phone. I held up my phone while opening the gate, the top of her hair bouncing as she came around the receiving area. "You rang?"

"That was me," she answered, eyeing my phone with a squint, unable to read it. Her hair was particularly stiff today, the hairspray she used tickling my nose. Alice worked as many years on the force as I'd been alive. She had a long sturdy face that exalted a do not mess with me build, which made her perfect to receive the street arrests. She'd toyed around with retirement once or twice, but always returned, saying that there wasn't anything out there to do that she hadn't already done before. I absolutely knew what she meant by that, and in a way it made me both excited and sad. It meant that I'd probably be working homicide the rest of my days. How many more cases would that be? Her lips moved as she read her name on my screen. "I suppose you knew that."

"You got something for me?"

Alice had been our station manager since before I became a permanent resident of the Outer Banks. While she tended to everything station related, I'd learned to use her as a source of informal station to station phone calls. Today's call was to a Chicago Police Department station where Jim Witney had been an officer for much of his adult life. She opened a spiral notebook and produced a pencil that had been hidden inside her hair.

"What is it?"

She glanced over her shoulder at the couple on the bench,

handcuffs jangling, the woman with stringy hair and deepest eyes pleading, "I need to use the bathroom?"

"You can hold it," Alice told her.

"But I can't," the woman complained and shook the handcuffs.

"After what we saw you holding up there!" Alice scoffed. She turned back to me, saying, "You know you can hold it."

"Who did you speak with?"

"The station manager," she answered. She shook her head. "And boy could that woman talk."

I felt like saying, I know what you mean, but kept that response hidden behind a grin. "About Jim Witney?"

"Well, first off," she began, her voice lilting like she was gossiping. "They only just found out that his wife had died. There was no mention of it before."

"That makes sense since we found out he was already here." Alice mouthed the word, *really*. "Uh-huh. He was already in the Outer Banks."

"I really gotta go!" we heard, the stringy-haired woman complaining. "Come on!"

"In a minute!" Alice roared, her voice steeped with aggravation, blood rising on her neck.

She turned back to me and put on a smile. "They liked him at the station. Said that he came in and did his job."

"The perfect officer?" The hospitals. The spousal abuse. Did nobody know? Alice tapped the page with her pencil. She was holding on to something. "What is it?"

She leaned forward, saying, "I hate to talk ill of someone."

"You won't be. This is part of our investigation," I assured her. She looked conflicted. "If it helps, he's a suspect in his wife's murder. We're also certain he abused his wife."

Her face brightened with understanding. "That makes sense. Over the years, there were several complaints filed against him."

She shrugged her shoulders, adding, "One pending, all the others dismissed."

We turned to the sound of tinkling, the stringy-haired woman telling Alice, "I told you I had to go."

"Are you kidding me!" Alice shouted, head rocking. She turned back to me and forced a smile. "Well, I have to deal with that."

"I am sorry that I kept you." I felt bad, but the notes were worth it. Alice tore the page, handing it to me, the bottom of it showing a large scribbling, the word, *Family*. "What's that mean?"

"Yeah, right, almost forgot. When the CPD station manager was talking about Jim Witney's wife dying here, she mentioned that it was good that he had family in the Outer Banks."

Muscles flinching, thinking I'd heard her wrong as the hairs on my neck stood. I knew for a fact that the Witneys did not have any family here. "Are you sure that you heard her right? She said it was good that Jim Witney had family in the Outer Banks?"

"A sister." Alice turned to walk away, adding, "A sister with a few kids. CPD station manager said that he traveled to the Outer Banks at least once a month. He'd been doing it for years."

"Years?" I stood there, my gaze fixed firmly on the puddle beneath the arrested woman, the ceiling lights gleaming from the surface like a mirage hovering above hot sand. "You didn't happen to get a name?"

"Of the sister?" Alice asked. I replied with a nod. "Station manager didn't know it."

"Thanks again, Alice." I opened the gate, the wood smoothed by years of hands that came before. Jim Witney was regularly visiting family in the Outer Banks. When we interviewed him, Jim Witney said that he'd never been to the Outer Banks before. That was a lie. Was it possible that he was one of those men with multiple homes? Multiple wives? Complete families in different states? My head blew up with the craziest ideas of what might be. That's how the investigating began. The crazier the better. It had to start with something. Multiple families. Why else would he have been coming here for years?

"Casey!" Tracy shouted, hands waving. Sherry waved along with her, joining in. They'd moved to Tracy's cubicle where her monitors showed the same pictures from Janine Scott. One of them was enlarged four maybe six times, the letters on the transom splotchy, colors inverted, the picture turned into a negative. She held her hands to present the monitor like she was Vanna White turning letters on the *Wheel of Fortune*. "Progress! We've got the beginning of a boat's name."

I squinted to make out the letters, reading it aloud, "Buoys and... is that the letter I?"

"We think there are two," Sherry said, holding up two fingers. She snapped her fingers, jabbing the air. "Tracy, Roman numerals."

"Could be," Tracy said, adding, "Once we figure it out, we can identify who the boat is registered to." Tracy clicked through a second series of images, the progression of sharpening shifting with animated colors.

"You know what, I think that says, *Buoys II Men*." I felt my stomach lift. They stared at the screen, not seeing it. "Boyz II Men? They were a huge band out of Philly?"

"There's too many letters in the last word," Sherry commented. She counted out the blurry figures, adding, "Six, not three?"

"You'll love this," I said, pinching my chin. "How about *Buoys II Seamen*? A very fitting name for a boat."

"Shit, I bet that's it," Tracy answered, tapping the keyboard.

"That might be!" Sherry smiled. The excitement of puzzle solving was a better look for her. Better than seeing her nervous and anxious. "We'll get started on tracking down the owner of the boat."

"I've got something too." I handed Alice's notes to Tracy,

explaining, "It seems Jim Witney has been visiting the area for a long time."

"Visiting?" Tracy asked, eyeing her screen, the work of image processing producing a name. "Why was he visiting?"

I felt a slow smile growing, the clue being juicy good. "According to his station manager up in Chicago, Jim Witney has family here, a sister with kids."

Tracy scowled and shook her head. "He doesn't have any family here. I checked for that."

"That's the suspect?" Sherry asked, excitement returning.

"Definitely." Before returning to my desk, I added, "I believe Jim Witney was in the water at the time his wife was murdered."

"A sister with kids," Tracy muttered, fingers tapping the desk while working the words like a puzzle. "Visiting for years."

"Do you know who I think he's been visiting?" I held my breath waiting for her to get it, the anticipation rising fast. When she shook her head, I answered, "Who lives here and has children? And whose husband travels?"

Tracy's eyes bulged as she blurted, "Janine Scott!"

THIRTEEN

Janine Scott wasn't as receptive to meeting with us on our second visit. The day had grown late and the daylight's blue skies ripened to the color of honeydew. There were cicadas trilling and tree frogs singing, a chorus rising from a swath of tall trees behind the Scotts' property. In a few weeks, the summer songs would go dormant with the season change. Other night life had come alive too. The winged varieties that Tracy didn't care for took flight in the dusky gold hour, tapping streetlights which flicked on one at a time. She shuffled her feet, eyes fixed on the fleeting activity while tapping her toe. We waited for a response to my knocking on the door, but there was no answer. Janine Scott was home though. Like our first visit, I could hear the children playing.

I hadn't given much consideration to the slut comments made by Tina Walsh when she explained her sorority house's carnal appetite for Jim Witney. But she'd also mentioned that Jim Witney and Janine Scott continued to have relations when the other women ended it. Could Janine Scott be the "sister" that Jim Witney's station manager told Alice about? Was Jim Witney the husband Janine Scott said was always traveling? A passing notion which had started small. It was one of those fleeting ideas with just enough barb to catch a bigger thought. Later, it turned into a working theory and compelled me to investigate.

The driveway had one vehicle parked in it, a plum color minivan that was at least twenty years old. Money, Janine Scott's finances, the state of her home. None of these were in question before. I don't know how much a Chicago PD officer makes up north, but if it's anything like the salaries in Philly or the Outer Banks, then every dollar must have been stretched to carry two homes. Rust ran along the minivan's bottom, and the rear quarter panel was bubbled, the paint chipped. Some of the roofing tiles were broken or lifted and needing repair.

The door opened suddenly, air lifting Janine Scott's hair. "What is it?" She wore no makeup and was dressed in pajamas that hung loose. Her children played in the downstairs area, running and shouting, a face appearing to look at us. She picked up a laundry basket which was heaping tall with freshly dried clothes. She began to turn around, saying, "Close the door after yourselves."

We were inside, Tracy shrugging her shoulders slightly and entering ahead, climbing the stairs. I followed, closing the door softly, the metal clacking. I looked around with a different lens on, the investigation deepening. I saw the house differently, smelled it even. The dust and the mustiness, an air-freshener plugged into a wall outlet to help curb the damp smell. If I could smell the home's secrets, what would they tell me? There was a hole in the ceiling above the kitchen entrance, a past leak in the roof. On the walls, the paint had been marred, the plaster gouged, an indentation that was roughly the size of a fist. My heart sank when I saw it. When we reached the top of the steps, Janine dropped the laundry basket, its thud against the floor quieting the children's play. A moment later, they resumed, the playful squeals and laughter rising up the stairs. Like actors to a stage, we resumed our places from the first visit, sitting when Janine Scott sat.

"Thank you for speaking—"

She shook her head angrily to interrupt. "What is it you want?" From the basket, she yanked a peach-colored bathroom towel and began folding it.

"Karol Witney." I could have jumped right into the questioning about Jim Witney, our main suspect. But if I was right about Janine Scott and Jim Witney, then there was a motive that had to be explored too. Her hands dropped onto her lap, the peach towel crumpling. A look of annoyance appeared. "Were you close friends?"

Janine Scott resumed folding the towel, holding the corner high to cover her face, answering, "I don't know. I mean, we were roommates in the house, the sorority house." She folded the towel by half, her face reappearing. "Honestly, we weren't like besties if that's what you mean. I really didn't know anything more about her than any of the other girls."

My throat itched, the smell of fabric softener tickling. "Would you have any reason to want her dead?"

Lips parting with a silent gasp. "What... what kind of question is that?"

"Well hello," I said before continuing. A young child appeared next to me. She was around three, younger than the boy and girl I'd seen before. She looked up and put on a big grin and grabbed my leg playfully. Her mother began to get up. "It's okay." The child tugged on my pants, eager to show me one of her toys. I knelt next to her, her mother kneeling too, and saw what had been a far-fetched idea. Until now. In the child's smiling face, I found the sapphire eyes of her father. The bright blue unmistakable. In their child's face, I found Jim Witney.

Janine Scott cleared her throat, her demeanor shifting and turning nervous. "This... this is my girl, Jemma."

"Hi there, Jemma." I wanted to playfully pinch one of her chubby cheeks but didn't. Instead, I searched the walls and corner table, as well as the old curio cabinet in the corner. All the pictures were of the children, a few with their mother too. None however, showed the father. I turned to Janine Scott, asking, "Your husband. The one who travels a lot. It's Jim Witney?"

Tears shined in Janine Scott's eyes. Jemma saw her mother's face and instantly pouted. "It's okay, baby." She lifted the three-year-old and glared at me. "There's been no laws broken, so what do you want?"

She was right. What Jim Witney did with Janine Scott wasn't a law-breaking offense. Not unless there was fraud executed along the way such as insurance claims or other means. But there was a broader motive, the murder of Karol Witney. I looked hard at the child who was old enough to understand the words I'd use. "Would it be best to speak alone?"

"You go on downstairs with your brother and sister," Janine Scott whispered in her daughter's ear. "The grown-ups have to talk." She lowered Jemma, arms stretching, the sleeve of her shirt rising enough for me to see a bruise on her shoulder. Tracy saw it too, shifting uncomfortably.

I waited until Jemma was down the first set of stairs, and asked, "Is there any reason you or your children are in danger?"

Janine Scott didn't understand the question until I dipped my chin toward her shoulder, the sleeve remaining bunched.

She froze a second, unsure of what to do or say. As she tried to cover the bruise, she answered in a shaky voice, "He's a good man."

"That's not what I asked you." My voice remained flat, almost callous. There was an immediate need rising for the safety and welfare of Janine Scott and her children. "Are you and your children safe?"

"We're safe," she answered, swiping the teary streak on her cheek. "It's the stress. He's got his job in Chicago and only gets down here once a month, sometimes twice."

"Funny, he said that he'd never been to the Outer Banks," Tracy scoffed, speaking openly. Her mouth twitched at the choice of words. "I didn't mean funny."

"It's okay," Janine Scott replied. "It's been a secret a long time."

"It must be very difficult, raising the children alone," I commented, sounding supportive. "And keeping a house?"

"My mom did it with less after Dad died. She helps us a lot." Janine's gaze drifted toward the ceiling, the stains. "But she's getting older now."

"Do you think Karol Witney knew about you and her husband?"

A pause. Janine twisted around toward a crying shrill. Laughter came next, easing her concern. When her focus returned to us, she shook her head. "She didn't know."

I motioned to the portraits, the number of pictures. "You don't think she wondered why he was coming to the Outer Banks so often."

She crossed her arms and pursed her lips. "To be honest, I didn't really care." She blew out a rushed breath, frowning. I sensed the anger. The jealousy. "Jim belonged here with me and his children."

"Was it his career?" Tracy asked. No answer.

Tracy handed me her phone, Jim Witney's official Chicago Police Department identification on the screen. I'd felt my phone buzz in my pocket, having gotten the same text message from Alice. She had contacted the Chicago station manager again. Beneath the picture was a home address I recognized as belonging to Karol Witney. There was also his parents' home address, along with a brother. "He was from Chicago?"

"It's his home," Janine Scott answered, her mouth pinched. "He always treated our place like it was a vacation."

"Is that what he told his wife?"

She grimaced at my word choice, her circumstance a troubling pain that may have gone on for years.

"I don't know what he told her!" she answered, raising her

voice. "For what it's worth, we were together first. Since freshman year."

Another towel. She dove into the laundry basket to continue folding. I couldn't recall if I'd given her a card before but took one from my pocket. It was a new card, the edge sharp, I handed it to her, asking, "For you and your children." My gaze lifted to her shoulder. "You can call me any time of day. It's your safety that is my concern."

Her face softened, the towel dropping to her lap. She shook her head, saying, "This isn't how I imagined my life. You have to know that."

"We do," Tracy answered. She was sitting at the edge of the couch. I could see the questions on her face. The same stirring in my head. Were we speaking with a possible suspect? Or a victim? There was a deep jealousy here, but there was also abuse, Jim Witney's violence extending to his family in the Outer Banks.

"When you're twelve, you dream about a husband and a home and having babies." She picked up a shirt this time, a faded stain on the front of it. She looked at us, adding, "I always fantasized. I even had a playhouse and dolls. You know. I never dreamed I'd be a leftover. That's what I feel like. A leftover."

She swiped at her face again, the words sad. Without knowing it, she'd answered my earlier question. Did she have any reason to want to see Karol Witney dead? Yes, she did. "With Karol Witney gone, your life would get better?"

"Oh my God! That's not what I meant," she answered sharply. She covered her belly instinctively to protect her unborn child. "You have to know that I would never do anything to risk my family."

"Look at it from our side," Tracy told her.

"But why would I do anything about it now?" Breath shuddering, she rubbed her stomach. Her head tipped back suddenly, saying, "The pictures on my iPad. That shows where I was during the dive."

She was establishing an alibi. "If you sent them all, the meta-data would provide a timeline."

"I did send them all. Every picture. You check them." She stood, shoving the laundry basket aside. "I think it's best you leave now. I know that I don't have to answer anything without representation."

She was pulling the lawyer card. I couldn't help but think of the similarity to what Jim Witney had done. "I was hoping we could finish—"

"Now would be best!" she interrupted, red heat rising on her chest and neck. "I know my rights."

We said nothing more as we followed her to the front door. I wrapped my fingers around the doorknob, pausing with thoughts of her alibi. While the iPad pictures showed she was snorkeling with her sorority sisters, what if she planned Karol's murder with Jim Witney? Was there a financial gain such as an insurance claim?

Before I could open the front door, the brass handle spun in my hand and air rushed toward me without warning. I jumped back, bumping Tracy as I did, the small foyer becoming crowded as a tall man entered the home. His eyes narrowed with a hard line forming across them. Blue sapphire eyes went through me like the sharp tip of an icicle. It was Jim Witney. He looked me up and down with a certain amusement. We knew his secret. His and Janine's. But did he think he had us beat? I grabbed Tracy's hand, my instincts taking over like Janine Scott's had. We walked around him, saying nothing until we were safely outside. His expression softened, confusion taking over as he glanced at Janine Scott and then back to us.

"Mr. Witney," I began, waiting for a reply. But he could only stare, lost for words. "First thing tomorrow, I'll need to meet with you."

He looked at Janine and the children gathering. "Tomorrow, detective."

"Tomorrow. For now, I am sure you two will have plenty to talk about." I couldn't leave though. Not just yet. Not with concerns gnawing at me. It was for Janine's safety. For her children's too. I looked deep into Janine's eyes and slowly gave her a nod, hoping she'd understand my meaning, as I began to say, "Day or night. Any time you—" but the door shut before I could finish. It was the last time I'd see Jim Witney and Janine Scott together. Alive, anyway.

FOURTEEN

There'd been a murder. There'd been an attempt made on my life and Tracy's as well. And now, there was a threat on Jericho's too. This was unlike any homicide case I'd ever worked. This wasn't the work of a serial killer. It wasn't a murder-suicide, a killing of a family member, or a hate crime. None of the homicides I'd investigated in my career resembled what was happening here. Was it greed? Jealousy? Wrath perhaps? Which of the deadly sins should we consider as a possible motive?

I only had the suspicions around Jim Witney to work with, given the history with his wife. His deceased wife. He'd lied to us about when he arrived in the Outer Banks. Did that mean he killed her? He had opportunity. But did he have a motive? And would he have attacked us to protect himself? These were the questions I couldn't answer. Not yet. Not without knowing more.

It was just past twilight, the sky brushed the color of rust. We parked south of Kill Devil Hills, not far from Nags Head. I had a few blurry pictures transferred to my phone and the crude drawings of the coin tucked safely in my pocket. There was one person Jericho said we needed to see, that they might know what we were dealing with. A part of me wanted to dive as soon as possible and find the coin. In the mayhem of saving Jericho from drowning, the coin was lost, and the disappointment of losing it burned.

I don't know where or when the coin went missing, but I imagined the daylight bleeding through the ocean and glinting off the gold as it fluttered back to the ocean's bottom. I could still feel the outline of it too, the weight of it in my palm, the precious metal tingling with danger. Someone had been with us every minute of this case. They were with me and Tracy after we'd visited Janine Scott. They were with us during our dive when they tried to kill Jericho. I'm sure they were with Karol Witney too. But why? If greed was the motive, then why not just take the gold? There had to more to it and I was determined to find out what it was.

I reached over to Jericho and curled a lock of his long hair around my finger, a rush of gratitude touching my soul. The slur in his speech was gone, but his memory was still chock-full of holes. He was already talking about diving again, the thought of it rattling my nerves. I'm sure he could say the same about me driving, Tracy and me still nursing bumps and bruises. But diving was different. It was a different kind of danger. I didn't know how to protect him, or us for that matter. We'd have to dive again to continue the investigation. For the next one, I'd enlist Emanuel to help. I was also thinking strongly about benching Jericho. Maybe have him sit out and stay on deck. But he was stubborn, and I could only hope he'd listen if I insisted.

I took hold of his arm to lead him up a steep walkway, our shoes grating on the pavement. He stopped halfway to take hold of my hand, lacing our fingers before continuing toward the foyer of a small house. It sat high on thick stilts, a sandy parking space beneath it with a pickup truck from the late seventies. There was a seashell garden lining the pathway which was edged by short solar lights that sprouted from between carefully placed rocks.

One by one the lights flicked on as daylight slipped into the night. Tree frogs and evening bugs came to life as well, their soft trills filling my ears. Wood steps creaked with the climb, the home's front door opening slowly with a familiar face smiling at us. I couldn't help but smile too when I saw who it was we were visiting. As Jericho had said, this was the one person in the Outer Banks who might shed some light on what I'd found.

His name was Peterson, an old crab fisherman who'd spent his life in the Outer Banks. He'd recently sold his crabbing business, trading his days of working on the water to manage a fishing pier. It wasn't the same pier as the scuba charter Karol Witney had gone out of, but that didn't matter. See, when it came to knowing anything and everything about the Outer Banks, I'd always gone to Jericho. He was my man. He was the guy with all the details. But Jericho had someone too. And that was Peterson. The two also shared a kinship that reminded me of a father and son, with Peterson always eager to share his knowledge, to pass it down to Jericho as if he knew he was going to see his last sunset soon.

The crab fisherman hadn't aged much since seeing him last. The lines on his face were deeper, maybe a little longer too. But he looked rested, the work on the pier a better fit for him. He was still tall and lanky, but no longer smelled of the crab he'd been fishing. The tufts of gray hairs that I'd normally see sprouting from beneath a worn fishing cap was now combed back neatly, a part running down the right side. He wore brown slippers and jogging pants, a button-down shirt with the top left open enough to show a faded tattoo on his chest. To look at him now, I would have thought he could pass for an investor, or a banker on vacation in the Outer Banks.

"Lass," Peterson said warmly, voice worn by the years. He used both hands to cradle mine as the faint smell of brandy chased a kiss on my cheek. He winked and asked, "Is this a social visit? I was just enjoying a nightcap."

"It's good to see you." My fingers turned cold when he let go. "I'm afraid this is police business."

A sigh. "Well, I guess that's okay as long as you don't mind if I finish my nip." He didn't wait for a response and turned to Jericho then, lightly clapping his shoulder. His wiry brows leveled with concern. "You, sir, look worn and tired."

"Hello to you too," Jericho said, eyeing the inside, eager for the invite. "May we?"

"Yes, of course." We followed Peterson into his home, the inside far distant from anything I would have imagined. There wasn't a shred of his career to be seen. No fishing memorabilia on the walls. No indications he'd been a crab fisherman. There was nothing that said we were in the Outer Banks, save for a framed map showing the barrier islands, the edges yellowed, the paper frayed. The rest of his place was made up with complimentary shades. There were whites and yellows and grays touching every wall and corner, the furniture selected made to match.

He led us to a couch with fat cushions, the pillows nearly swallowing me whole when I sat. There was a small fireplace in the corner of the room, the tips of the flames vanishing into heat. There was a large screen television mounted on the wall, the screen dark. A reading chair and table sat across from us with a light focused on the seat where Peterson had left a book open, a pair of round spectacles on the table. He closed the book and sat down with us, his glass of brandy in hand. "So, what brings you two to my home on this fine evening?"

From my pocket, I took the drawing, opening the sheet of paper, and held it between my fingers.

Peterson studied it, a flame shining in the corner of his eyes. He placed the brandy glass down, the thin glass tapping hollowly.

"We were wondering if you could tell us anything about what this is."

"A moment," he instructed, voice gravelly. Peterson exited down a hallway, disappearing into its dim light, a cough bouncing from the walls. On his return, he held up what looked like an old album, the outside made of leather, the pages between them spaced oddly, sandwiching more than family pictures. He paused before re-entering the room, demanding, "What is shown in my home, stays in my home?!"

"Certainly—" I began to say as he stood in front of us, straining to keep the album balanced with one hand. He shooed at Jericho, motioning for him to make room. Jericho did as the old man said, making space between us enough for Peterson to sit. He opened the book's cover, the scent of aged leather and dusty pages tickling my nose. I expected to see a family portrait. A collection of photographs showing a younger Peterson perhaps. But this wasn't a photo album. This was a collection of money. It was a curated hoard of green and gray paper that showed the faces of dead men, their names long forgotten. There were dates from centuries before and denominations that I'd never seen before. He turned to the middle of the album, a flash of silver and gold appearing. On a few, I saw markings that were like the ones in my drawing.

I pointed at a coin, saying, "That woman on there, I think she is on the one I found."

"Ahh, this one is a favorite. It's a big part of my retirement." He ran a finger over the coin, the skin on his arm like crepe paper, creasing while he removed it from a protective sleeve. Turning it over, back and forth, he said, "This is part of my 401 and my IRA and whatever else 'em banks are naming retirement accounts these days."

"This one is dated 1861. Twenty dollars." Peterson's coin had the same golden-orange coloring as the one from the ocean. It wasn't a bright gold that I was used to seeing. From my phone, I showed him the blurry pictures, eyebrows bouncing between recognition and confusion. "I wish I'd gotten a better picture."

"It is gold," he commented, but didn't sound assured. "You think it look liked this one?"

"Not entirely." I studied the woman's head stamped on the front, the word LIBERTY near her hairline. I counted thirteen stars bordering the circumference, the same thirteen I'd seen on my coin. "Her face and the stars. They look the same. May I?"

When I held out my hand, he placed the coin into my palm, saying, "That is one ounce of gold you're holding."

"I'm guessing it *is* worth more than twenty dollars," I said jokingly, having read about coins having a numismatic value along with the raw values.

"Considerably." He flipped the coin over; it had an eagle stamped in the middle. The diameter of the coin was similar, as was the front. But the back was entirely different.

I pointed to the drawing. "On the back of the coin we found, there was this kind of shield made of stars and stripes."

"A shield? It didn't have an eagle?" Peterson frowned, questioning what I'd drawn. He ran his fingers over the words, TWENTY D, and the UNITED STATES OF AMERICA. "What about these?"

"Those are close. The TWENTY D was there, but the word UNITED was missing." I flipped the page of my notebook, showing him what I'd drawn from memory. His jaw going slack as he gripped his chin. "On the coin we found, it said CONFED-ERATE STATES OF AMERICA."

"Do you think it was real?" Jericho asked. "Or someone made it?"

Peterson puffed a short breath as he glanced at me, and then Jericho. "I've been collecting coins my entire life. United States currencies dating back to the eighteenth century. The coin you said you had, the one you're describing"—a broad shrug—"it doesn't exist."

"Doesn't exist?" I didn't understand what he meant.

He flipped through pages of his album and tugged on a loose sheet. There was a coin printed on the page, the back of it listing a denomination at a half dollar. I sucked a fast breath when I saw what was in the middle. "That's the one. That's the shield I saw. See the stars and the stripes."

"This one?" Peterson's frown deepened.

"And the other stuff around it. That's what I saw." This picture had all the same markings, and even had the lettering for the CONFEDERATE STATES OF AMERICA. I couldn't help but hop up and down, nodding. "That's them." When Peterson didn't share in the excitement, I drew in a breath asking, "Confederacy? As in the Civil War?"

"That's the CSA, the Confederate States of America. And they did print money before the war," he answered, a whistle riding on his breath. "They even tried minting coins. Only two denominations, a few made was all."

"The CSA," Jericho said, searching my phone's screen for any resemblances. The pictures were too blurry, and no amount of filtering had helped. "The CSA had their own mint?"

"They did." Peterson lifted his head, voice turning boastful. "By the way, the name of the printing plate engraver was A.H.M. Peterson. He comes from the line of New Orleans Petersons."

"Is that so?" I commented, wondering how common the name might be.

"That's right," he exclaimed. He nudged Jericho's phone, adding, "You can giggle or gaggle the name *A.H.M. Peterson*. Do whatever it is you kids do on them things."

Jericho was already typing the name and included the words, *plate engraver*. When a face displayed with text, he chuffed a short laugh and showed Peterson the screen. "Old man, I do think there is a resemblance."

Peterson gazed at the screen, putting distance to help him see the phone. "Some Louisiana blood high up in my family tree. It was my great-grand-pappy who come up the Intracoastal Waterway from New Orleans. He'd worked one of 'em flat-bottomed barges when he was just a sprout." His expression turned solemn, the frown returning as he pinched my drawing with a slight shake. "Like I said though, there never was no third denomination. No twenty dollar dies made or coins minted. Especially none that was gold."

"Any idea what this is?" I moved the page to face the photograph of the half dollar. "There's a lot of similarity."

Peterson pawed at his chin, the tips of his yellowing nails scratching. There was quiet for a moment, his speaking to himself. "It's like they used the Lady Liberty die and made another for the reverse?"

There was a sense of awe growing, a mystery building. "Maybe this was a new coin? Its date *was* 1865."

"If it helps, here are some more coins with CONFEDERATE STATES OF AMERICA." Jericho held his phone for Peterson to see.

The old crab fisherman shook his head. "Those are real enough, but they are called re-strikes." When we didn't understand what he meant, he clarified, "Anniversary coins and collectibles."

"Which means they're not the original minted coin?" Jericho asked. "They're made later?"

"Yes, sir. With the Confederacy, there'd only been a few of the hand-minted coins. None ever got circulated." Peterson repeated, "Nothing in the year 1865 either."

"That was the end of the war? Wasn't it?"

"Uh-huh. May thirteenth of that year." Peterson must have recalled something, his eyes growing wide. Fingers trembling slightly, he covered his mouth, asking, "Where did you say you saw that coin?"

"It was off one of the wrecks we were diving—"

"Which wreck was it!?" Peterson interrupted abruptly, but then shook it off. He sat back, the seat cushion gushing air. "It doesn't matter. Around these islands, the ocean floor is littered with shipwrecks. Centuries of them piling on each other."

"What are you thinking?" Jericho asked, a slow smile building. There was an energy buzzing in the air like when climbing a rollercoaster. I felt it. Jericho felt it too. Peterson certainly did as well.

"It's 'em tropical storms that just blew through here. One was almost a hurricane?" Peterson spoke fast, hurricane sounding like *hurrikan*. "They'd come early this year, didn't they?"

"They did." I glanced at Jericho while Peterson went on muttering about the storms, his voice turning hoarse.

When he quieted, his gaze lifted toward the ceiling where a fan paddled with a soft whooshing sound. "Waypoints! You got 'em?" Peterson lowered his head sharply. There was a fierce look of concentration, his stare falling on me. "You marked where you were? You ain't shared it with nobody!?"

"We marked it." Jericho's earlier smile was gone. There was concern in his voice now, its tone contagious and making me worry. "There was another boat at the dive site."

"Another boat!" he exclaimed. "They know you got the coin?"

I shook my head. Nobody knew about the coin. "Peterson, what is it?"

"Couldn't be," he mumbled, fingers drumming against his chin. "Could it?"

"What!?" we nearly shouted in chorus.

"The Confederate States of America. The CSA!"

Peterson placed his collection on my lap and stood. His hands shook as he poured himself another brandy, the bottle clinking against the glass. His color was wrong, not that it had ever been great. But now it was pale with a clammy sheen. He gulped the glass and cringed deeply, the cords on his neck rising. We said nothing while he poured another and spoke. "There was a story told to me by my pappy when I was a lad. I was 'leven or twelve is all. The story was told to him by his pappy, a story about my great-grand-pappy, the one who'd come up here from Louisiana."

"A story about this coin?" I wanted to keep the focus on our visit. He cocked his head annoyed. "Sorry. Please, continue."

"Pappy had more stories in him than a goose-down pillow got

feathers. Most of 'em gone from my head now, but not this one."
The bottle clanked his glass again, the brandy gurgling as it
splashed the bottom. "My great-grand-pappy was a young'en after
the Civil War. He'd grown up around men who'd fought in the
war, and around men who'd done other things, including things
with gold. It's about a treasure!"

"Big enough to kill for?" Jericho asked.

Peterson's hands dropped, his jaw slack. "It was big enough to
create a new nation and continue a war!"

I shuddered at the thought, the magnitude of what Peterson
declared. I grabbed Jericho's hand, clutching it. The case
suddenly felt massive. It felt overwhelming. Worst yet, it felt like
we were one move away from putting everyone's life in danger.

FIFTEEN

The air in the room vanished, the flames in the corner fireplace sucking it in with one deep gulp before shooting it up the chimney. I knew criminals. I knew what they were made of, and what they were capable of doing. I also knew how to catch them. But I didn't know anything about treasure or the types of crimes occurring when the stakes were riches such as the kind Peterson was talking about. How could we protect anyone?

I moved my hand across the doodles of the coin as if to hide it from the world. It was the world that frightened me. If word about gold got out, the rumors would spread like wildfire. It'd burn rampant through the islands like a plague. It wouldn't stop there either. It'd reach the mainland and then travel up and down the coast. That was just the surface contact, the part to expect immediately. It was the online news that would bring the masses to the Outer Banks and clobber the shores with enough machines to change the face of our small home. There was only one way I could think of to solve Karol Witney's murder and to protect our islands. We had to find it first. That way, we'd find who else was hunting for it. I looked at Peterson, his posture listing, balance tipped by the brandy he drank. That is, if the treasure really existed.

"A treasure?"

"I know that story." Jericho moved closer, answering, "Casey, it's just a story. There's never been proof that it exists."

"Coins. Gold bars. Jewels. Ain't never been proof that it didn't exist neither," Peterson countered, pointing his finger, brandy sloshing in the bottle. "The way my grand-pappy tell his boy the story, the war was about ended and some Confederate soldiers loaded up the treasure to take it south. The president of the Confederate States was Jefferson Davis, and he'd planned to take that treasure to Mexico and give it to 'em. Give it all to the Emperor, Maximillian the First."

I held up my hand as though we were in history class. "Why would he give a treasure away?"

His voice scratchy, Peterson answered, "Davis was never going to yield to the North. There was no secession in his mind. His idea was to get support from Mexico. He already had support from the queen."

"The queen?" I asked, his story turning muddier, the credibility thinning. "Of the United Kingdom?"

"That'd be Queen Victoria." Peterson cocked one brow, adding, "Think about it. Who would benefit from a divided United States?"

I glanced over to Jericho to see that Peterson had his attention.

"Jefferson Davis was going to create a new Confederate States, a new nation."

"There could be some truth to this, but Jefferson Davis was captured in Georgia." Jericho showed me a map that included drawings of wagons and horses and a large camp where the ex-president's days of freedom had ended in the month of May. "There was no gold with him. But Davis's wife did have a Confederate coin in her purse. Just one though."

Peterson touched the tip of his finger to his nose. "That's right.

Because the treasure never was with Davis. It was in Virginia."
Peterson waved east toward the ocean, brandy sloshing again. "Ya
sees, the treasure went by boat. That's the story passed down from
my great-grand-pappy. They loaded one of 'em ships with the iron
cladding on the hull. Sailed her from Virginia out the shallow
mouth of the Chesapeake Bay. From there, they went due east a
hunerd miles to the deeper waters."

"An ironclad ship?" Jericho asked, Peterson nodding. "The
Confederate Navy?"

"That's right. Some was taken by the Union—" Peterson
began and waved his hand at the ceiling. "Some others
disappeared."

"Wasn't there a story of the treasure being in Richmond,
Virginia and sailed out of the James River?" Jericho asked, interest
growing. "It was lost forever?"

"That was a decoy." Peterson stabbed the air with his finger,
knuckles bulbous. "The treasure was never in Richmond. They
loaded the ship in the Potomac and sailed it out of the Chesapeake Bay."

"Sailed it all the way to Mexico? From Virginia?" My knee
bounced with ideas of undiscovered riches. His story taking me
back to the days of watching movies with Tracy's father, the
ones like Indiana Jones where every treasure belonged in a
museum.

An exacerbated nod. "Only, they was carrying all that weight
and a storm blew them shallow, and it run that heavy ship
aground during low tide."

"If that's what happened, a storm could have ripped the ship
open like a tin can," Jericho said, pinching and zooming the map
on his screen, lips pressed tight with focus. "Your great-grand-
pappy from Louisiana. Who did he learn this from?"

"'Twas there!" Peterson shoved a gnarled finger near his eye.
"Said he'd seen an unflagged ship stuck a mile from shore. Wasn't
marked Union or Confederate. He saw it destroyed too, the pieces

of it getting swallowed in the storm's rage. Men came ashore, dressed in Confederate army uniforms."

Thoughts returned to the diver who'd attacked Jericho. Why didn't they take the treasure? Doubt sprouted in the back of my mind, rooting into Peterson's story. While it was magnificent, there were so many like it already. "Wouldn't it have been found by now? I mean, it's been over a hundred and fifty years."

"When my kin was helping the survivors, he said that another ship got blown in by the same storm." Peterson held his glass high like he was toasting the lost souls. "Sank her right on top of that iron beasty."

"Wait? Another ship?" Jericho questioned. "You mean the wreck we were diving?"

"That's right." Peterson finished his brandy, waving his glass at the fire, a spray burning instantly with a flash. "The wreck you were diving is the one my kin seen sunken on the top of the Confederate ship."

"What about the men?" I asked, looking to poke holes in his family's story. Deep inside, I wanted to believe the old man. And why wouldn't I. Less than forty-eight hours earlier, I'd been on the ocean floor and had held a gold coin in my hand. A coin that Peterson said should not exist. "Were there any survivors?"

"The end of the war is what happened to them." He dropped into his chair with a grimace, sipping at an empty brandy glass. "Prison I'd imagine. Union army was everywhere by then. The war was over, but that didn't stop them. Men was still fighting men. Men was still dying too."

"The storms this year," Jericho said, sitting near the edge of the couch. I could tell he was all in on this story. The possibility of it anyway. "You think the storms moved the wreck we're diving?"

"Storms have a way of shifting the sands. Make things appear and disappear in an instant." Peterson sighed deeply, his cheeks rosy. The glow on his face was from more than the brandy. It was family pride. He winked at us, adding, "Storms have a way of making the sea cough up her secrets too."

"That's one very big secret," I commented.

Peterson's look shifted like the sands he spoke of. The pride was replaced with concern. "Lass, you say someone was murdered? They try killing your beau here too." He sat up and pinned an elbow on a knee, cradling his chin. His wiry brow rose with understanding. "That woman on the news. This about her? The one who died in a diving accident."

"It wasn't an accident," Jericho answered. He nudged my arm, adding, "Yes. They tried to kill her beau too."

"Whoever they are, they went after me and Tracy also."

Peterson made a tsk-tsk sound, his eyes drifting in thought. He held up a finger. "But why didn't they take the treasure for themselves? Why kill that girl and go after you?"

In my head, I saw the old wreck where we'd been diving. I saw the fish swimming around the structure, the sands lifting and falling when I fanned them in search of clues to Karol Witney's murder. And I also saw Jericho adrift, his arms and legs hanging limply, his tank's regulator gone from his mouth. "Maybe the killer is protecting the area because they don't know where the treasure is."

"They only know the vicinity," Jericho added.

"It's just sitting there—" Peterson began, reeling back with eyes like marbles. "They know the Confederate treasure is real! We've gotta go—"

"Hold on, old man," Jericho warned. "The only thing we know for sure is that someone killed a diver and tried to kill me."

I nudged Peterson's collection, his retirement slipping from my lap. "We don't know exactly what I found. Just that it has similar markings."

"But it's gold," he winked. "Gold is a powerful persuader. I think I'll take my chances with a dive."

I tapped my badge, fingernail striking the tin. "My metal is the only persuasion you need." When he didn't get my meaning, I leaned forward. "I can hold you without cause for forty-eight hours; seventy-two if I believe you're a danger to yourself."

A weak smile appeared as he settled back in his chair. It was a threat he knew I'd never act on. He also knew it meant that I was in charge. "Fine, I'll stay put, lass." He wagged a crooked finger, adding, "One condition."

"What's that?"

"When you dive for it, I need to be on the boat."

"We can do that," Jericho answered. He tapped the album, saying, "But don't get your hopes up. Could be there's only that one coin."

I couldn't help but think there was a treasure, the story sounding real. I know I wanted it to be true, and that wanting could shade what was real. A single lost gold coin was one thing. We were going to work the hard evidence. Someone killed Karol Witney and they'd gone after Jericho. Like Peterson said, gold is a powerful persuader.

SIXTEEN

Jim Witney guilty. From the moment I woke up, those words were on the tip of my tongue. Dusty sunbeams slanted through the room, the bands swimming across the sheets like spotlights. Eyes gritty and heavy, I yanked the covers to pull them over my head. I had another minute in mind, just one more before the day got away from us. Our apartment was on the beach, the window opened a crack, very faintly; a wind chime tinkled in the distance. Hushed laughter. The patter of little feet. Shadows darted across the sunlight. They were here. I could feel them climbing the bed. I peered from beneath the cover to find Thomas and Tabitha armed with pillows, a battle continuing from the evening before. I grabbed and hugged and kissed them both before getting up. They minded me for the moment before their attentions turned to the lumbering giant next to me. Jericho pretended to be asleep. He lured them closer and closer before jumping up with a roar. The room filled with shrieking laughter, a pillow fight with tickles taking over the bed.

I left them to play, my head already in the day. We were close to solving Karol Witney's murder. I was sure her husband was guilty. Then again, there might have been a bias since I already knew he was guilty of abuse. To make a case in front of a jury, the district attorney needed hard evidence and motive. Tracy and Sherry made progress with some online sleuthing. They'd also made a couple of carefully placed phone calls to help establish a motive. There was a life insurance policy. *Until death do us part.* That was the vow taken, and with his wife's death, Jim Witney had a claim on the hundred-thousand dollars. It wasn't a lot of money, but having visited with Janine Scott twice, their family growing, every penny would help.

We had a motive, but we lacked any hard evidence. I texted the district attorney about the insurance policy. I also texted her about how Jim Witney drove to the Outer Banks, staying off the highways where license plate cameras were in place. And explained that we confirmed his travels using cell-tower pings to show he was in the Outer Banks when his wife died. She replied with a comment about it being circumstantial evidence, that it wasn't enough, and we needed something concrete. That meant a face to face with the charter boat's owner, the captain, and any staff.

"Your phone," Jericho said, his hand appearing in the bathroom. On the screen, I saw two new text messages, a third causing it to buzz.

"Thanks." I took the phone and his hand, gripping it hard enough to pull him closer. He was wide awake, the children made sure of it. His hair flopped to one side and there were fresh pillow marks creased on his cheek. "Love you."

"Love you too," he mumbled, pinching the sand from his eyes. "I'm going to make some coffee."

"Add an extra scoop," I told him.

He turned and was gone, my phone buzzing with a fourth message. There were text messages from the medical examiner's office as well as directly from Samantha. She was on her way to the beach near my apartment where a body had washed ashore. While a beautiful beach paradise, the shores of the Outer Banks could be treacherous to the unsuspecting. It was the midnight swimmers who dared the darkness and the inky black waters that we often discovered dead the next day. This could be that, but death would always be suspect until it wasn't.

"Extra scoop," I heard echo in the hallway, my focusing on the messages. This had to be more than an accident, otherwise I wouldn't have been alerted. More than midnight swimmers, their courage warmed by the evening cocktails they'd drank. This must have involved foul play, or the suspicions of foul play. I perked up and typed,

Not a drowning? Signs of foul play?

Her response started, three dots hopping one after the next like a trumpeter's fingers rolling through scales. She stopped, the dots disappearing, their absence leaving me more curious. When it resumed, her text response came with a photograph and the words,

This was sent by the couple who discovered the body.

The phone rang, the screen showing her name. "Samantha?" I answered, concern edging my voice. "This must be serious if you're calling me."

"You know me too well," she chided, the moment fleeting. "I've got some bad news to share."

I gripped the bed, saying, "Who is it?"

"It's not confirmed yet, but take a look at the photo I sent."

In the picture was an open wallet, brown leather with creases, the seams starting to become undone. It had been placed against the dark grains of wet sand, the toes of someone's foot next to it. In the left side pocket, there was a clear plastic protection, but it was fogged, an indication beneath which had been waterlogged. I couldn't make out the face, but in the text field there was the name "Officer James Witney." A breath gushed from my lips, the bathroom sink taking my weight in a lean. "Shit! That's our suspect."

"I know," she replied. "I'll know for sure when we're on site in twenty minutes."

"Okay. Send the coordinates to me and Tracy." I was at a loss. Especially having seen Jim Witney with Janine Scott the day before. Who would want Jim Witney dead? "We'll be there!"

The sky was thundery gray, clouds heaping in tall stacks that swallowed every ounce of morning sunlight. The grim colors matched the way I felt, our case going sideways. Samantha had said the body was near where I lived. She was right. It was less than a few miles from our apartment. If not for the equipment, I could have walked to it from my rear door. I drove though, chugging a coffee, trying to convince myself it was anyone other than our suspect. But try as I might to find someone's face other than Jim Witney, I couldn't. It was him. My lead suspect was dead. There was no mistaking who it was lying in the ocean surf, foamy seawater tumbling around his body.

Samantha and Derek were already on location when I arrived, the medical van safely parked away from the moving tide. There were patrol vehicles with balloon-like tires that were made spongy for driving in the sand. Three of them were parked at the edge of the crime scene, yellow and black tape strung from bumper to bumper. Red and blue lights skipped in Samantha's eyes, flashing silently while she struggled to position herself next the body. She found her footing, gaze locked on Jim Witney, frustrations ebbing like the receding surf. She offered me a hand, our balances clumsy with shifting weight.

Water raced back into the ocean a moment later, stealing the sand beneath the body and our feet. I shifted with a hand on Jim

Witney's hip, bracing him. He'd rolled once that I saw, and
perhaps a dozen other times before we arrived. His head and face
had been beaten by the rough surf, leading me to think he'd been
in the water for hours. There was sand everywhere. It plugged his
nostrils and ears and had filled his mouth. There was sand caked
in his eyes, their sapphire colors bleeding through enough for us to
see they'd begun to film over. His hair was a tangled mess with
sand throughout it, nesting deep against the scalp. His skin was
gray like the clouds, the touch of it cold beneath my gloved
fingers.

"I'm not seeing anything?" I spoke the question aloud,
searching Jim Witney's face and neck and head.

Samantha stopped and looked up, answering, "See what?"

"Any signs of trauma?" I searched the area behind his head,
probing with my fingers. "Something that'd give us a possible
cause of death?"

She drove her fingers through his hair, commenting, "His skull
is without injury." She sat back, resting on her feet and surveyed
the body. "Whatever it was, I don't think we'll figure it out here."

Our bodies pivoted with another wave, both of us grabbing
hold. "A few more minutes, I want to get some pictures."
Samantha followed my gaze to beyond the patrol vehicles where
Tracy approached with her camera gear in hand. To my surprise,
she enlisted Sherry Levin's help. The IT staffer trudged through
heavy beach sands, carrying a crime-scene investigation case. She
was IT and I had nothing against that, but Sherry wasn't Nichelle
who'd gone out of her way to become an investigator. Was Sherry
following the same path?

"Got here as soon as possible," Tracy said, the wind beating
against the arms of her windbreaker which flapped loudly. She
assessed the conditions and immediately began firing picture after
picture. "Any talk about cutting the field assessment short and
moving to the morgue?"

"I think we might have to," Samantha answered. She held up

her hand, offering it to Sherry. "Name is Samantha, medical examiner. And this is Derek, the assistant medical examiner."

"Sherry," she replied, her eyes disappearing in a squint, a hand shading against blowing sands. She shifted to her right to see the body, the wind carrying the first indications of decomp toward her. "Sherry Levin."

"Morning, Sherry." She waved briefly at me as the color drained from her face. "Are you okay?"

She half shook her head, Tracy taking the crime-scene investigation case while I led Sherry to a spot closer to the patrol vehicles. When we were safely outside the path of the wind, I motioned for her to breathe again. She did, her color returning. "It's... it's my first time," she managed to say.

"Yeah, that first time can be tough. It's nothing like you'd expect." I moved close enough to block the view of the body, and asked, "Sherry, do you have an interest in crime-scene investigation?"

"Oh yeah sure! I'm like this really huge fan of the television shows." She'd answered immediately, sweeping the hair in front of her eyes. She peered around my shoulder and gave the body a hard stare, questions firming in her eyes. Clearly, her expectations of what we do and what was reality were not compatible. "I mean, that's why I took the job at your station. I was a fan of Nichelle's blog, her online stuff. You know?"

A slow nod. "Tell you what." I turned us around, leading her away from the scene another five feet, taking us behind the hood of the center patrol vehicle. "How about you observe and watch what we do and how we work."

"Uh-huh," she answered, tugging on her fingers. "Ma'am, I mean detective. Thank you."

"Of course." She'd get an eyeful, I was sure of it. Tracy joined me, walking alongside. When the winds promised to hold our conversation, I asked, "Did Sherry ask to come?"

"This was all her," Tracy replied. I slowed when stepping into a cloud of body decomposition, the weather not cooperating. "Sorry, I should have called first."

"Well, we need another investigator. Maybe we can train her." Sand peppered our faces, carried on a sharp wind along with the smell. I looked over my shoulder to see it hit Sherry, her shoulders jumping as she gagged. "That is, if she can stomach it."

"There's not much decay. Eight, maybe nine hours?" Tracy asked when we returned. The changing smell of a corpse was our first useful tool to measure a time of death. I agreed with the assessment. She checked the time on her phone. "We saw him about fifteen hours ago."

"That means Jim Witney would have died around midnight?" We moved close enough to see his face, my gaze falling briefly to the muted sapphire colors beneath the sand in his eyes. I knelt carefully, the tide eagerly devouring the sands. I considered the presence of insects to help further establish the time of death estimate. But it wasn't insects that had found Jim Witney's body. There were sand fleas and crabs, Derek and Samantha tackling the scourge. I flicked one from Jim Witney's right shoulder. It landed on its back with a plunk, a black and white shorebird with a long red beak tackling it immediately. "Lividity and rigor?"

"Early stages." Samantha's hair blew flat against her scalp, her eyelids closing to guard against blowing sand. The winds coming off the ocean were gaining, giving us minutes before compromising the site. "Very early."

"Guys, hold on?" Sand disappeared in a sudden wash that swallowed everything, the surf's white foam racing. "We can't stay."

"No kidding," Derek said, losing his balance, his thin hair dancing like a candle flame. "The tide is rising, and the wind is blowing at us."

As if to make a point, mounting waves crashed with a thundering roar. "I'm calling it," Samantha exclaimed, hand raised. "We'll meet back at the morgue."

"Body bag!" I yelled over the crushing surf. "Better yet, lift and shift?"

"Lets!" Samantha answered, stuffing her hands beneath the body. Derek nodded as he did the same. I positioned myself to help lift his legs, a gurney next to the medical examiner van our target. "On three."

We froze when a breath spilled from Jim Witney's mouth, sand tumbling in a dribble down his chin.

"Perfectly normal," Derek reminded us.

When the body was on the gurney and secured in the medical examiner van, I closed the rear door, the latch clacking. "A few hours?"

Samantha brushed her hair back and looked exhausted, the morning still early. "At least," she answered breathlessly. "I need to do a collection, clean the body... I'm not even sure how to deal with the sand."

"Derek knows." This wasn't the first body I'd seen to the morgue where sand had been an unfortunate complication. "One of my first cases. Ask him."

A nod. "I'll see you in a few hours."

Tracy and I returned to where the body had been discovered. Crime-scene tape snapped as it whipped and twisted in the harsh wind. Two officers continued working through questions with the couple that had reported the body. Tracy made herself busy with pictures, which I ended with a short wave. She looked up, expression filling with uncertainty. As a wave crashed around her feet, she began to understand. If there'd been any evidence here before us, it had surely gone out to sea. The sands had blanketed flat since removing the body, the impressions of our feet and Jim Witney washed away as if we'd never been. The sand has no memory. Our being there was already forgotten. If there were clues to discovering what happened to Jim Witney, they'd have to be found with him.

"Hello?" I shouted, a crashing wave stealing my voice. I recognized the phone number, the call from the owner of the *Buoys II Seamen* charter, Terry Nichols. He also acted as the boat's captain and was anchored on the shipwreck the day Karol Witney died. "Sir, can you hear me?"

"Yes, ma'am, I—hear you—" he answered, the line breaking. "—calling about the—girl—died?"

"That's correct. Your boat was there," I said, shuffling across the sand in search of a better signal. "Sir, can you tell me who was on the charter?"

"I can hear you now," he said, his voice suddenly booming loud enough for me to hear a southern twang. "Please, ma'am, call me Terry."

"Only if you call me Casey," I told him. "About your charter that day?"

"Strange day. There was only the one guy," Terry answered. "A northern fella. I think his name was Tim?"

"Jim Witney?" I asked, yelling over the waves again.

"Jim. That sounds right," he confirmed. "But I never got a last name. He only dove an hour or so."

"Do you have a last name?" I asked, confused. "How was the charter booked?"

"They paid in full; I've got the receipt in my hand. A credit card."

"Perfect, his last name would have been on the card," I said, feeling an itch of confirmation nearing. "Can you read it to me."

"Well, it was a woman called it in, ma'am." Paper rustling. "Says here, name was Janine Scott. Chartered it for the day."

"Sorry, did you say Janine Scott?" That couldn't be right. Janine Scott had paid for the Rutledge brother's boat.

"That's correct. Janine Scott."

SEVENTEEN

We didn't see Jim Witney until sometime in the early afternoon. The skies remained gray, but the rains had tapered to a drizzle, a light mist beading on everything. I must have carried the dampness from outside, the morgue feeling more uncomfortable than usual. I layered three lab coats, borrowing one of Derek's XXXL sizes. He was big, but not that big. He layered too. When I opened the doors, thick rubber sweeping across the floor, it was temperature that was the first point of discussion. Jim Witney's body temperature had dropped substantially more than the expected 1.5 degrees Fahrenheit per hour. Samantha stood over him, a body thermometer plunged into his body, a perplexed look on her face.

"You mentioned seeing him earlier?" Samantha asked, the thermometer's probe sliding free, overhead lights glinting off the metal. She stepped down from her stool to enter the measurement into a computer tablet.

"It was yesterday, early in the evening." I went around the other side of his body which was bare of the dress shirt and slacks, all clothing removed and tagged. Derek handed me a sheet, the contents listed, which included Jim Witney's wallet, a keyring with car FOB and house key, and one half-used stick of lip balm, strawberry flavored. Nudging Tracy's arm, her gaze fixed on the body, taking the pictures we did not take on site. "Check it out, his car?"

"He had his car keys," she replied, face bright with understanding.

"Alice forwarded a report. Witney's car was found parked near the Avalon fishing pier."

Her focus narrowed on the listing. "It was late and already dark. He left Janine Scott's house after we were there?" A nod. "Why a fishing pier?"

"Fishing?" Derek said, asking. Heads turning. "They're open from six in the morning until midnight, every day."

I motioned to the bag of clothes and the list of belongings, "Business attire? I don't think he was dressed for fishing."

"It's a public place," Tracy said, her phone showing the Avalon pier's website. "Shoot, their webcam is down so that's no help."

"What if he went there to meet someone?" I raised my phone, showing it to Derek. "Did you find a cellphone?"

He shook his face, mouth turned down. "Just what's listed." He hoisted the clear plastic bag, the clothes still wet and littered with sand. "Do you want me to search it again?" he asked, pinching and squeezing it.

"Would you, please." An image popped into my mind, Witney's hand in the interview room. He had his phone then, a bigger model. But was it too big for a back pocket? "If it was on him, it'd have to be in the front pocket of his slacks."

"Uh-uh," Derek muttered while fishing through the bag, frosty air rising from the top of his head. "Washed away probably."

Samantha looked up at us, saying, "We removed enough sand to fill a child's pail. Doubtful anything electronic would be salvageable."

The body refrigerator's motor kicked on with a low thrum. "What about the cellphone tower pings?" I looked to Sherry when asking. She stood next to Tracy, the pink in her cheeks returning. "Like Tracy did to figure out his path from Illinois to the Outer Banks."

"I can do that!" Sherry answered excitedly, perching a laptop on a nearby autopsy table.

Derek made a tsk-tsk sound, commenting, "We keep a clean house," and rolled a steel tray toward her. Sherry fumbled with the laptop, lifting it, moving backward, uncertain what he meant. He offered a gentle grin when reaching her and lowered the tray to her height. She caught on, returning his smile.

"Forward us the last known coordinates," I instructed and returned to the body, the cause of death still a mystery. There were bruises on the knuckles of his right hand which looked to be a few hours old, possibly a day. His right arm was sleeved in tattoos, the colors limited to a few, the images a myriad of police badges and logos, some appearing to be historic. Aside from the bruising on the right hand, there were no other obvious signs of trauma. I went to the end of the table, a shadow beneath the cloth covering his middle. The other side of his body also presented without indication of injury, even though he'd likely been in the ocean for hours. "I'm not seeing anything that stands out."

"We've still got the full autopsy to perform," Samantha said, motioning for me to join her at the front.

Jim Witney's face was empty of expression. Images of his children surfaced in the memory of our first visit. The eldest girl had the same color hair, the same waviness too. On Jim Witney, Derek had combed out the grains of sand and washed it thoroughly. Though the shine was absent, the waves remained. It was the sapphire color in his eyes that told me Janine Scott's children were from Jim Witney. Only now, the color was nearly gone, covered by the filmy cloud that comes with death. His jaw was slack, the lower part askew, his tongue swollen and jutting through his teeth. Samantha gently nudged the chin, bone on bone grinding slightly. She commented, "It's a fractured jaw and some broken teeth."

"With the bruising on his hand, the broken jaw could indicate a fight?" Tracy asked, her camera flash turning his face ghostly white.

I lowered my face close to his, decomp wafting beneath my nose. "I don't think so."

"No?" Samantha asked.

I peered up to see she'd raised a brow, egging me on to continue as though she were speaking in my head.

She raised her other brow, encouraging me. "Go on, tell us."

With my back straight, I carefully lifted Jim Witney's hand, the rigor mortis protesting. "These bruises here, they're almost a day old." A memory crept to the front of my mind like a shadow passing before my eyes. Tenth grade. Soccer practice. The grass was dry and brittle, Philly was in a late spring drought. Sheila Donahue took an elbow to the side of her face. It was an accident, and I thought it'd broken my arm. But it wasn't the bones in my elbow I heard break. It was her jaw. "Water-ice."

"Water *ice*?" Samantha blinked, her eyelids fluttering. "I'm not following."

"It was a schoolmate of mine. She had a broken jaw. I'd put my cup of water-ice on it during practice, thinking it was just a bruise. Cherry flavored, it was hot that day. Muggy too, and the cup was sweating."

"Water-ice, you mean flavored ice." She shook her head. "It wasn't just bruised though."

I pointed to the sides of the jaw, gently touching Jim Witney's face. "On my friend's face, it had swelled immediately. I mean, like instantly. There was also a really dark purplish-blue color. That's what told us it was broken."

A grin. "Can you tell what happened here?" Samantha asked, Tracy's camera ratcheting through more frames.

"The broken jaw and the missing teeth. That happened after he died."

"Hm," Tracy grumbled. "While he was in the surf?"

"Must have been." Given the amount of sand, the time in the ocean, there may have been additional broken bones. All occurring post-mortem. My breath caught when I saw that beneath his chest, lower to the right side of his back, there were two burn marks, the distance between them identical to what was found on Jericho's back. "Tracy!"

Footsteps approaching, Tracy switched to a macro lens and ring flash. She fired a handful of pictures, asking, "That's from a shark deterrent tool? The same kind Jericho was hit with."

"It is." The burn marks established a link between whoever it was that attacked us, and Jim Witney's murder. Thinking aloud, I began to rattle off what we knew. "Found dead in the surf. Presumed to be in the ocean considerable amount of time. Was he diving?"

"There wasn't any evidence of a dive," Samantha answered.

I shook my head, seeing an image of his body as it was discovered. "No, there wouldn't be. He was in his street clothes." Maybe he was subdued? But then what happened to him? "Samantha, how about X-rays? Were there any other notable injuries?"

"Thought you'd ask for them," Samantha said and tapped a keyboard, the adjacent wall turning bright with the black and white images.

I wasn't a doctor but knew enough to recognize old fractures and broken bones. I couldn't help but search Jim Witney's skeleton for the same, hoping to have seen a few, hoping to have known he'd felt the kind of pain he'd inflicted on his wife. Karma is ofttimes a mild thought. A wishful one at best. And unfortunately, I was left disappointed.

"Detective? Do you see it?"

Samantha liked to challenge me but surprised me with this one. Heat rose on my chest and neck. I felt like I was standing in front of a class and reading a report I'd only dodged my way through. "Afraid to say, I can't see a thing wrong."

"Decapitation," she replied. A subtle gasp rose from behind me. The idea of it seeming impossible.

I faced Jim Witney to look at his neck which was intact and without any signs of injury. Samantha's face was fixed with a grin, waiting for me to guess as to how.

"You're serious?"

"It's a first for me." Her grin widened. "Its formal name is atlanto-occipital dislocation."

"You're talking about an internal decapitation?" I guessed, recalling a case I'd read about once a long time ago. Her grin turned into a smile. "Really. That *is* the cause of death?"

"With a name like that, you'd think it would be. But surprisingly no." Samantha tapped through a series of X-rays until showing a side-view of Jim Witney's head and neck. "The ligaments attaching Mr. Witney's skull to the spine were severed. His head is still attached though."

"He didn't die instantly?" Tracy asked, taking a picture of the area.

"Seawater was found in the back of his throat, enough for me to suspect that he'd drowned," Samantha answered. "When we perform the full autopsy, the lungs will tell us more."

"Drowned?" I returned to Jim Witney's body and pulled my gloves tight. With his shoulders in my grip, I asked, "May we?"

"Of course." Samantha motioned to Derek, the three of us shifting the body, rolling Jim Witney until he was face down. His head moved freely, swiveled loose, which I might not have noticed if not for Samantha's finding. Samantha's eyebrows were drawn together. "What are you looking for?"

"An injury like that would have inhibited movement. His arms and legs?"

"Compromised, yes," Samantha answered while plugging in hair clippers. "I suspect he may have been unconscious."

I ran my fingers across the back of his skull, finding an injury not easily visible. The clippers buzzed, Samantha motioning for me to stabilize Jim Witney's head. A band of hair was removed, the shearing close enough to the scalp to show what shouldn't be there. "What caused that?"

Samantha ran the clippers until we saw all the injury. She put the clippers onto an instrument tray, a metal-on-metal plunk. Stepping away from the body, she answered with a faint southern lilt, "I haven't the slightest idea what would have caused that."

"Tracy, get this." She did as asked, strobe light flashing as I placed a medical ruler next to the injury. It was in the shape of a crescent moon, the fingernail kind, a smile pressed into Jim Witney's skin.

Slowly motioning with my arms to reenact a strike, I asked Samantha, "Is it possible to be struck hard enough to cause an internal decapitation?"

Eyes wide, she replied, "That is exactly what I believe occurred." She came to my side, running a finger in the groove. "A quarter to half millimeter depth at the apex of the arch; I think the edge of the instrument used was swung with such force, it caused the injury."

"An inch higher and a blow like that would have caved in his skull." I moved the ruler to run perpendicular to the injury, camera flash whining with a recharge. "Whoever did this, did so with the intent to murder him."

"That's where the seawater comes in," Samantha commented. "Think about where his body was discovered."

"Already there. Jim Witney was on a boat when this happened."

"The treas—" Tracy blurted, catching herself.

A groan rolled deep in me. I kept it to myself but tipped a brief look in Tracy's direction.

Derek heard her though and asked, "He was treasure hunting?"

"We saw him last night," Tracy said, red faced as she busied herself with picture taking.

"Huh. That's a typical tourist move"—Derek shook his face—"wouldn't be the first in here who died trying to find treasure."

I unfurled Jim Witney's right hand, the bruising possibly a defensive wound. Thinking aloud, "He was at Janine Scott's house. From there, a boat? Possibly defended himself from an attack?" The sequence didn't work. Not with the injury to the back of his neck and head. I motioned to it, asking Samantha, "Conscious?"

Her lips curled downward, answering, "Very unlikely. Even if he was, the impairments would be immediate."

"Meaning, Jim Witney collapsed?"

"At once," she replied.

"Let's say he collapsed and was thrown overboard where he was picked up in the tide." I ran the tip of my fingers across his knuckles, the bruises with a slight abrasion. "If his limbs were impaired, drowning occurred right away."

"I have a chart of the tides," Sherry said, her voice soft, mouse-like. Heads turned, the attention making her shrink for a moment behind the laptop. She peered over the screen, a question on her face. "Want to see?"

"You don't have to ask," I invited, waving her closer. "Let's see what you have."

"I have a timeline too." Her map showed the tidal flow along with pins dropped to indicate where Jim Witney's body was found. She pointed to the beach and pressed a button, the tidal chart reversed. "Using an approximate weight of one-hundred and eighty pounds, he could have been in this location."

The circled perimeter was a half dozen miles wide. "That's a rather large area," I commented, trying not to sound disappointed.

Her eyes jumped, growing wide. "There's a lot of variables like buoyancy and water salinity, the temperature, winds—"

"Don't get me wrong, the vicinity helps," I interrupted, heart sinking. I recognized the area immediately. Peterson and his crew were anchored there, taking guard over a treasure that may or may not exist. My throat felt thick with concern. It was impossible though. Could Peterson have been involved? "Good work, Sherry, send it."

"His hand?" Samantha asked, seeing that I was holding on to Jim Witney's fingers.

I looked down and dropped his hand as though a spider were crawling up my arm. "It's the bruising," I said, shifting the discussion and hating the idea that was haunting my thoughts. "I suspect they occurred while he was at Janine Scott's place."

"We should check on her," Tracy said, taking a picture of his knuckles. The whites of her eyes were big with understanding. "Right? See if she is okay."

"There's the kids too." The thought of more abuse sickened me. But we knew Jim Witney's history. My insides stirred with an idea as I picked up Jim Witney's hand again. "It'll give us a chance to ask her about the *Buoys II Seaman* charter."

"Right. Why charter both?" Tracy asked, the question remaining unanswered.

With thoughts of abuse, I saw images of the first victim, asking, "Samantha, did you create an impression of the handprint on Karol Witney's leg?"

"Of course," she nodded. "I've made it a standard practice."

"What's an impression?" Sherry asked, eyes narrowed on me with questions.

Samantha held her hand in front of an overhead light, fingers splayed. When she placed a sheet of paper in front of it, the shadow of her palm and fingers showed.

"Like a tracing?"

"Close," Samantha said. She pinched her fingers and closed her hand into a fist, adding, "But a little more complicated when the hand's imprint isn't flat."

"That took a lot of measuring," Derek commented and rolled

his eyes toward the ceiling. He looked at me, assuring, "We got it though."

The screen behind me changed to show multiple images of Karol Witney's leg, the raised skin around her ankle and the distinctive markings of fingers and a thumb. There was a reconstructed image, the handprint made to appear open, which was what I needed. "Can I get a print of this?"

"Already have it," Derek answered, handing me a copy. When he saw that I was questioning the printed sheet, he commented, "It's measured to scale. A one-to-one match."

"One to one." But that couldn't be. I held it up, the light bleeding from behind while I pressed my hand in place. "This would never fit."

"Fit?" Sherry asked and puffed hair from her forehead. The wheels on her tray stand squealed as she wheeled herself next to Jim Witney, gaze falling to his hand. Any nerves around death she'd had before, were gone. "Is that too big or too small?"

"Too small," I corrected her. With the printed sheet placed across his middle, I lowered his hand above.

"It couldn't have been him," Tracy said, voice breathy as she flashed off a series of photographs. "Way too small."

"Samantha, look at this." She joined us at the autopsy table, Derek leaning over her shoulder. "Look at his fingers. Even his palm is too big."

"What's that mean?" Sherry asked.

Confused disappointment settled like a cloud while I lowered Jim Witney's hand onto the table. "It means that he wasn't the one who held Karol Witney beneath the surface. He didn't kill her."

"Then whose handprint is that?" Sherry asked from the screen, arms crossed.

"I have no idea." It was the only answer I could give her. The only answer I could give anyone. And I hated it.

EIGHTEEN

Footsteps thundered amidst the squealing laughter, the roar of Alice's voice echoing from the front of the station. A bittersweet smile curled from a corner of Janine Scott's mouth, her children playing happily with Tabitha and Thomas. It was growing late in the day and Janine was alone. She'd no idea of what was next to do or who to talk to about Jim Witney's death. After speaking with the medical examiner, Janine Scott decided to come to the station. Samantha texted a warning, a heads-up that Janine Scott was on her way. Selfishly, this worked out. I had no less than a dozen questions to ask after discovering Jim Witney could not have killed his wife. Who else had motive and opportunity? Would Janine Scott's life improve if Karol Witney wasn't in the picture? But the biggest question had to be about chartering two boats the day Karol Witney died.

"Your mom?"

She shook her head, heartstrings pulled, her eyes puffy and red, her hair pinned sloppily, some of it hanging loose. She wore bathroom slippers and sweatpants and an oversized T-shirt with the faded face of a purple bear, the context of which was lost on me.

"Can she come to help?"

"I called." She dabbed her eyes, pinching at the corner of one. Her hands plunked into her lap, a sorrowful and woeful look on her face. "She's up north."

"I'm sure she'll return."

"I... I didn't know what to do?" Clearing her throat. "Or if you needed me to do anything?"

"Such as?" I eased into my chair curious if Janine Scott had come in with something in mind.

Before she could answer, Jericho popped his head into my cubicle, a sheen of sweat on his face. He held a bag of juice boxes and pretzels and other snacks. "I wanted to make sure it was okay?"

Janine Scott mouthed a thank you and picked up the snacks, flipping it over to read the back. "Peanut allergy." When she'd seen enough, she thanked Jericho again.

"How are you holding up?" I asked, the evening plans for a sunset date with the kids abandoned.

He popped his head in again, a flop of hair dangling, a haircut needed. "Red-Light, Green-Light." He shook his head, adding, "They're too good."

Janine gave him a smile before returning her focus to me. From behind her, Tracy waved her hand briefly, just enough to catch my attention. My phone buzzed with a text message from her. "Do you need to get that?" Janine asked. I shook my head and waited for her to answer my original question. She pursed her mouth, wary of what to say, answering, "He didn't live with us. Not officially..." voice breaking, "but he is the father of my children and a husband to me, even if it wasn't formal."

I leaned forward, tipping my head. "Please know that I am sorry for your loss." Looking toward the frantic patter of feet and the echoing laughs. "And I am sorry for their loss as well."

"I just want what's right for them." Janine shifted and crossed her legs.

"As do I."

Tabitha's voice lifted above the others, the sound of it filling my heart.

Janine scowled. "The medical examiner said that she'll be contacting his family in Chicago?" I gave her a nod, the formality an established practice. Her voice lowered with what sounded like a growl. "I don't think they know."

"Know?"

A blur flashed, children racing by my desk.

"Them. I don't think Jim has ever told his parents that they have grandchildren."

I kept my eyes fixed steady, her emotions swinging. "That may be something you will have to do."

"I guess so." She lowered her head, a tear dropping to her hand. My seat back creaked as I fished a fresh box of tissues from my desk, finding them tucked beneath a blanket of unread intra-office memos. "Thank you."

While she wiped her eyes, neck and face covered in red blotches, I glanced at Tracy's text message, a squeeze touching my lungs as I did my best to hide a gasp. "Again, I am sorry for your loss." I tapped the case file on my lap, the folder's cover fresh with the newly printed letters and numbers, as well as the name, "James Witney." "But I have to ask you some questions."

"I don't know anything," she answered at once, shifting nervously.

"That's okay, but if I could ask first?"

"He came home and then left," she grunted, offering answers before I could ask. There was a sudden nervousness in her eyes, gaze darting around the station. When her focus returned to me, she nodded, "That's all."

"Let's take a step back." I motioned with my arms, mimicking a deep breath. She followed along, which was good. "Now, when we saw Jim Witney, it was last evening at your house. What time did he leave?"

Her lips tightened, shoulders rising. "About an hour or so later, I think?" She leaned forward, "He was really hot about something."

"Hot? He was mad." A hesitant nod. She flinched at a child's yell. Thomas's perhaps. "Was it because he saw that we were talking to you?"

"It wasn't because of you. It was a phone call." A pinch. That's what it was. A pinch in my gut, Tracy listening, and Sherry sitting next to her. They heard mention of a call and disappeared behind her cubicle wall, the thin sound of keyboards keys rattling. Janine Scott's face changed with an ashamed, or perhaps an embarrassed look. "Jim... he raised his hand and punched the kitchen wall really hard."

"It was with his right hand?" I asked, opening the case folder enough to remove a picture of Jim Witney's bruised knuckles.

Janine leaned forward, eyelids peeling. She shook her head silently.

"Hit a stud and knocked one of the pictures off the wall." An unexpected grin flashed with a soft chuckle. "He told me that he thought it was broken. I told him he probably deserved it."

"What happened after that?"

"The back of his left hand is what happened." Her face emptied, every muscle flat. Her eyes seemed lifeless as she ran the tissue across her face, concealer appearing on cottony white. Along her jawline there was a fresh, narrow bruise, the shade's red eclipsing an intensely dark blue and plum purple. "It would have been worse though, but our oldest intervened."

"Intervened?"

Eyes narrowing with a sharp frown, she answered, "I hate that she knows to do that."

I understood, stomach feeling heavy with a growing sympathy for her children. "It means she is aware of your situation." Janine fumbled with the tissue, pulling at the parts marked by the concealer. Secrets like hers can never be hidden for long. Eventually the blemishes of what's beneath will surface like a bruise. As bad as I felt for her, I had to ask the hard questions. "What happened next?"

Shoulders rising, forehead wrinkling. "He was gone."

"Janine." I tilted my head. "Did you have anything to do with his death?"

"Wha—" She looked hurt at that, tipping her head toward the children playing. She pressed a hand over her heart and exclaimed, "I'd never! He's the father of my children."

"And you want what is best for them," I challenged. These were the questions we always ask. They were also the few that solicited surprising results. My focus shifted to the bruise, a sign she'd been abused by Jim Witney. "Given your circumstances, your status, would you and your children be better off without him?"

"I don't see how," she answered, sincerity in her voice. "Truly, I mean that."

"Life insurance?"

"He never put my name on anything." She shook her head, continuing. "Like I said, I don't even think his parents know we exist."

If what she said was true, that eliminated a financial motive. I eased back, chair creaking, silence descending between us. A moment passed and she pawed at her arms while I considered the direction of questioning. I couldn't help but stare at her hands, stare at the way she wrung her fingers one at a time. Karol Witney? Were Janine Scott's hands the right size? I slipped the sheet of paper with the handprint from the folder, finally breaking the quiet and asking, "Would you place your right hand in the air for me?"

At once, the tears and nerves vanished. She fixed a cold stare on the handprint and asked, "Do I need a lawyer?"

I glanced at the paper and then back to her. "You tell me."

"We'll see," she said, lips tight as she held up her hand like she was taking a pledge. Only, this wasn't the kind of pledge one does for allegiance. Instead, it was to determine if she'd been the one who killed Karol Witney. With the station lights shining behind, I placed the sheet against her fingers. Hesitantly, she spread them to match what was drawn, my heart sinking a little as she finished. A part of me was hoping to see a perfect match. It wasn't. Like her lost love's hand, Janine Scott's was far too large. There was no way she'd inflicted the bruise on Karol Witney's leg.

She let out a heavy breath but sucked it in, relief temporary.

"Janine. What can you tell me about *Buoys II Seamen*?"

Her lower lip disappeared. Gaze returning to the front of the station and her children. "I don't know what that means." She was lying. I could hear it. Heck, I could smell the fib like it was a rotting piece of meat. I sometimes think there is a sixth sense that detectives are born with. We hear the lies. We see them through the body language. I'd even say that we probably sense them on a level that is primal. She looked directly at me, adding, "I really don't."

"We spoke to the captain of the charter. He gave us your name." I held up my phone to show her a picture of the *Buoys II Seamen* charter boat's schedule. It was set for the same date and time as the one she'd planned for her sorority sisters. "Janine. You chartered a boat with the Rutledge brothers. You also chartered the *Buoys II Seamen* boat. Why did you charter two boats for the same date?"

"Right. Yeah. I forgot about that one." Her complexion changed, its color a pale yellow, almost green. She nodded and gulped the air like a dying fish. "That boat was just a backup. You know, in case we had too many girls show up."

My detective senses were tingling. Without a doubt, Janine Scott was lying about the boat. Maybe I could trip her up? I took a breath and commented, "I suppose that's reasonable, given the boats only hold a limited number of people." Janine took a shaky breath, color returning to her face. But I wasn't done. I neared the edge of my seat in a lean. "Only, the dive boat you guys were on, it wasn't at capacity, was it?"

Janine Scott's eyes bulged. "I... I don't remember—" She lifted her head toward her children's laughter and the footsteps approaching. They were deep and reverberating, a pair of uniformed officers arriving to stand between my desk and the front of the station. She eyed them up and down, gaze fixing on their utility belts and hands while they waited for my instructions. "—in case some of the girls canceled."

I jabbed my keyboard to wake my computer screen. The pixels came alive, rendering a picture of the sorority sisters. It was one of the photographs from Janine's tablet. In the background, there was the second dive boat she'd chartered. "If your dive boat wasn't at capacity, then why would *Buoys II Seamen* have left port? They were already paid, and the boat was fueled. Surely, they would have stayed docked to save on expenses?"

Her color was gone. For a moment, I thought I'd have to grab my trash bin for her. When her chin began to quiver and the overhead lighting glistened from her wet eyes, I knew I had her. There was no talking out of it. In a soft voice, she mumbled, "Karol was already dead." I had to move my chair closer to hear Janine's whispering. "Detective, I'm begging you. Please don't... don't take my babies from me."

"Janine? You said Karol Witney?" I ignored her plea, homing in on the mention of the victim. From the corner of my eye, I saw Tracy's shadow on her cubicle wall with a shadowy telephone cord dangling from the station phone in her hand. Tracy heard Janine's plea and knew exactly what to do. In the background, there were Tracy's soft words calling North Carolina's Child Services. Janine's attention shifted to Tracy's voice. "Janine, Karol Witney was already dead?"

"Huh?" Janine asked and gulped at the air again. She motioned that her insides were threatening to gush. I snatched the trash bin and handed it to her. "Could I get some water?"

"Ma'am" A bottle appeared in Sherry's small hand. She lowered it from the adjacent cubicle. "Here you go."

"Thank you." Janine Scott followed the voice to find the bottle, taking it and twisting the cap, plastic snapping. She took a sip and when ready, she went on to explain, "He couldn't keep up the travels. The being married part while trying to raise our kids with me. He said he wouldn't divorce her either... said that it was best to make it look like Karol had an accident."

"You planned the murder of your sorority sister: Karol Witney?" I needed to hear Janine say it.

"Uh-huh." She gulped water from the bottle, a gurgling sound filling my cubicle. She swallowed hard and wiped her mouth, breath shuddering as she tearfully asked, "What happens now?"

"I'm going to have you speak with the district attorney," I told her, the revelation unprecedented. Could the DA file attempted murder charges if Karol Witney was already found dead? The handprint absolved both her and Jim Witney of any physical involvement, but a murder had been planned. Janine Scott set up a weekend for her sorority, chartering boats for them and for Jim Witney to use. When Jim Witney entered the water on that day to kill his wife, he must have discovered she was already dead. What else did he see? Who did he see? As for Janine Scott, I didn't know what charges the DA would come up with. I didn't think she cared though. She was only interested in what was going to happen to her children.

"Ma'am, we'll have to contact Child Services. I suggest you contact your family and a lawyer."

NINETEEN

The talk with Ms. Welts and our adopting Thomas and Tabitha was fresh on my mind. Peterson rolled off the side of the boat, going in headfirst. His wetsuit was mottled with rubbery patches, the material aged a light shade of gray like the curls in his hair. A breaking splash dispersed, but my thoughts of Thomas and Tabitha continued. They deserved a mother and father who would be there no matter what. I couldn't help but feel as though our profession contradicted their needs. Then again, I'd lost a child once before and my being a cop had nothing to do with it. So what do I know.

What I did know was that we still had a homicide to solve. Two homicides now that Jim Witney, our lead suspect, was dead. The mystery of what happened to his wife, Karol Witney, still lay beneath the ocean's surface, a missed clue hidden amongst a treasure Peterson was certain existed. I felt my responsibilities stretching like a rubber band, its heating from strained tensions. Jericho felt it too. Maybe less, but it was there. In my heart, I knew we were the family for Thomas and Tabitha. We had to make this work.

Tracy leaned over the rail, elbow brushing mine as the old crab fisherman sank into the blue sea. The shape of his body faded quickly beneath the breaking foam, air bubbles rising from his regulator. He was good, which meant it was our turn. I gave Tracy the go-ahead nod as a cast of butterflies danced in my belly like a chorus line. Diving always came with a swarm of nervous excitement, but there was a deeper fear here. I only had to look at Jericho and think of Ms. Welts to know what was at stake.

The boat rocked with a swell, the calm slipping with a change in the ocean's tide. The winds were working against us this morning, blowing opposite of the outgoing tide which raised the swells to make for rougher waters. We could handle the sea. I wasn't worried about that. The boat was teamed with two dive captains today, Jericho and Emanuel sharing the responsibilities. It was with my insistence that Jericho stay above, sitting out this dive, a decision that didn't come easy. It made me feel like a coach benching a star player. Although his ego was bruised and he grumbled and pouted some, I sensed there was some relief even if he'd never admit it.

With Emanuel and Jericho staying on deck, they would be our eyes and ears for this dive. They were our protection. This one wasn't like the last. All of us felt the heavy worry. Deep and gnawing, it covered us like a shroud. I saw it in Emanuel's eyes. On Tracy's face too. The emotions still raw from nearly losing Jericho. Peterson had only heard about what happened and was underwhelmed by the threat of any danger. I could tell that he had a fever growing. A gold fever. There were flashes of rich excitement in his eyes whenever he spoke about the war and of the theories about a Confederate treasure. The fever touched his voice. His step as well. It took twenty years off his age, and in any other circumstance, I'd want to catch that fever too. But not with Karol Witney's case. I couldn't help but think that Peterson was a liability. That he was adding a danger to our dive.

Jericho trusted him and convinced me to keep Peterson on the team. I had my reservations, but both Emanuel and Jericho assured me the old crab fisherman was up for the task of leading the dive. Risk or no risk, they also pointed out that we needed him. I didn't have the experience. Neither did Tracy. Peterson did. He'd been the one who'd first taught Jericho how to dive. That didn't stop me from worrying. I wish it had. I hoped it would. We'd make it work with Peterson. I warned though, if his gold fever did anything to steer us toward trouble, then he was gone. The question remaining was whether we were alone?

The horizon was empty of other boats, a crisp line set in the east where clouds climbed into the sky like slow rising steam. The sun was halfway to midday, its shine muted. The western shores had the same landmarks as our first dive, the coordinates saved. I recognized the outcrop of a jetty extending the tip of a southern island where fishermen stood in formation, lines draped from poles. Tracy turned away from the sea and gripped her mask while I held her vest, lowering her. She shoved the regulator between her lips, teeth squeaking against the mouthpiece, and gave us a thumbs up.

"Safe dive," Emanuel told her, raising his voice. He clapped her shoulder gently, his care for her endearing. "Get in there then."

"See you in there." A smile flashed beneath her mask, the regulator blocking some. She tipped backward in perfect form the way we'd been trained. I faced Emanuel, eyeing Jericho at the wheel. Voice shaky, I exclaimed, "My turn."

"Like you've been trained," Emanuel commented, helping me move into position. I placed my butt on the edge of the boat, the tank's weight pulling me from behind. One of the flippers got snagged, forcing me to lift it. The moments before a dive were awkward. The amount of gear and the positioning. "You good to go?"

"Uh-huh," I mumbled and gave him a thumbs up. I glanced at Jericho once more and tipped backward. The fall was further than before, the timing of a swell lifting the boat. When I hit the water, I rolled immediately, and then sucked a breath from my tank, the needle on the air gauge pegged in green. Tracy and Peterson were waiting, hands waving as they swam in place. The visibility was less than before, limiting us. I held out my regulator, squeezing it to let out air, a bubbly twister spewing. Both nodded and then turned away, each of us taking to a section of the wreck.

I reached the bottom with muscles straining, a strong current pulling me sideways. It was like a cold river inside the ocean, its size narrowing with cooler temperatures. Kicking until my legs burned, I came free of the current and made the descent. I didn't stop until the wreck was in sight, the timbers jutting from the ocean floor, standing tall like a ballerina's pirouette. The ancient wood had been reshaped by time, the edges which had once been squared by a carpenter's plane had turned soft and been worn down and rounded by decay.

My focus shifted to the sands around the wreck, to anything that resembled gold. When the water cleared, the cloudiness dispersed, I saw all the ship's remains, its ribs still fastened to the keel, which I thought of as its spine that ran from bow to stern. Was this the same ship Peterson's great-grand-pappy witnessed in the storm? Did he see this one sink? Or was this the other ship? For all we knew, these could be the bones from one of a dozen ships that had the misfortune of sinking at these same coordinates.

I backed away to get a better look. To see if this was one ship, or a heap of tinder in a pile, pushed together by the slow movement of tides and currents. Two? It wasn't the finding of gold that had my heart beating faster, it was another ship. Legs kicking, I swam along the spine of the first ship, a school of fish swimming alongside me. A second ship sat perpendicular to the first, a portion of it buried beneath the keel. Peterson was there already, pointing down and waving sporadically. Was it the hurricanes? Did the storms spit up the ocean's secrets like he'd said?

Bubbles glided across my face as I pitched downward and carefully kicked my feet. I didn't want to stir too much sand and disturb Peterson's search. Beneath the surface, everything moved differently. His hands were pruned, fingers like gray sausage. I preferred to wear gloves and didn't have the years of crabbing to callous my hands. Together we waved away the sands around us, carefully revealing more of the sunken ship. It was an iron post, rusted to a burnt orange that looked as if it would disintegrate when touched. I moved on to the other side of the ship, the port side which angled downward.

I followed the ocean floor's drop into deeper waters, the daylight bleeding from the surface dimming. I peered up at where Emanuel and Jericho waited and guarded our dive, the sun blocked by clouds. Our boat looked tiny from here, like a toy boat made for playing with in a tub. When the clouds passed and visibility improved, I fanned the sands to reveal more of the wood structure. There was another iron spike buried in wood, the rust threatening to dissolve it entirely. Most metals have a short life in the sea. Anything made with iron was apt to disappear over time. But not gold. And that's what glinted as the visibility brightened.

My heart leapt into my throat, bubbles racing in a fountain. I buried my hand into the sand and wrapped my fingers around the cool metal. It wasn't a coin. It was bigger, the edges smooth. It was oval shaped and thick with a lip around the edge. Was it gold? The metal was duller. It wasn't as yellow or as shiny like the coin. And for the size of it, I expected it to be heavy. It wasn't. There were no markings other than a letter C and S. Were these someone's initials? I shoved the find into my bag, the netting floating around my leg. Peterson might know what it was.

When I reached him, he had his hands clasped together, a hazy cloud of blood around them. It was a cut from one of the metal posts. There was blood in the water and a look of rookie embarrassment in his eyes. I'd seen a school of sharks swimming near us, but they were blacknose sharks, the smaller of sharks found around the islands. I plucked the regulator from my mouth and squeezed it, air bubbles rising in an alert for Tracy to see. We had to go up. We couldn't risk dangers of blood in the water.

I emerged inside a swell, floating in it until seeing Tracy's head break the surface. Peterson came next, hands above his head, blood seeping through his fingers and running down his arm.

"Sorry, lass," he said, spitting the regulator from his mouth. "Fucking thing bit me."

"You got bit?" Tracy asked, voice pitched as she steered around in a circle.

"We're okay," I yelled out and pushed against Peterson's rear, shoving him while Jericho and Emmanuel lifted. Tracy continued staring wide-eyed at the surface as though expecting a great white to suddenly leap out at us. "It's just a cut. I'm playing it safe."

"These dives are cursed," she said with a frown and whisked her mask from her head, wet hair threaded in the strap. "I was making some good progress."

"My fault!" I heard Peterson holler. He continued grumbling, scolding himself. "Stupid old man."

I followed Tracy, smacking her bottom to hurry it up, the idea of a shark taking hold of my leg suddenly feeling like a real threat. She looked back at me with a broad smile, saying, "Now look who's scared."

"It's fine. There's nothing that's going to bite you," Emanuel chided, lifting Tracy with little effort. His eyes bulged suddenly as he screamed, "Except that one!"

I spun around, gripping the ladder hard, knuckles shattering. There was nothing but ocean. Lots and lots of ocean. And laughter. "Got you, lass," Peterson said with a smile.

Jericho laughed too, but saw my bag, his expression turning serious. "You found something?"

I lowered the tank to the floor, careful not to squish a toe, and knelt while bodies circled around me. "It's not a coin. Too big. Not sure it's gold either."

"Saints be with us," Peterson said under his breath, the metal in my hand. I rubbed my fingers over the letters C and S. "It's not gold, but it's a great find."

"It's brass?" Jericho asked. He knelt next to me. I turned the object over, the metal thinner when seeing it in the daylight. The backside of it was blemished by melted metal where chunks of metal were soldered onto it. These were smaller pieces, three pointed, their purposes unknown to me. "I think I know what that is."

I nudged Jericho's arm. "Aren't you the know it all."

"A belt buckle?" he asked and looked to Peterson.

"It is. A very good one too," he said, eyes wide with delight. Emanuel crowded from the other side, pressing a gauze on the wound.

"A good one?" I asked, thinking it in poor condition.

"Handmade, and rare to find them with all three posts." Peterson gripped the gauze on his hand, frowning at Emanuel's crowding. "They did what they could with what they had but lacked the machining."

"The CS, Confederate States?" Tracy asked.

"It is. Some later buckles are CSA." Blood dripped onto the deck where it bloomed like a rose.

"You'll need a few stitches," Jericho said while rubbing his arm. "Tetanus too."

"I found this on the ship beneath the other ship." I stood up to strip and get dry, handing the buckle to Jericho.

"There was a man who died wearing that," Peterson said, gaze drifting toward the sea.

"I never thought of it like that before," Tracy said, following the old man's gaze. "It's like a graveyard."

Peterson nudged his chin west toward the islands. He lifted his head higher as though he could see the mainland from where we were. "Most of the countryside was covered with bodies. Lass, it was the deadliest war this country has ever fought."

Rubber squelching against my skin, I kicked the suit off and began to towel my arms. "This find gives some credibility to your great-grandfather's story?"

"It most certainly does!" Peterson said, straightening his shoulders. "When we going back in?"

There was a spark on the horizon before I could answer, light bouncing off glass. It was far, but through the haze I saw the outline of a boat. Jericho saw that I saw and commented, "They've been watching for about thirty minutes."

"No boat numbers either," Emanuel added. "They anchored and started watching us."

"Pish-posh, this is our claim!" Peterson belted, his fist raised to hammer the air as blood ran down his forearm.

"Easy does it, old man." I grabbed a towel, handing it to him. "Nobody is going back in the water until I know we're safe."

He didn't put on a face of disappointment like I'd expected. Instead, he nodded slowly and asked, "If there's no objections, I'm keeping my guys on this spot?"

I wasn't sure how to answer. There was Peterson's safety along with the safety of his crew. From the corner of my eye, I saw Jericho and Emanuel trading looks, both uncertain as to how best we should reply. "No objection," I told him. Daylight shimmered on the ocean's surface, a flash of light striking Peterson's face as his focus shifted to his cellphone. In that moment, I realized that it didn't matter what I'd say to him, or whether I'd approve or not approved what he planned to do. Peterson had the fever and was going to proceed with whatever he had in mind. I closed the distance between us and took his hand, the open wound in his flesh pulsing. Wrapping the towel around it hard, applying pressure until he looked at me, my caring what happened to him, I warned, "Just don't get yourself killed over this."

He put on his best smile, answering, "Lass, I am like the alligator of the sea. Strong, tough skinned and resilient." Peterson winked slowly, bracing my shoulder with his good hand. He looked directly at me, leaned closer, saying, "This sea would never turn on me."

I gave his arm an affectionate squeeze. "It isn't the sea that I'm worried about."

TWENTY

The morning and afternoon were gone and the investigation shifted to the station. We weren't a few hours from the day ending when the text messages poured in like a rainstorm. They were from Peterson, a dozen or more. They were also from Jericho and Emanuel too, filled with concerns about Peterson. Finding the Confederate States of America belt buckle was like putting a flame to the fuse of dynamite. That fuse lasted less than ten hours.

Jericho's face was blood red with frustration, Peterson wagging a knobby finger at him. The sight of them arguing took my breath. Emanuel stood nearby and lifted his chin when he saw me pull up to the apartment. It was twenty minutes past dusk, the daylight dimming with clouds brushed orange and red and purple. The stars were appearing too, faint like an afterimage, but they'd grow bright as the day faded into tomorrow. On the eastern horizon, there were red warning lights that shined from buoy markers. Red was the color for this evening, Peterson stepping closer to Jericho, the old man's posture threatening. I'd never seen him like this, the fury and the bitterness in his face giving me pause. And from the painful look on Jericho's face, I don't think he had either.

"What do you suppose that's about," Tracy asked. I threw the car into PARK, but she didn't wait for a reply. Her door swung open, and she shuffled from the passenger seat, calling, "Hey, guys!"

"Tracy, maybe—" but she didn't hear me. I grabbed my gear, finding Jericho's eyes through the windshield. In that instant, I saw that it was bad. He relaxed some then, eyes shifting to say he had it under control. I offered a subtle nod, clutching the door and shutting it with purposeful weight. Metal on metal clacked loud enough for even Peterson to hear with his bad ears. "What's going on?"

"Lass! I have to tell you!" Peterson began, voice raised, some of the words riding on a toothy whistle. He spun in my direction, blocking the path to the apartment, turning away from Emanuel and Jericho. "I want to dive! Tomorrow morning!"

"Okay, a minute." I wanted us inside, seeing the next-door neighbors craning their necks, a couple who I'd only gotten to know recently. They must have heard the heated words and come outside to investigate. They stood on their patio, each cradling a bug-eyed dog that looked more like a wingless bat than canine. I offered an apologetic wave. "Sorry for the noise."

"About the dive!" Peterson clamored, ignoring my gestures to go indoors. "We have—"

"Please!" I finally scolded. He stopped mid-sentence, gray eyes frozen. It had been a long day and the last thing we needed was a 911 disturbance call made to our very own station. Alice would never let that one die.

"But—" Peterson pleaded.

"Nope!" I raised a hand, demanding his silence. To my surprise, Peterson listened. His face went soft, the hard creases relaxing. For the moment, it was quiet, save for the yip-yap coming from the bat-dogs. When Peterson nudged his upper lip, his elbow bending, I snapped, "Not another word! Inside. Now!"

Tracy was doing everything she could to contain a laugh, the kind that gets in you like a relenting itch. Lips tight. Jaw clenched.

She masked it well enough by asking, "What's this about anyway?"

"Gold," someone muttered, feet shuffling as we filed through the door. It could have been Peterson or Jericho, or even Emanuel who answered. But the sheer mention of gold abruptly removed Tracy's smile. From the looks Jericho and Emanuel were trading, this was serious.

"We'll discuss it at the table." I could feel the anger like it was heat from a fire. This was deeper than a disagreement. Gold meant greed, and the thought of friendships threatened turned my gut sour. Greed was like a disease. A contagious one. I was beginning to regret our visit to Peterson's home. I think somewhere deep, I was starting to regret ever seeing that damn coin in the first place.

"Jericho, please," Peterson began to say, his words diffused. He went to Jericho, head down, and wrapped his long fingers around Jericho's shoulder. "I am sorry for my behavior. Sorry for arguing with you."

The corner of Jericho's mouth rose as he gripped Peterson's arm. "We've got the boss here now. She'll make the call."

Peterson turned to plead his case, saying, "Lass, we have to keep diving. That treasure isn't going to find itself."

I looked to Jericho, eager to hear his side. "Like I told him, I think we should wait. This morning's dive was a bad idea." The agitation in Jericho's voice sounded worse than I thought it should be. It had me thinking that his near-death experience was weighing on him. Maybe it had him feeling vulnerable? Afraid even? I wasn't used to seeing him like that. He ran his fingers through his hair, seeming to resign the argument. "Casey, it's your call."

Before I could answer, the heat in Peterson's voice returned. "I ain't going to let it alone! We can't let them steal it out from beneath us. How about me and the girls dive the site!" Peterson turned to me, focus narrowing. "What do you say, lass?"

My gut cramped with the idea I'd been considering. It cramped because it went against Jericho's opinion. But it was necessary. Jericho made a face when he saw my eyes. That look turned to disbelief, his arms crossing. I wasn't sure how best to say it and blurted, "I agree. We should dive again. Right away."

"Hot diggity!" Peterson yelled, slapping his hands together. In the small space of our kitchen, the walls echoed like canon fire. Tracy flinched and Emanuel cocked his head, confused. Peterson shifted his cap, wiry grays sprouting beneath it. He held up two fingers, instructing, "We'll use both boats. I've put a couple sand blowers on mine—" facing Jericho, hand perched on his shoulder, he asked, "You know how to use one?"

"Sure, I mean, you point at the sand and blow," Jericho answered curtly, frustrations stewing. Peterson heard it, but didn't care, the potential of riches too powerful. "Casey?"

"Let me explain." Emanuel and Jericho traded a disapproving look, questioning the decision. I urged them to sit, sliding one of the chairs from beneath the table. Emanuel was first to accept the invitation, chair legs creaking, Tracy followed. Truth was, fatigue was plaguing my legs and feet, the day growing long. I grabbed bottles of water from the counter and plunked them onto the table, taking to the closest empty seat. Peterson eased into the chair next to me, snapping a bottle from the table, movement spry. Jericho was reluctant to join us and stood half in and out of the room. "Please?"

He agreed but didn't join us at the table. Instead, he took to the counter in a lean. He snapped the cap of a water bottle, asking, "Why the rush?"

A deep breath. "Jericho and Tracy already know about it, but Jim Witney was murdered yesterday." A low murmur. Bodies shifting.

I looked squarely at Peterson, a sinking sensation in my belly. I would never have thought him to be a suspect, but in this career, I've learned to never underestimate people. He caught the stare, a hand bracing his heart immediately. "Me? I was with my sister after we met. Got back late last night." He crossed his chest like it was a blessing or a Scouts promise. "Swear it."

"We'll verify with her." I knew his sister, a history teacher at one time. After retiring, she'd gotten bored and became the town's librarian. I also knew her to be righteous and honest. We'd verify Peterson's story with her. For now, we had a dive to plan, as well as my explaining the reasons behind it. "To complicate things, we also have evidence that excludes Jim Witney as the suspect in the murder of his wife, Karol Witney."

"Jim Witney *was* there though," Tracy commented. She opened her laptop and showed a picture of the dive boat, the fuzzy lettering on the transom, *Buoys II Seamen*. "Only, that dive boat was chartered by Janine Scott."

Peterson raised his hand, pointing at the air as he spoke. "Do you think it was that Jim Witney fella who attacked you guys?"

"Possibly, which is why I want to dive tomorrow." I sensed Jericho's concerns. Saw it on his face. It was enough to sprout my own case of nerves and make my skin feel too hot. To say I felt anything less would be an understatement. I held my bottle of water firm, trying to hide a twitch in my hand. "Janine Scott is in custody. She confessed that she and Jim Witney had planned to murder his wife. Only, Karol Witney was already dead by the time Jim Witney reached her."

"Already dead?" Jericho questioned, lips on the water bottle, his voice thin. "Do you believe her?"

"I do." That answer surprised him. I quickly added, "Samantha had evidence to clear him."

"The handprint on Karol Witney's leg?" he asked.

A nod. "And it doesn't match Janine Scott's either."

"A real Cinderella glass slipper," Jericho commented. There was levity in his voice, tensions lifting.

"We're clear to dive tomorrow morning," Emanuel said with eyes on Jericho, seeking approval. His gaze shifted to me. I nudged a chin toward his phone, his adding, "The tide and weather actually work in our favor."

"Double hot dog," Peterson snapped. He clapped his hands, wringing his fingers, adding, "I'll print copies of the tidal times too."

"No need, old man," Jericho told him. He dragged a chair to the table, spinning it around to sit with his chest resting against the seat back. "We *giggle* and *gaggle* everything online now."

"Huh"—The whites in Peterson's eyes grew when seeing the number of screens at the table—"I suppose you do." Being old troubled him for a second, but the excitement of the dive won, a toothy smile appearing. He belted a wicked snicker, saying, "You can bring as many of 'em gadgets you want!"

Laughter filled the small space, the sound of it like medicine to break through the troubles. I leaned back, my hand on Jericho's arm and looked at my team, including Peterson. While it was good, I sat up and asked, "What's next?"

"Navigation," Emanuel said and showed a chart on his phone. He swiped the screen, clearing it, his expression changing just as fast. "About this Witney guy. He might be dead, but that doesn't mean we're safe. Whoever killed him and his wife, they're probably who attacked Jericho and went after you and Tracy."

The lighthearted moment was gone. "I know." My throat closed around the true intention of the dive. "That's why we're setting a trap."

"A trap!" Tracy exclaimed. Eyes darting around, bodies shifting again. When the commotion settled, Tracy cleared her voice, asking, "What kind of trap?"

"Peterson, the report your guys sent earlier today said that the boats are still watching?" He gave me a hesitant nod. While he was all in on diving for treasure, I could see that the mention of setting a trap didn't sit well. "I believe that whoever killed both Karol and Jim Witney will come after us." I looked at Jericho, adding, "Like they came after you."

"You didn't answer the question though," Tracy said, a troubled look in her eyes. "What kind of trap?"

"I don't know yet," I confessed. "We've done stakeouts. Surveillance of an area, witnessing a crime, making arrests for crimes in progress—"

"Yeah, but how do we set anything like that up beneath the surface?" Jericho asked, his voice edged with concern. He got up before I could answer. His head lowered as he began to take baby steps. Back and forth he walked, the heels of his shoes scraping. I knew the look. It meant he was thinking about it. His eyes beamed with an idea. I just hoped it was the same one I wanted to suggest. He clapped his hand against his chest, saying, "We are the bait!"

"Yes! Exactly what I was thinking." I turned to face Peterson, asking, "What is it you do when you bait the water?"

"You mean chum it?" he asked, looking perplexed. He regarded it a moment, and his face turned bright with understanding. "You want to chum the water to catch a shark."

"Only, in this case, our shark is a murderer."

"That means, we're the chum?" Tracy asked, face twisting around the idea.

"We're the chum," I answered.

The patter of fingers against phones and tablets, as well as the tapping of laptop keys descended between us. The sense of team was there, the vibe turning positive as we worked a brainstorming session. And as the conversations grew thick with details, I heard Tracy quietly mumble to herself, "I don't want to be chum."

TWENTY-ONE

Early sunlight beamed through the ocean surface, its long fingers nearly touching the wreck beneath us. Sea life lazily swam in the bands of light, a school of silvery fish shimmering. In my head, I heard the word chum, and felt the tone of Tracy's concern. This morning, we *were* the chum. The bait. But would the sharks come? Were they treasure hunters? Were they the ones who killed Karol and Jim Witney? I paddled my feet and swam into a river of Jericho's bubbles, following, wondering how he was doing. This was his first dive since being attacked, the thought of it making me shiver. His eyes were set deep behind the mask, his skin a bloodless color. I squeezed his arm and motioned to the other side of the wreck, the place where I'd found the gold coin.

The temperature dropped suddenly as I passed through a strong current. It lifted me effortlessly like a butterfly caught in a breeze. Too far in fact, the distance growing between me and the wreck. Jericho saw it and turned to help, but I corrected the course, kicking hard until I swam clear of the current. His figure turned dim, the visibility dropping to less than fifteen feet. Maybe less. My arm brushed a school of silvery humps that swam around me. They had marble-sized eyes and watched as I moved. When they determined I wasn't food, or that I wasn't tasty enough, they turned and were gone. I focused on the sands around the old ship, kicking again, the bottom within reach.

There was no gold this time. Not on this trip. But I couldn't help but look. Fanning the waters, grains lifted and fell in slow motion, I uncovered a rusty piece of iron, the timber around it mostly disintegrated. The ship's wood may have preserved the spike, but if touched, I was certain it would fall apart. In the salty water, it didn't take long for iron to melt like cotton candy.

In the distance, I saw our muscle. I saw Emanuel and Jericho strategically positioning themselves, both dolphin kicking with swift maneuvers. In a moment they'd put themselves out of sight, making sure to be hidden while me and Tracy looked like gray seals to be preyed upon. The distance to Tracy made my stomach twist. Then again, the plan of setting a trap that involved my daughter gave my insides a squeamish squeeze. Above us, the silhouette of our boat rocked steadily, tipping silently from side to side. Peterson and a mate who worked for him were on board, keeping guard, fingers poised against the radio button which was tuned to the Marine Patrol who were out of sight and standing by.

A wildcard. Peterson had become a wildcard. A risk and danger to the team. But we needed him. I couldn't shake the sight of Peterson's face. The fury in his eyes. The rage. The disease of greed making him someone I didn't know. Someone I didn't want to know. What would have happened if I had sided with Jericho yesterday? This morning might have looked entirely different. Before any mention of treasure, I would have trusted Peterson with my life. But now? I hated feeling that way about him. Jericho and Emanuel agreed. Especially Jericho. He'd known the old sailor the longest and saw the changes too. For now, we placed Peterson where we knew it was safest, up top, while we acted as the bait. Down here, we were all law enforcement set to execute an investigation through to its conclusion. That was our priority. Not a lost treasure, or the promise of gold. If Peterson were with us, I think the possibility of riches would be too much of a distraction for him. Greed *is* a disease, and sadly, it wouldn't have been the first time it endangered lives.

We were in position, adrenaline climbing. Even with the wash of cold water, sweat teemed on my skin, turning it itchy inside the dive suit. I glanced at my tank's air level, the needle sitting in green. I gave the regulator a short squeeze, bubbles spewing to glide over my cheek with a subtle tickle. This was a stakeout. As simple as that. It was a stakeout, which meant we were waiting. This wasn't my first stakeout, but it was the most dangerous. With most stakeouts, we're huddled in an unmarked car, or our knees are squashed against our chest in the back of a van. Not here. In the ocean, we didn't have conversation or food and drink, or even a deck of cards. Instead, we were inside the world's largest aquarium waiting for something to happen. Tracy had seen my bubbles and knew to keep looking, making sure I was okay. Pointing to the wreck, I motioned for her to play like she was searching it. She waved a hand, acknowledging, sand kicking up in a cloud behind her.

I gave her a thumbs up, following the lead, and proceeded to make like we were treasure hunting. Jericho swam across the bottom, dolphin kicking until he cleared the wreck. He let gravity take him in a slow drift toward the sandy floor, where he started working in a shaded area, remaining unseen. We started at the shipwreck's four corners, coordinating efforts to work our way inwards. While the activity was fake, if I was right, then it should stir more than sand. It should stir the sharks into attacking. Fish swam in and out of view, curiousness bringing them close enough to plant a kiss. An orange fish with a white stripe swam near my face, forcing me to shoo it away. It was more zealous than the others, following like a stray cat while I fanned the seafloor.

After ten minutes and seeing nothing but more fish, the team's attention to the wreck was shifting to treasure hunting. Playacting to bait a potential strike only works if the sharks are watching.

What if they weren't watching? What if Peterson was right and they'd come in the night and taken the treasure? If that's what happened, then there wasn't anything to protect. Nothing to kill for. I signaled to Emanuel who was closest. He spewed bubbles from his regulator to catch Jericho's attention. Tracy lifted her head when seeing the same. When I had their attention, I pointed at the wreck, or what was believed to be two shipwrecks. It was time to dive for treasure and find out if what Karol and Jim Witney potentially died for was still here.

I went deeper, slowing my air intake, swimming carefully as I maneuvered around the first wreck, the one that was known, the one closest to the surface. Arms waving, I descended until I was above another wreck, the unknown one. There was more of it now, the sands shifting again since our last dive. This might be the Civil War ironclad ship Peterson believed was here. From the pictures we'd seen, what remained was only a shell lying perpendicular to the wreck on top of it. What I knew to be the ship's keel and frame looked like the spine and ribs of a carcass left to rot. The Civil War wreck had died on its side, the iron cladding that Peterson talked about was completely gone, disintegrated by the years of saltwater washing over it. If Peterson was right, then these were the remains of significant history, the ship's untold stories thought to be lost forever to the sea.

Jericho stayed hidden, but Emanuel emerged, somersaulting gracefully, and spinning around to swim up next to me. He'd been diving these waters almost as long as Jericho and Peterson. I fanned the sands to show him more of the second ship's keel. His voice boomed, the trumpeting filled with excitement. It was contagious, quickening my heart; I heard it thudding in my ears. Emanuel was hearing it too, and from the look in his eyes, he knew that this second ship was a discovery.

Peterson said something about the seafloor giving up her secrets. I think he was right. She gave up a big secret. That alone was hugely significant and needed to be reported to the appropriate historical societies and organizations. But there was a clock on the Civil War wreck now. It had slept undisturbed for nearly two-hundred years. The storms had pulled the blanket of sand away from her remains, exposing what had been preserved. Without protection, the tides would erase her from history, decay washing away a molecule at a time until the last of her was no more.

A shine. A band of sunlight struck the sand and reflected light into our eyes. I heard Emanuel's voice trumpet again, the sounds of elation bending in the seawater. His fingers disappeared into the seafloor, sands swallowing his palm and wrist as he dug deeper. His eyes bulged when he latched on, muscles thick like ropes across his arm. Blue lightning. It flashed across my face, a commotion stirring around me. Emanuel's head lurched back, his regulator falling from his mouth. It was the attack that we'd planned for. But we'd fallen prey to the same distraction that plagued Peterson. Greed.

Swim! The voice in my head screamed. I kicked my legs at once, the seafloor rising enough to douse visibility. I kept it up until the burn in my thighs threatened to stop my heart. For the moment, there was safety in the sand, a place to hide while I swam away and around, arms aching when spinning. I held a place in the sea like a hummingbird above a flower, my fingers brushing across long strands of seagrass as Emanuel's lifeless body appeared. I was behind him and took hold, shoving the regulator into his mouth, our attacker gone.

They must have swum opposite of me when the sands clouded the site. Bubbles raced over my face, the stream of them rising frantically. I squeezed Emanuel's regulator, filling his mouth with air, forcing the seawater from it. His eyes sprang open, his hand covering mine as he breathed deeply. He'd only been dazed and was becoming alert, another blast of blue lightning appearing from above.

Our attacker swam across our heads, covered head to toe in a black dive suit, his eyes invisible behind the mask. The prongs of a shark deterrent tool jutted forward, arcing like an electric spear. We didn't move fast below the surface. Every motion was an effort with the depths pressing against our bodies, the currents battling. I swam sideways, avoiding the strike, an arm jerking me backward suddenly. The space between me and the attacker filled with black and white, Jericho's suit appearing, his arms and legs tangling around the attacker's body like a squid. Emanuel was quick to jump in with me, the three of us ascending on one, stealing the weapon, their mask and their regulator.

When I saw the face, I swam backward with surprise. He was frozen in place by Jericho's and Emanuel's grasp, his mouth puckering like a fish, desperate to breathe. Jericho wouldn't let go, his eyes darting from my hand to the dangling regulator, telling me to give our prisoner air. The shock of who it was held me in place with icy fingers that refused to let go. It was Shawn Rutledge, the owner of the dive boat, *The Wanderer*. Jericho's muted voice pleaded to let him breathe. I picked up the regulator and placed it in the older Rutledge brother's mouth, letting go when I felt the touch of teeth on rubber.

The lump in my throat was like a rock. If Shawn Rutledge was here, then where was his brother? Where was Tracy? I spun around, breathing heavy and fast, my insides filling with an electrical pulse that'd rival the shark deterrent tool. The stirred sands stole the visibility, making it impossible to see. Frantic, I waved forward, swimming to where she'd been. That's when I saw her. That's when I saw Patrick Rutledge holding a speargun to her neck, a faint puff of blood coming from a cut in her neck. The bubbles stopped. I stopped.

TWENTY-TWO

Every muscle was stuck as though they'd turned to stone. Tracy's breathing was fast, bubbles rising in a thick stream. Her eyes were big and shining with fright behind the mask, darting from me to Jericho and Emanuel. Nobody moved, the gurgling sound of our breaths rising to the surface. I dared to raise my hand, waving subtly to Emanuel and Jericho. They eased their grips on the older Rutledge brother, Emanuel holding the shark deterrent tool. The younger Rutledge brother jerked his arm suddenly, pressing the tip of the spear into Tracy's neck. She winced, eyes narrowing behind the mask, the expression of terror ripping into me as though the spear's cold metal touched my heart.

"Wait!" I tried yelling, voice garbled by my regulator. I held both hands, fingers splayed, pleading to him to stop. Bloody puffs clouded around the wound, floating upward like small balloons, stretching oblong with tails. The cut in Tracy's neck wasn't deep. It wasn't life threatening. And it was nothing compared to what would happen if her captor pulled the trigger. I'd only used a speargun once before and had underestimated its raw power. They were simplistic in design. A short metal spear poised on a shaft and a thick rubber band made taut. The only time I'd used it, the rubber band had enough energy to propel the spear through a fish that was as thick as my thigh. We'd fished for our meal that day, but it was the last time I said I would ever use it.

I lowered my arms, paddling steadily and closed the distance between us. I had no idea what I was going to do when I reached Rutledge, my mind homing on a counterattack of some kind. I'd do anything to remove the tip of the spear from Tracy's throat. That's the thing about a speargun. They're a single shot. One only. And then you have to reload it. I'm sure Patrick Rutledge knew that. He had a utility harness around his calf, a half dozen more spears waiting. He wouldn't be able to get that second or third if I was on him. I'd make sure of it. It was his eyes that told me so. They were filled with the kind of sweaty desperation that said he wanted to be anywhere but here. When I was within ten feet, I sized him up. He wasn't much bigger than me, leading me to think I could take him, hold him long enough to slip an arm between him and Tracy. An earthquake shuddered inside my skull. Blood mixing dangerously with a toxic dose of a mother's protective instinct. Patrick Rutledge didn't know that, but he would.

The wildcard. Seawater whooshed past me, a black and white figure appearing suddenly like a ghost in a graveyard. I jerked my head back with a sharp gasp seeing Peterson, his gray eyes beaming from behind his mask. I knew the old wet suit too which was patched with the same pale, rubbery goo Jericho used. The fisherman drove himself between Tracy and Rutledge, his shoulder knocking the young man's jaw, the speargun wavering aimlessly. It was the opening I needed and took hold of it, Rutledge overpowered two to one. Bubbles and sand clouded the chaos, arms and legs in a twisting spin like sharks rolling to their death. I swam headfirst into it, the speargun's cold metal clutched in my hand, fingers straining around the shaft behind the arrow. I had one goal, get it away from my daughter.

Tracy's screams were shattering. It didn't matter that we were more than twenty feet below the ocean's surface. I'd know her cries anywhere. There was a sudden starry bright silence, pain rifling down my spine, the side of my face struck fiercely. It might have been an elbow or a fist. Not that it mattered. Senses dazed, my regulator was gone, torn away, teeth collapsing in a biting grind that cut deep into my lower lip. The air hose was wrapped around one of the men, the force of their fight sucking me into a spinning calamity. We were three bodies tangled as one, grunts and cries mixing with the endless flush of air spilling out of our regulators.

The blood came. It wasn't the puffy cloud that could be shaken away with a wave. It was billowing and came without pain. I kicked ferociously, nabbing hold of Tracy's arm, jerking her away. She helped with my regulator, the worry for me grooved deep by a frown. I sucked the air and arrested the ache in my chest. The bloody cloud grew, forcing us to swim. But I only got another couple feet before my arm wrenched back, the speargun still tight in my grip. The spear was gone, the attached rope threading a path to Rutledge and Peterson.

Peterson hung on to the end of the rope, his body undulating like the fish I'd caught, the spear running through his side. The sight of him stole every ounce of my strength. In the fight, the speargun had gone off, striking the old man. Emanuel swam next to me, blowing past us, his arms stretched wide, swallowing the younger Rutledge. Patrick Rutledge was done. His face was blue, his eyes half-lidded, the battle lost. Tracy was gone from my side, swimming to Peterson, her arms sliding between his, hugging him tight enough to carry. I cut the line to the speargun, dropping it, the fisherman's life becoming priority.

———

There was blood mixing with the seawater. Small streams of it ran across the deck of the boat and was spilling over the side. We had the Rutledge brothers in custody and Peterson's mate on the radio and Emanuel at the helm, the heading set to return us back to the Marine Patrol station where an ambulance was waiting.

"I... I don't know how to thank you!" Wet hair hung in clumps, the ends dangling in front of Peterson's gray face. He put on a smile and nodded toward Tracy, blood coating his teeth, his breath wheezing like a leaky float. "How did you know?"

He choked back a cough, the wound serious enough to have us motoring Emanuel's boat as fast as it would go. Peterson looked at me, his focus lazily wandering to Emanuel, Tracy and Jericho, a laugh chortling. "You didn't think I'd let you guys keep the treasure all to yourselves?" His laugh abruptly ended with a ragged cough. "Did you?"

"Old man," Jericho said, voice breaking. "You know that what's ours is yours. Forever. You understand!"

"Now now, lass," Peterson answered. Tracy swiped errantly at her eyes, pressing around the wound, the entry and exit filled by the spear which had gone straight through his side. The blood in his mouth and the graying look of shock told us the wound was bad. Possibly life threatening. Peterson touched Tracy's cheek, gaze turning distant. "Now now."

"Guys!" she wept. She looked up at us, yelling, "Do something!"

"We're almost there!" Emanuel hollered from behind the wheel.

"Old man, don't be fooling!" Peterson's mate yelled. He cupped his hand over the radio, relaying status.

"I didn't mean for it to go off!" the younger Rutledge brother exclaimed. His face was cramped with rigid concern and watering eyes. "Really, I—"

"Shut it!" Jericho yelled, kneeling next to Peterson whose chest rose and fell slowly. "Come on, Tracy. Let's give him room."

The boat deck dug into my knees while I wiped Peterson's face dry and took hold of the bandages to resume pressure. I glanced over at the older Rutledge brother, his face was stone, empty of feeling as he stared coldly at Peterson.

"Lass," Peterson whispered. "You save me a piece of it, won't you?"

"Of course." I put on my best smile, daring to look at where the spear entered his body, the wetsuit cut away. The dead don't bleed. I wiped around the wound. Wiped it twice and then a third time. His bleeding was slowing terribly. I leaned forward and kissed his forehead, tears stinging as red and blue lights flashed bright from the shoreline. "We're almost there."

"Is he?" Emanuel yelled and looked over his shoulder.

"Alive, but we have to hurry!"

Emanuel faced forward as Jericho joined me and took Peterson's hand.

"Hang in there, old man. Or you get nothing," Jericho demanded.

Peterson replied with a weak smile, eyelids staying closed, his color white like a sheet.

A bump. Ropes thrown. Seawater sloshing against the hull. A calamity of footsteps, wet rubbery kisses planted on the deck as a team of paramedics raced around Peterson. They jostled him, pushing and shoving and hoisting him onto a gurney. "Take it easy," I scolded, Jericho taking my arm.

The boat's abrupt motions brought a fresh wave of life into the old man's body. His eyes sprang open and rolled around until he saw us. His gaze drifted to the sea where much of his life had been spent. There was a hard glow on the ocean's surface where the sun dipped into the west. It was lower in the sky these days, the season racing toward winter. Peterson raised his hand, pointing at the southern skies, and saying, "It's God's finger."

"Finger?" I questioned. A paramedic covered Peterson's face with a mask and whisked him to shore before he could explain. I turned to face what Peterson saw, a bolt of lightning splitting the sky with thunder clapping the air. There were heaping clouds colored black and blue, the sight of them ominous. Threatening even. "God's finger."

"That was supposed to be a small storm. Insignificant," Jericho answered gruffly. A cold wind blew through us, lifting my hair and forcing me to close the front of my jacket. The sea tumbled and turned, a thick sheet of rain and hail pummeling the surface. This wasn't like the storms we'd see busting humid days in the middle of summer. We were past that. This was an early autumn storm, the kind born from a tropical depression that occurred a hundred miles away. And in its travels west and north, those miles added up, building and building until it was ready to crack open on top of us. That's what it was about to do. Crack open with a thunderous crash. "We have to get moving."

"You'll be at the hospital?" I asked, knowing it was the only place he would want to be. Jericho gave me a nod, slinging a rope from the boat's cleat, ambulance lights flashing urgency in his eyes. I looked to the Rutledge brothers, knowing the business I'd attend. "I'll deal with these two."

TWENTY-THREE

Rain drummed against the building, torrents of it coming in waves. When joined by the winds, a pause washed across the station, conversations silenced as chins lifted, saucer-sized eyes rising to search the ceiling. I joined in, looking up, the roof groaning with the threat of lifting away. At one point, I'd expected we'd get carried up into a funnel cloud like Dorothy's house. Only, this wasn't *The Wizard of Oz*. It was the Outer Banks, and this was a shattering storm that had been terribly underestimated. By tomorrow, North Carolina's emergency services would be in place to help clear downed power lines, flooded roads and whatever else the storm had planned for our barrier islands.

I lowered my phone, the last of the reception bleeding with a static rasp. Peterson was in his first hour of what was expected to be a five-hour surgery. He'd live. But he'd lose a spleen. The spear had gone straight through him and had missed every other major organ. Jericho was already home, guarding our place and taking care of Tabitha and Thomas. My heart was with them. My soul too. And I'd be on my way there just as soon as we finished with the Rutledge brothers. If remorse were a sickness, I'd say the younger of the brothers was fatally ill. There was a trash bin next to him, the interview room stinking of what he'd discarded in it. A sweaty sheen made his face glisten in the room's bright lights, his older brother glancing uncaringly.

Tracy stayed with me, bringing her laptop into the room, wincing at the stink as she took her seat. Steam rose from the coffee I sipped, my focus locked on the brothers, deciding whether to separate them. From the looks of the younger one, any movement might send him to the hospital. His hands shook, the cuffs jangling, the clamoring metal grating on his older brother's nerves. I could use that. I could use the stewing impatience and get them talking. Before asking any questions, I had to know which of the two killed Karol Witney. From the size of him, I had to think it was the younger one.

"Hand, please." I held up my right hand, fingers spread. They traded a look, one waiting for the other before following my direction. When they hesitated, I urged, "Go on."

"Like this?" the younger Rutledge asked, coughing and spitting into the trash bin.

I nodded and lowered my hand onto the table. When they began to do the same, Tracy tucked a copy of the handprint Samantha gave us beneath the older brother's hand. The younger brother caught on and fit his fingers and palm inside the outline, the tips jutting from the pen marking, too big. Neither of their hands were a fit, and he commented, "That's a tiny hand."

"So it seems." Disappointment shortened my breath: the older brother was right. Both had large hands, thick and calloused, the tops of them marked indelibly by a life at sea. They were not our suspects in the Karol Witney murder.

"Can we go now?" Shawn Rutledge asked, the audacity of his question catching me off guard.

I sat back, astounded, trying to think of how best to answer without sounding sarcastic. "Come again?"

The older brother dragged his handcuffed hands across the table, shoving the handprint. "Karol Witney?"

"It is," I answered, stomach clenching as images of Peterson hit me. "We have a colleague in surgery with a life-threatening injury. That's assault with a deadly weapon."

"Oh fuck," Patrick Rutledge said with a deep groan, head dipping beneath the table. When he returned, I replaced the handprint with a new picture. It was the back of Jim Witney's head, hair shaved partially to show the crescent-shaped injury. Metal rattling, Patrick Rutledge reacted immediately, a hard stare fixed on his brother. "You said you only knocked him out!"

"Stow it!" Shawn Rutledge snapped, glaring at his brother, the younger sibling shrinking in his seat. Beads of sweat stood on the older brother's forehead. In my experience, a nervous perspiration can tell a lot. The look on Shawn Rutledge's face told me he had no idea that we'd discovered Jim Witney's body. Perhaps nobody was supposed to have ever discovered it. He swiped at his eyes, asking, "Who's that supposed to be?"

"I want you to tell me about your meeting with Jim Witney." When the two of them said nothing, I fibbed, emphasizing, "We know he was on your boat."

Color returned to Patrick Rutledge's face. Blood red splotches glistening. "How—" An elbow. Shawn striking his brother before he could say anything more.

"Patrick, would you prefer to speak with us alone?" I asked, interested in only the truth. Both men were going to prison. There was no way for them to avoid it. What determined how long they'd remain guests of the North Carolina penal system was entirely based on what they decided to say or not say now. Patrick shrugged with uncertainty while side-eyeing Shawn. I leaned forward, asking, "I promise to work with the district attorney."

"Shouldn't we have a lawyer?" Shawn Rutledge asked. They'd been mirandized, their rights clearly spelled out. "I mean, for what happened today."

"We can notify a public defender for you?" Tracy asked.

They both nodded, the distance to the truth growing. I gave

Tracy the nod but redirected the questioning. I opened the folder with pictures of their boat. "The air tanks." I showed them one of the photographs I'd taken from our initial visit with them. It was the bottom of a nitrox tank, yellow, the paint chipped, its bottom ridged, the pattern and shape matching the impression on the back of Jim Witney's head. I placed the pictures side by side, asking, "What can you tell us about this?"

"Shawn," Patrick pleaded.

Shawn's focus remained fixed on the pictures, his upper lip twitching.

"I promise that whatever you can tell us, will help you."

"We only want to know what happened," Tracy added.

"It was an accident," Shawn muttered. He shook his head, the hard look he'd held breaking. Shawn gave his younger brother another look, defeat showing before he continued. "That Witney guy came onto our boat and threatened us. He said he'd make sure we'd lose everything."

My stomach jumped into my throat. "Jim Witney threatened you."

"The guy was a cop and said that he would make sure we went to prison for his wife's death," Patrick said, voice rising. Shawn jabbed his eyes, fists digging as he rubbed them. Patrick gave him a brief look, gaze returning to us, the freedom to speak his. "He said since he was a cop he could make all kinds of trouble and that we'd go to prison for decades if we didn't tell him where the gold was."

The mention of gold hit me like a cold wind. I held back any reaction, asking for clarification, "You mean Karol's gold?"

Patrick squinted in disagreement. Shawn looked up and shook his head.

There was gold, but was it Karol's? I followed up, suggesting, "Karol Witney found gold when she was diving."

"Not the dead girl. The other one," Shawn answered, his eyes bloodshot and puffy. He bit his upper lip and jabbed a finger at the picture of Jim Witney, adding, "I only meant to knock him out so I could get him off our boat. He was going to destroy us."

I saw confusion on Tracy's face. I felt the heat of it too, the explanation puzzling. I thought of separating the brothers again, but first asked, "Let's back up a second. What did you know about the dive boat, *Buoys II Seamen*?"

They traded a look, Shawn answering, "Good people I suppose. They're a competing boat, but we get along." A shrug. "We've never had a problem with them if that's what you're asking."

"Janine Scott?" I was fishing, trying to connect the dots of this case.

"The woman who chartered *our* boat?" Patrick asked, bracing his chest. Another shrug. "We didn't have issues with her."

They didn't know. "What would you say if I told you Jim Witney was on the *Buoys II Seamen* boat during the dive when Karol Witney was killed?"

"What? They were anchored near the same wreck," Shawn said. He tapped his brother's arm. "Did you see anyone else down there?"

"Uh-uh! I swear it." He cocked his head with a squint, adding, "But I wasn't looking. I was working with the sorority sisters."

Handcuffs scraping metal, Shawn bumped the picture of the handprint, mouth twisting. "Maybe he killed his wife and tried to frame us."

"He didn't kill his wife," Tracy told him, voice flat. She looked at him, the bandage on her neck wrinkling. "And it doesn't sound like he was framing you for his wife's murder. It sounds like he was trying to blackmail you."

"That gold," Patrick mumbled, eyes glazed and fixed on Tracy's neck. There was defeat and exhaustion. How many days were they guarding that spot in the ocean? The look on his face pulled a heartstring, a sympathy. But I only had to tell myself that these were the men who'd attacked us and nearly killed Jericho. "I wish we'd never seen that fucking gold."

Chair legs bumping, Shawn delivering a kick beneath the table. "Stow it."

"Shawn. You already mentioned the gold." He shook his head. I lowered my chin, quoting him, "When you told us, 'The other one.'"

His lips thinned, his answering, "It was all her idea. She said there was more. A lot more."

There are times when a revelation is subtle like a butterfly passing in a breeze. And then there are times when it strikes you like the storm tempting the structure of our station. That's what it was like now, the force of the revelation nearly blowing me over. "Tina had the gold?"

"Fucking thing was a small brick—" Patrick began to answer, his voice an echo in my mind, bouncing off the images of her house. Her place was ransacked because they were looking for the gold. "—I seen letters on it when she dropped it on our deck. She didn't think we saw. But we did."

"CSA," I told him. He looked astonished like a ghost had just slapped him upside his head. "You two tore apart her place looking for it?"

"Tore apart her place?" Shawn asked, answering with a question.

A second revelation. "Jim Witney did it. That's why he went to your boat with demands."

"She told us she'd give us a cut. Said it'd be fifty-fifty, split even," Shawn said, shifting tiredly, shoulders slumped. "But said we had to guard the site from anyone else. That we'd get the rest of the treasure after the dust settled."

"Did Janine Scott see the gold when Tina dropped it on the deck of your boat?" I asked, picking up the sheet with the hand-print. How big were Tina Walsh's hands? *Cinderella's glass slipper*, I heard Jericho say in my head.

"She was there," Patrick answered. He jumped out of his chair, slamming a hand against the table. "She told him! She told the cop about the gold and our boat. That's how he knew about us."

"I believe you're right about that." The door to the interview room opened. Standing in the doorway was a balding man in his fifties, a brown suit and tan trench coat, his eyeglasses spotted with water, his head dripping.

"You're their lawyer?"

"I am," he answered with a cough. "Where can I get a cup of coffee?"

"We'll take you," I said, beginning to lead him from the room.

From behind me, I heard the younger Rutledge brother ask, "What happens to us?"

I didn't turn around, my sight on visiting Tina Walsh's house, but answered, "You'll have to speak with your attorney."

TWENTY-FOUR

There were eyes glaring through the window, rain pummeling the glass and drenching us. It was later in the afternoon, but it might as well have been early evening, the storm thick with dark clouds that had parked over the islands and stalled. I was soaked from head to shoulders, water dripping into my eyes and running down my face. I ran my hands across my pants, drying them before cradling the butt of my gun. I'd unclipped the safety holster, uncertain of what to expect when Tina Walsh opened the front door of her house.

Red and blue patrol lights flashed silently, joining the occasional lightning when it splintered the sky. We had a warrant in hand for Tina Walsh's arrest, suspicion of murdering Karol Witney. We also had a warrant to search the property and seize any evidence in the case that proved her guilt. I'd need the latter to make the district attorney's case. We had the witness testimony from the Rutledge brothers, their claim to what Tina Walsh returned to their boat with. But that wouldn't be enough. A jury of her peers needed irrefutable evidence to conclude she was guilty.

The front door eased open, Tina Walsh's eyelids fluttering

when a spray of rainwater struck. She swiped errantly and kept her body hidden where I only saw her face and a hand, fingers clutching the door. The handprint from Karol Witney's leg was in my bag, tucked in a folder, protected from the weather. I held up the warrant, an officer shoving the door. It didn't move, Tina's weight pressing from the other side.

"Is that legit?" she asked, scoffing at our request while assessing the myriad of law enforcement parked in front of her home. Her lips curled in a pout, and she stepped clear of the door. "I suppose you wouldn't be here if it wasn't."

I didn't ask to enter her house. Not like before. We marched in this time, backed by the law, where I focused immediately on her hands, searching for the possibility of any weapons. There were none. "Tina Walsh. Warrants have been issued for your arrest and the search of your property."

"Arrest?" she asked, lips in a pout while eyeing an officer approach. Her gaze lifted to the staircase along the wall, her mouth disappearing in a thin line.

"Tina! You don't want to—" I began, but my words were cut off by a sudden run. I didn't hesitate, shoes slapping against the wood, the stairs creaking in pursuit of our suspect. A cat. Calico I think it was. It arched its back and fluffed its tail, scurrying in response to the chaos approaching. I hurdled the furry figure, running toward a bedroom door. Tina Walsh slammed the door, but I caught the bottom of it with my foot, the sharp pressure threatening to break bones in my toes. I winced and yelled, "Tina, what are you doing? There's no place to go!"

A scream. The door gave way, its edge splintering when I shoved it open. The curtains across the room were blowing wildly, the window opened. On the windowsill there were pale fingers clutching the wood, another scream rising. "Help me."

"Take my hand!" My voice was swallowed by a clap of thunder. I grabbed her wrist before she fell, her upturned face filled with fright and glistening wet. The drop beneath the window offered nothing but a pavement and a promise to break bones. She was smart to have run to this room though, the officers still on the other side of the house. Behind the pavement was the field, mud and tall grass that was darkened by the storm: it offered a path to escape. Was her plan to jump? Perhaps. And perhaps she was having second thoughts. I squeezed my hold of her, the rains blowing sideways and pummeling my face and chest. It drenched my arms, running down my hands and fingers, the grip slipping. "Tina, listen to me! You need to climb."

Tina's hair was flattened against her face, rainwater pooling in her eyes. She tipped her head, pools spilling as she glared at the ground. She shook her head and cried up at me, "I can't go to prison—"

"Help me!" I demanded, her weight surprising. She might have been smaller, but she was thick with muscle. Tina Walsh knew how to use them too. She grunted a yell, hoisting herself up and reaching inside. That's when I should have braced myself, but she was fast. Much faster than I'd think anyone could be when hanging from a window. Her free arm lashed out like it was a coiled snake, fingers grabbing hold of my collar, clutching it with enough force to pull me clear outside.

We fell together, tumbling clumsily through the air, head over heels, the house passing my eyes in a blur. There was a moment when I felt weightless, felt the pit of my stomach lurching into the back of my throat like we'd dropped from the top of a roller-coaster. That moment ended with a crash, the breath in my lungs gushing violently. Silence descended as the stars took flight and zipped across the sky, long tails vanishing. I couldn't suck in another breath, my insides cramping like it was turning to stone. An edge of darkness surrounded me with a threatening tease.

"Casey!" I heard distantly, Tracy's voice in distress, a door slamming shut. There were hands on my shoulders and rain peppering my face as a low, thundering rumble stirred my senses. "Stay still, we'll—"

"Get me up," I grunted, wheezing sloppily as spittle ran down the side of my neck. Her face came into view with her big, baby-blue eyes filling with shock and objection. She shook her head, the stars clearing, the gray haze lifting. "My hands! Tracy, help me!"

"You shouldn't," she urged, her face blurred, stretched and pulled in a macabre sight. Footsteps descending, Tina Walsh rounded the back of her house and ran into the field. I got to my feet, Tracy's concern rigid in a hold on my arms.

"I'll be fine." It was a lie. I was hurting inside, thinking there was a cracked rib, the pavement keeping its promise. Each breath made me wince, but I had an idea of where Tina Walsh was headed. "Get some patrols over to the neighboring property."

"I can do that." Tracy was gone from my sight as two officers followed me into the field. The rainy sky had grown darker and threatened to steal our sights altogether. But I remembered the edge of her property, the overgrown trees bordering it, the outline of their shadowy figures showing me the way. Beneath them, I saw Tina Walsh entering, saw her white shirt disappear. "Tina!"

A scream. But it wasn't like the escape from the second floor of her home. This time she was scared for her life. "Help—"

"Officers, stay close." The soles of our shoes sucked against thick mud as tall grass whipped our legs. We entered the thicket of trees, breaking branches, trudging through until we stopped at a swelling river. The crevasse that Tracy had fallen into during our first visit was filled with stormy runoff, a torrent of rainwaters flooding the narrow space between the properties. A thick sycamore tree had fallen, its trunk the width of a small car. It hung precariously across the gully, bridging the pass with its roots exposed on one side where the grounds beneath had washed away. On the mottled bark, there was a pale arm and a hand like I'd seen in the house, petite fingers clutching one of the branches. "Tina!"

"Down here!" she cried. A crash, a bigger tree getting swept by the runoff. The sudden wash of land from the storm turned over the earth, throwing the stench of boggy mud into the air, the humidity of it like soup. "Hurry!"

The tree bark was wet and loose, a rope needed. But there wasn't time. I took hold of Tina's hand, an officer taking hold of mine, linking us together to try or die trying. Another officer remained as close to land as he could, folding the crook of his arm around the base of a tree root.

"Climb!" I screamed, rushing water pouring over Tina Walsh's head. For a moment, she was gone, her body swallowed by the muddy water. I had only her arm and pulled like I'd never pulled anything. It was a tug-of-war and Tina Walsh was the rope. The storming river jerked Tina's body, dragging her closer to death, our bodies lurching forward. We pulled back, straining, the officer on land hollering. An arm appeared on the downed tree. And then a shoulder. Slowly, her body rose from the flooding waters. "Climb up, Tina!"

"I'm trying," she screamed, coughing and gasping. But fright has a way of making you weak, stealing every ounce of muscle. I saw that now and thought Tina Walsh was going to let go. My insides tensed and I drove my legs around the fallen tree. The trunk was strong but wouldn't hold much longer. When her grip on my hand loosened, I dared to let go of the officer holding me, swinging my arm around until it landed on her shirt collar, doing to her what she'd done to me earlier.

"Up!" I yelled into the sky as lightning split it open in a frightful show of power. Every muscle stiffened with a single heave, Tina's chest collapsing against the fallen tree. She lay still, disbelief on her face, her gaze wandering. Stormy waters rushed around us, the tree's last hold turning loose with a sudden shift. Was she actually thinking of running? I leaned over, jerking an arm free and slapped a handcuff around her wrist. The officer next to me joined, the two us working together, dragging Tina to safety where we collapsed in the mud. "Tina Walsh. You have the right to remain silent... Anything you do say may be used against you in a court of law..."

I toweled the soaking rain from my head and chest, a station issued jacket draping my shoulders as a chill settled enough to give me a shake. It was the cracked rib that bothered me most, each stiff breath reminding me it was there. Tina Walsh had come out of the chase with a few bumps and bruises, one of her eyes puffy. There were a handful of scratches that stretched from her hairline to her chin, the skinny branches of the sycamore leaving its mark when she tried to cross it.

"I've never seen it flood like that," she commented, her stare empty. "Not in all the years that I've been living here."

"There's flooding in a lot of unsuspecting places," Tracy explained, her laptop open and perched on the edge of Tina's couch. Days earlier, we'd sat on that couch to ask questions about the death of Karol Witney. There were no suspicions that Tina Walsh could have been the murderer at that time. That'd changed now. "Casey?"

The home looked amazingly neat. Every bit of it that had been ransacked was tidied, mended, and repaired. To look at Tina Walsh's place now, there was no knowing that someone almost destroyed it. "Tell me why you ran?"

"I dunno," she answered without looking at me. Her focus stayed fixed on where I stood. My shoes were outside, but my wet feet had puddled on her hardwood floors. "Would you mind?"

"No problem," I answered, moving to a throw-rug. "You understand you have a right to an attorney?"

"I understand my rights." She looked deeply into my eyes and added, "There were no laws broken when I ran? I feared for my life is all. That's my excuse. I didn't know you were the police and thought this was a home invasion. I mean, that's reasonable enough since my place was trashed a couple days ago."

"Okay. We can play along. You understand, we've already got a warrant for your arrest."

"A warrant?" she asked, eyes rising to meet mine. "On what crime?"

"The murder of Karol Witney." I motioned to the officer guarding her. He removed the handcuffs. Tina didn't know what to make of the gesture but immediately rubbed her wrists to rid them of the metal-on-bone fatigue. "I just need you to place your hand here."

Tracy presented the sheet with the handprint, the corner edge of it wavering. "On here, please," she insisted, all niceties in her tone gone.

"What, like just put it there?" Tina asked as if the instructions were difficult. They weren't. A shrug, "Sure, I can do that."

She offered a hand, the opposite one, an immediate mismatch.

"Your other hand, please," Tracy instructed.

"Oh." Tina smirked as she slowly aligned her fingers with the handprint. And though she was fidgeting all the while, it was a perfect fit. She scoffed and spit, "That doesn't mean shit. How many people have the same size hand as me?"

"I know," I admitted, hiding the pain as I desperately needed to take a deep breath. "We also have the testimony of the Rutledge brothers. They've stated that when you came back from the dive without Karol Witney, you'd dropped something on their boat's deck."

"Oh yeah?" Shoulders rising. Tina shook her head, asking, "What did they say I dropped?"

"Gold." I moved around the room, still feeling amazed at how remarkably well she did to clean up the mess. I faced her, adding, "The same gold that Janine Scott saw you with. And the same gold that Jim Witney was searching for when he tore your home apart."

"What gold?" she asked firmly. She had a look and tone that was convincing. It could be very convincing to a jury, which concerned me. "I don't know what you're talking about."

"It was the gold that Karol found while you were diving." I circled around the room to where shadows from her fish tank danced on the wall. During our last visit, a stack of unpaid bills was on the table. They were gone. While the bills might be missing, I was certain the debt was still very much her burden. "You saw the gold in Karol Witney's hand and saw a way out of your financial problems. That's why you took it. Only, she fought back, and you killed her."

"I'm sure that's a great story." A smirk appeared. "There's no proof of any of it."

"Uh-huh." The sound of her fish tank filled the room as the talking ceased. The fish swam back and forth, moving somewhat erratically, darting to the surface, expecting food. I picked up the small canister of flakes, asking, "May I?"

Another shrug. "Yeah sure. I needed to feed them anyway."

"I used to have a goldfish named Howie. He'd swim at the surface when he wanted food too." Tracy looked at me, her expression odd. She'd never heard about the past adventures of Howie the goldfish. "That was a long time ago though. I really loved that guy. I mean, as much as a person can love a pet fish."

"Yeah. Fish are easy," Tina said, her gaze fixed, impatience setting in.

"Your place does look great." I continued to make small talk while pinching fish food and dropping it onto the surface. One by one, the fish approached, eagerly eating what was offered. "It really is amazing how good. I mean, I would have thought you'd still be restoring it, with all that damage."

"I know how to clean and fix things," Tina commented and began to fidget. She was uncomfortable and I knew exactly why. "Wasn't as bad as it looked."

"No. It was as bad as it looked." Her posture changed as I

moved around the tank. It was as I expected, and I could almost sense the madness building in her. "It was bad. Right, Tracy?"

"It sure was," Tracy replied. I could see that she was wondering where I was going with this.

I held up a finger, adding, "There was one place Jim Witney didn't search. It was the only place left unscathed by his handiwork."

"Please, do tell," Tina snarked, continuing to play it coy.

"Where else would you hide gold?" I asked, and carefully dunked my hand into the fish tank, bubbles rising between my fingers. The water level rose and spilled over its lip with a splash. Tina's face was like stone. There was no grimacing or complaining about the floor now. And that was enough to tell me I was right. I followed the bubbly trail coming from the plastic chest with the lid that opened and closed, taking hold, and lifted it out of place. Beneath it, the golden letters CSA appeared amidst the tank's colorful stones. "The answer is a treasure chest."

"Care to tell us what really happened to Karol Witney?" Tracy asked, the look on Tina Walsh's face sullen with defeat.

"Do tell," I added, borrowing some of the suspect's snarky words.

She shook her head, whispering, "God, I hated that fucking bitch."

I slipped a latex glove over my wet fingers, the CSA gold in view, ears perked toward Tina. Fingerprints can survive days in water and I didn't want to add my own. "Was it because of the gold?" I asked, knowing that wasn't the only answer. When you present the wrong answer to a stubborn suspect, they'll almost always feel compelled to correct you.

"No!" she scoffed. "She stole him is why!"

"Jim Witney?" Tracy asked, her reacting as though watching a soap opera. In a way we were. "You had more than a physical relationship with him?"

"That's right! It was just us back in college. Until I joined the sorority," Tina answered. "He loved me first and I loved him."

"You still love him?" Tracy asked, focus trained on the drama.

"I never stopped." Tina nodded and fought her tears. "But he never looked at me again. Not like he used to."

"Was it your plan to kill Karol Witney that day?" I asked, searching for premeditation.

Her gaze swam like the fish as I removed the gold and placed it in an evidence bag. Her words drifted too, dreamily, answering, "It just... just happened. I saw the gold first, but she was closer and got to it before I did."

"Karol picked up the gold before you?" A lazy nod. "She had it like she had Jim Witney."

"Uh-huh." Tina Walsh stood and said, "I think I'm done talking now. I don't have anything else to say without a lawyer present."

EPILOGUE

Karol and her husband, Jim Witney, were gone. Their remains flown back to Chicago. I'd been through a half dozen calls, working with the medical examiner's office and Samantha on the logistic of it all. There were cemetery plots being prepared and family services planned. There were mothers and fathers and sisters and brothers that had been tasked to make the remaining arrangements, including what their loved ones would wear to their graves. There was also the matter of assets and what to do about the custody of Janine Scott's and Jim Witney's children in the Outer Banks. As suspected, his mother and father never knew of the life their son had south of their city. They never knew they had grandchildren.

Sharing their father's sapphire eyes, I suspected his children might be casting a gaze on Chicago's falling snows this coming winter. Their time in the Outer Banks was ending abruptly. For the time being, they were moving to their grandparents' home and their mother was facing time in prison. The DA had no choice but to file charges against Janine Scott. There was a law broken. A few in fact. It was likely that she would take the recommended

plea bargain and accept a prison sentence and supervisory proba-
tion to last a period of five years. That wasn't her only problem
though. North Carolina's Child Services had become involved.
They'd done so at the request of Jim Witney's parents and their
attorneys. Yes, attorneys. There was wealth in that family. I didn't
know what the children's future looked like, but expected a turbu-
lent back and forth custody battle that might last years. It
saddened me to know the hardships that awaited the children
with the sapphire eyes.

There was no plea bargain for Tina Walsh or the Rutledge
brothers. Tina Walsh had confessed to us, the motive a surprise, a
spur of jealousy that was deeply rooted in her, dating back to their
time together in the sorority house. But once Tina Walsh had a
lawyer, she tried denying what was said. That included her
arguing that the handprint we lifted from Karol Witney's leg
could have been from anyone. She was right. However, the handprint was a perfect match and would work well for the DA at trial
as supporting evidence. It was the gold she took and hid in her fish
tank that closed the case against her. There were fingerprints
recovered from the surface. Two were found to be from Karol
Witney's left thumb and index finger, proving she had possession
of the gold prior to her death. Tina Walsh's fingerprints were also
recovered. Maybe she thought the water in the fish tank would
wash them away? There'd been cases I'd worked where we recovered prints after being submerged in water for more than two
weeks. Or maybe she never considered fingerprints at all.

There was the SUV also. The one that struck us. Tina Walsh
tried to argue that it had been stolen but we knew it was her
behind the wheel. We also knew she'd learned where we were
from Janine Scott, phone records showing a conversation taking
place after we'd left the Scott residence. We'd found the SUV
later. Rather, Alice and her work with the patrols discovered it
parked in the abandoned property next to her house, the wind-

shield cracked, the license plates removed. The damage to the front driver-side included scuffs with the same color paint matching my car, the hit involving more than bumper to bumper.

The Rutledge brothers faced attempted murder charges for the attacks against Jericho, Tracy and Peterson. The district attorney wanted to charge them with premeditated attempt to kill. However, it was impossible to prove what their intentions were beyond protecting a treasure in partnership with Tina Walsh. The DA decided to file assault charges against the brothers instead, coupled with manslaughter charges against Patrick Rutledge for the death of Jim Witney. Video evidence from a neighbor's doorbell showed that it was Jim Witney who had trashed Tina Walsh's home. He'd learned of the gold bar from Janine Scott and had threatened Tina and the Rutledge brothers.

Greed is a disease. That was something I'd never thought of until working this case. I didn't know Tina Walsh and the Rutledge brothers. I didn't know if they were good people before greed intervened. But I'd like to think that maybe they were. That they were the kind of people their friends called in the event of an emergency or when in need of a favor. Was it the gold? When I'd had that moment with it clutched between my fingers, I'd felt something electric. I think Tina must have felt the same and believed the riches of it would make her problems go away. The brothers too. Even Janine Scott. The greed spread amongst them. An infection. An incessant itch of what was possible. What was truly possible was the saddest of outcomes: their lives ruined.

It wasn't surgery or the attention of a hundred doctors and nurses. It wasn't the attentive round-the-clock care of a hospital. And it wasn't the riches promised by a treasure that had eluded historians and hunters for nearly two-hundred years either. What

Peterson needed more than anything were two little souls, our Thomas and Tabitha. Every chance we had, we took them to his hospital room. It was about the only time I saw a shine return to his eyes and a smile show on his face. Brief as our visits were, they were the best hope of his finding a way back to his old self.

His recovery had been painful and slow, and as much as I hated to admit it, our visits only did so much to help. Peterson was a man of the world. He was about being outdoors and around the sea, his first love. If he wasn't fishing or diving or sailing her, then he was working the docks. Perhaps the sea was his only love. As he'd tell it, she'd scorned him and taken back what he thought was rightfully his. *God's finger*. That's what Peterson had called the storm before losing consciousness. It was like God's finger had run across the second shipwreck and erased it from history. The ship and its treasure were buried beneath a mountain of sand once again.

The waters around the wrecks had shallowed enough to warrant new markers, placed by the Marine Patrol, along with notifications broadcast by the Coast Guard. They didn't know what lay beneath all that sand though. Only a few of us did. The case had been documented, the district attorney briefed along with the Chief and half the station. It was only a matter of time before word of treasure ran through our small part of the Outer Banks. From there, it would spread to the northern beaches of Carova and to the southern-most tip of the islands. The treasure hunters would come then, filling the hotels and motels and every available bed and breakfast. It's happened before, and it'll happen again.

For Peterson, what had been the promise of fame and riches was gone. Snuffed like a candle flame. The lively flicker I'd seen in Peterson's graying eyes was gone also. At one point, two days had passed without his speaking a word. He faced the hospital room's dirtied window and stared at the sky. When he did speak, his words were sparing and mostly in riddle about how storms urge the sea to give up her secrets.

"If it's buried, can't you still dive for it?" I said, asking, his eyes weepy.

Peterson slowly closed his eyelids and shook his head. I dared to cover his hand with mine and carefully squeezed his fingers. I didn't like his color or the sullen look on his face with his cheeks sunken and his eyes set back in his head. He'd lost weight and was borderline anemic, the skin on his arms thin to the point of seeing the blood vessels beneath. When he shook his head, I challenged him.

"Why not? I mean, you mentioned having the boats and crew, along with those sand blower things. Sure, it would take a lot of time, but couldn't you get down to the second shipwreck? Pick up where we left off?"

"It's 'em government folk," he said breathlessly. "It doesn't matter how much the sea hides it from us, 'em bureaucratic yahoos lay down the law and put restrictions on the site. Nobody allowed now."

"Yeah, I heard something about that." I'd only just learned of a federal interest. But this sounded like an intervention, my heart sinking for him, the ideas that were racing in my head suddenly gone. It didn't matter how deep the sea buried the Confederate ship, if the government was involved now, they'd take control. Cringing, I had an idea of what might soften the blow. "Confederate States of America. Wouldn't the treasure have belonged to them anyway?"

"Mayhap it does. Mayhap it doesn't," he pouted and shrugged, nodding subtly. On his lap, he pushed open a copy of *People* magazine. Pages fanning, he shoved a knobby finger across an article with pictures of a massive treasure that had been discovered off the coast of the Bermuda Islands. An older couple stood behind tables covered with jewels, a centerpiece showing a gold cross adorned by emeralds and rubies. There were strings of pearl necklaces, some of them as thick as ropes. There were chains of chunky silver and gold too, as well as coins piled in heaps, sunshiny metal glowing on the couple's smiling faces. From the title and opening paragraph, I gleaned the couple had discovered the riches accidentally while they'd been snorkeling. "A storm washed through 'em islands and the sea gave it up."

"This is amazing," I commented with a pinch of jealousy. Peterson wasn't the only one who wanted to dive again. "What happened to the treasure and the couple?"

"Bermuda took custody like 'em *govment* folks we got will do." He jabbed another finger, adding, "But for 'em, they got themselves in magazines and on the tube. A big finder's fee too. Enough to retire three lifetimes worth!"

"I am so sorry we didn't get it before the storm did." It wasn't often that I was lost for words. I did have something that might cheer him up though. An evidence bag's plastic crinkled when I hoisted it from my bag, the weight shockingly heavier than expected. His eyes lit up when he saw the gold, fingers clutching the air. I handed him what Karol Witney had discovered, what Tina Walsh had killed for and hidden in her fish tank. "I thought you'd like to see it before... before it's placed into evidence."

Peterson scoffed, sounding his familiar wicked snicker. "Govment folk ain't gonna let you keep it no how. Don't matter who got murdered." He held it close to his face as if trying to smell it through the plastic. Faint sunlight struck the bar through the hospital window, shining a beam of gold light on his ailing face. Bushy eyebrows rising with a toothy grin. "I could make it disappear."

"Old man!" I laughed. When his smile faded and his grip tightened, I thought for a moment that I was going to have a fight. I gave him a hard look, speaking without words to tell him to reconsider whatever it was he was thinking. "Peterson?"

"I know 'em government folk will take it." He held it against his chest, adding, "But it's good to have it a spell. Don't you think?"

"Yeah, it's good to have it for a spell." The soft patter of shoes echoed from the hallway, followed by shouts of laughter and squeals. I leaned forward, telling him, "You have some visitors."

"Pappy!" We heard as Thomas and Tabitha stormed into the room holding the handle of a wicker basket, its size making them tip sideways. When the children came to live with us, Peterson had been first to the apartment. With no objections from us, he'd introduced himself as Pappy, the name sticking fast. Other than Tracy, he'd been back more than anyone, ofttimes bringing gifts, anything with a reminder of the sea that was his life. "You like chocolate?" Tabitha asked, the word chocolate sounding like *chalk-lit*.

"What about Twinkies?" Thomas asked as he brushed hair from his eyes.

"Chocolate and Twinkies?" Peterson asked them, grinning happily. He cocked his head, the tip of his finger bouncing between Thomas and Tabitha. "Did you two make this basket for me?"

"Uh-huh! The *chalk-lits* was my idea," Tabitha answered.

I hoisted the basket to the end of the bed, my eyes growing. Like the gold, it was heavier than expected. Jericho let out a laugh, Tracy joining, the two trading a look that told me they'd let the kids build the basket unsupervised. Tabitha climbed onto the bed, plopping her tiny body at the end of it, the corners of her mouth crusty with chocolate. "I had a bitty bite."

"I got you boxes of Twinkies," Thomas declared, a soft burp slipping from his mouth. He covered his lips with a short laugh, nose wrinkling. "I ate one."

"You kids can have as much as you'd like," Peterson told them, the gold in his lap entirely forgotten.

I slipped it from his hands, his attention drawn to the children. The look on his face told me that this was the real treasure in his life. He just didn't know it. Or maybe he did. I wanted to think it was, my heart swelling for him and the playful laughter filling the room. I knew this to be true for me. For me and Jericho. I knew that this was our family, that this was my treasure. And I wouldn't trade it for all the riches in the sea.

A LETTER FROM B.R. SPANGLER

Thank you so much for reading *Our Sister's Grave*, Detective Casey White book 10. If you did enjoy it, and want to keep up to date with all my latest releases, just sign up at the following link. Your email address will never be shared and you can unsubscribe at any time.

www.bookouture.com/br-spangler

It seems like yesterday when I submitted the very first Casey White book to Bookouture. Ten books later, what started with one has grown into a popular series. Thank you to the amazing team at Bookouture and to the readers who have made this possible.

What happens after book 10? What mystery will Casey and the team tackle next? How about little Thomas and Tabitha? We'll find out soon.

Want to help with the Detective Casey White series and book 10? I would be very grateful if you could write a review, and it also makes such a difference helping new readers to discover one of my books for the first time.

Do you have a question or comment? I'd be happy to answer. You can reach me on my website or through social media. I've included the links on the next page.

Happy Reading,

B.R. Spangler

KEEP IN TOUCH WITH B.R. SPANGLER

www.brspangler.com

facebook.com/authorbrianspangler
x.com/BR_Spangler
instagram.com/brspangler

PUBLISHING TEAM

Turning a manuscript into a book requires the efforts of many people. The publishing team at Bookouture would like to acknowledge everyone who contributed to this publication.

Audio
Alba Proko
Sinead O'Connor
Melissa Tran

Commercial
Lauren Morrissette
Jil Thielen
Imogen Allport

Data and analysis
Mark Alder
Mohamed Bussuri

Cover design
Head Design Ltd

Editorial
Claire Simmonds
Jen Shannon